RAISING HOLY HELL

A Novel

BRUCE OLDS

Picador USA

Henry Holt and Company

New York

www.picadorusa.com

Picador® is a U.S. registered trademark and is used by Henry Holt and Company under license from Pan Books Limited.

For information on Picador USA Reading Group Guides, as well as ordering, please contact the Trade Marketing department at St. Martin's Press.
Phone: 1-800-221-7945 extension 763
Fax: 212-677-7456
E-mail: trademarketing@stmartins.com

Library of Congress Cataloging-in-Publication Data

Olds, Bruce.
    Raising holy hell : a novel / Bruce Olds.—1st Picador USA ed.
      p. cm.
    ISBN 0-312-42093-5
    1. Brown, John, 1800–1859—Fiction. 2. Harpers Ferry (W. Va.)—History—John Brown's Raid, 1859—Fiction. 3. Antislavery movements—Fiction. 4. Abolitionists—Fiction. I. Title.

PS3565.L336 R35 2002
813'.54—dc21
                                      2002066770

First published in the United States by Henry Holt and Company

First Picador USA Edition: August 2002

"Powerful and urgent . . . the story moves with unswerving momentum. Fury animates the book, which means to speak about the country today." —*Select Fiction*

"Olds can be both dazzling and overwhelming. . . . Doesn't necessarily provide all the answers, but does raise some great questions . . . Imaginative and unusual." —*San Francisco Chronicle*

"A creative and compelling first novel. Great storytelling at the hands of a skilled and poetic writer."
—*The Star Ledger* (Newark)

"[A] powerfully imagined historical novel."
—*Houston Chronicle*

"A devastating vision of an uncommon man . . . Olds's haunting first novel plumbs the fiery soul of abolitionist John Brown, re-creating the alluring passion of fanaticism. . . . Plunging dangerously into the American past, the novel forces the reader to confront Brown's unique brand of passion. . . . In every way, a superb piece of historical fiction." —*Booklist* (starred review)

"John Brown's body all but rises from the grave in this energetic, multifaceted . . . story at once fact-filled and power-packed. A provocative, compelling view of the man and his time." —*Kirkus Reviews*

"In Olds's fiery, compelling new novel, John Brown's body . . . is up and about wreaking havoc. This is no ordinary telling. . . . Bitterly eloquent." —*Library Journal* (starred review)

"Olds offers a fascinating study of slavery in the United States and of one of its most ardent opponents. . . . A remarkably complex portrait of a paradoxical zealot."
—*Publishers Weekly* (starred review)

to,

    for,

        and because of,

Susan Silkwood

Raising Holy Hell is a work of fiction, some of whose characters, settings, situations, and events were lifted from history, reconstituted, and redeployed.

And some of whose were not.

Spiritual combat is as brutal as the combat of men: but the vision of justice is the pleasure of God alone.

—Rimbaud, *A Season in Hell*

If war is not holy, man is nothing but antic clay.

—Cormac McCarthy, *Blood Meridian*

Raising
Holy Hell

The old man awakens before daybreak. He detests this hour—its wanton indolence, its longueurs and inertia, the intolerable absence of industry—but it has been his habit since boyhood and he is by temperament not one disposed to change his ways.

He arises with a start to the familiar taste of sea salt, an ocurrence he finds neither alarming nor unpleasant, but reassuring, even oddly arousing. This morning, as most mornings of late, his gums are bleeding; he is lipsticked with blood.

His bib of albumen beard—an affectation of recent manufacture got up to sidetrack manhunting federal marshals and overzealous bounty hunters—is brindled with blood as he unspoons himself from his wife before sidesaddling from bed to shuffle his way across the darkened bedroom, down an eccentrically tapered corridor (taking care to sidestep the buckled patch along the right-hand wall), and into the lusterless kitchen.

The price on his head this Monday morning is $3,250, a portion of it authorized by President Buchanan himself.

Lingering before the back door, he takes a moment to knuckle the tangles from his eyes before cocking an ear and glancing back to confirm that the rest of his household still is abed. Then, squaring his shoulders, he inhales sharply, rises on tiptoe, and unsnags the leather strop from its knag out of child's-reach high on the wall. When he opens the door the blast of air is as the swack of a two-by-four. It is deep winter high in the Adirondacks, and the earth which has been frosted shut-tight for months is socked in beneath a yard of starlit snow.

1

When the old man steps into the snowlight, he is unshod.

Head down, shoulders bunched, he churns his way through the thigh-high snow with the labored strides of a hiker bucking an invisible hill.

His feet punch chimneys in the ice-lensed surface.

Although the route is familiar to the point of routine—past the privy house, down the millrace, across the barnyard—the foray is literally staggering. By the time he unlatches the barn door and ducks inside he is so winded that he props himself by a bale of hay and doubles over at the waist trying to catch his breath.

Only then does he realize that the cold has cut him off above the ankles; he can no longer feel his feet.

Enflanneled in darkness and assailed by cold, he manages to locate and light the coal oil lantern hanging by the horseshoe U'd into the rafter armslength above his head. When the lamplight sifts down it discloses shins snaggled with blood where the snow's crust has abraded skin.

Ignoring his wounds he reaches behind his neck and draws the nightshirt over his head before dropping to his knees on the straw-strewn floor. In his right hand he clutches the leather strop: eighteen inches of untanned oxhide cleated with knots, tapered to a V, and attached to a stub of broomstick. He has given this instrument a pet name. He calls it "the divine persuader."

He begins. Twice straight back over the right shoulder, twice across the chest and over the left. The leather barks. Knots bite. Right, and right again. Left, and left. The pace quickens. Oxhide blurs. His face flushes as he chuffs fitfully through clenched teeth.

O my God, he prays, shutting his eyes in surrender to the felicity of the pain, *behold how I suffer with them held in bondage, how I remember them that are in bonds as bound with them.*

O Lord, behold how I bask in the blood.

O my God, lend me the strength of thy arm that I might deliver them from their masters who defile and debauch the land with their blood.

O Lord, behold how I bask in the blood.

O my God, give your sword into my hands that I might cleanse the land of their blood with the blood of those who have shed it, mindful that without the shedding of blood, there can be no remission of sin.

O Lord Jehovah, behold how I bask in the blood of the orlop.

His back colors. White becomes pink, pink carnation, carnation rose, rose red, red ruby-red. At last the macerated flesh rifts, tugs apart, bursts open. Blood fantails the air as steam brumes from the freshly opened wound in the dead cold of the barn.

He moans in sweet release.

Weeks later he will finger the keloid weal.

Sensing the bloodspill cool upon his back, he smiles—uplifted, *blissful*—eyes bright-wet with the light of the radiance.

On the floor of the barn the blood of the flagellant lies pearled just there upon the straw.

I have heard it said, and would not disagree, that when one contrasts the beautiful, rich color; the fine, tough musculature; the full, broad features; and the gracefully frizzled hair of the Negro with the delicate physique, wan color, sharp features, and lank hair of the White, one is inclined to believe that when the latter was created, Nature was pretty well exhausted—but, determined to keep up appearances, She pinched up his features and did the best She could under the circumstances.

—ANONYMOUS

Though the effects of black be painful originally, we must not think they always continue so. Custom reconciles us to everything. After we have been used to the sight of black objects, the terror abates, and the smoothness and glossiness or some agreeable accident of bodies so coloured, softens in some measure the horror and sternness of their original nature; yet the nature of their original impression still continues.

Black will always have something melancholy in it.

—EDMUND BURKE, "On the Sublime and Beautiful"

A Devill he was. Blacke within and full of rancour. But white without and skinned over with hypocrisie.

—THOMAS ADAMS, *The White Devill* (1614)

Human skin is composed of three layers.

The outermost layer is the Epidermis.
The Epidermis is composed of four layers.
The innermost layer is the Basal.
The Basal contains Melanocytes.

Here is where it gets ticklish.

The Melanocytes manufacture pigment.
    This pigment is known as Melanin.
    Melanin is brown in color.
    Everyone has the same number of Melanocytes, give or take.

Here is where it gets sticky.

The Melanocytes of some people manufacture more Melanin than
the Melanocytes of others.
    The Melanocytes of native northern Europeans, for example,
manufacture less Melanin than the Melanocytes of any other people
on the face of the earth.
    This accounts for the color of their skin.
    Approximately white.
    The Melanocytes of native Africans, on the other hand, manufac-
ture more Melanin than the Melanocytes of any other people on the
face of the earth.
    This accounts for the color of their skin.
    Approximately black.
    It would appear that all men are not created equal.
    Some have Melanocytes that manufacture a Kilimanjaro of Mel-
anin.
    Others have Melanocytes that manufacture a mere foothill.

Here is where it gets ugly.

Those with Melanocytes that manufacture lesser amounts of Melanin feel that their Melanocytes are superior to the Melanocytes

of those with Melanocytes that manufacture greater amounts of Melanin.

Here is where it gets grotesque.

Those whose Melanocytes manufacture lesser amounts of Melanin feel that not only are their Melanocytes superior, but that this superiority extends to their whole person—body, mind, heart, and soul.

In turn, they feel that not only are the Melanocytes of those whose Melanocytes manufacture greater amounts of Melanin inferior, but that this inferiority extends to their whole person—body, mind, heart, and soul.

Whence, one might ask, did this feeling arise?

As it possesses no basis in science and is unsubstantiated in rational fact, it is perhaps not unreasonable to assume that it arose out of thin air.

In other words, it is prejudice.

Here is where it gets twisted.

The prejudice of those whose Melanocytes manufacture lesser amounts of Melanin is so overweening that they believe it confers upon them the right to engage in any manner of behavior—however brutish and depraved—toward those whose Melanocytes manufacture greater amounts of Melanin.

Including their wholesale enslavement.

In the beginning God created the heavens and the earth. The earth was without form and void, and darkness was upon the face of the deep, and the Spirit of God was moving over the face of the waters. And God said, "Let there be light," and there was light. And God saw the light was good, and God separated the light from the darkness.

God called the light Day.

And the darkness he called Night.

The Blood of the Orlop

"One night about the last of August came in a Dutch man-of-warre that sold us 20 and some odd Negars."

We read this entry in the journal of Captain John Rolfe written in 1619—the year before the *Mayflower* lands at Plymouth Rock—in Jamestown, Virginia; America, New World.

Liken it to reading an eyewitness account of the dawning of creation. Only this—these "20 and some odd Negars"—is the dawning not of creation, but of something very like its opposite.

In time, these first 20-and-some-odd will be joined by another 500,000-and-some-odd, which by dint of natural propagation will swell to 4,000,000-and-some-odd (half of them chattels) by the eve of the Civil War.

The name assigned the numbers is the Slave Trade, coincidentally known as the African or Guinea Commerce, and those being traded are labeled Black Cargo or Contraband. They are in fact neither slaves nor commerce nor cargo nor contraband. They are human beings, many of them tribal warriors, not a few of them tribal chieftains.

They are:

Wolof and *Efik* and *Mandingo* and *Kru*.

Ibo and *Serer* and *Yoruba* and *Ewe*.

They are:

Fanti and *Fula* and *Fon* and *Fetu*.

Papaw and *Quaqua* and *Kom* and *Bantu*.

They are:

Ibibio and *Mende* and *Ovimbundu*.

Coromanti and *Dahoman* and *Ashanti* and *Mbundu*.

All captured, abducted, or in some manner coerced from their homes in the African bush.

All driven like a remuda from the interior to the coast in a "coffle," strung one to the other by leather collars or yokes attached to a long leash or chain.

All crowded into a warehouse—a "slave trunk" or "barracoon" —there manacled for weeks to an iron girder or "bilbo" embedded in the earth to await arrival of the "slaver"—a brigantine, barquantine, brig, schooner, sloop, clipper, or frigate modified to feature a raised stern to facilitate the easy clearance and enhance the field of fire of the quarterdeck-mounted swivel guns configured precisely to enfilade the main deck in the event of revolt; thicker rails to deter deathjumpers; wider beams and deeper holds to accommodate a surplus of "cargo."

All stripped naked.

All shaved hairless.

All branded—men on right breast, women on right buttocks— with a red-hot iron or engraver's tool bearing the insignia or initials of the ship's financier.

All herded naked aboard the slaver—the *Desire*, the *Peace*, the *Good Fortune*, the *Rainbow*, the *Sunrise*, the *New Day*, the *Black Joke*—and "tightpacked"—"belly to buttocks" in case of the men, "arse-by-tit" in case of the women—belowdecks.

All shipped westward across the Atlantic convinced they are bound for *Jong Sang Doo*, "the land where the slaves are sold," to become property of the *Koomi*, the "slave eaters" who will consume their flesh after having first scooped their eye sockets clean with a spatula.

The voyage takes six to seven weeks. Unless there are headwinds and high seas. Then it takes longer. Often twice as long. Those in the trade call it the Middle Passage. More than one in ten of the "cargo" fall victim to it.

They die of:

Fever, distemper, typhus, scurvy, scabies, measles, dysentery, and smallpox.

Crew-administered poisoning when it is discovered that they have contracted smallpox.

Hunger.

Thirst.

Fright.

Throwing themselves overboard, starving themselves to death, cutting their own throats, strangling themselves with their chains.

Murder, when they are caught taking it upon themselves to die of any or all of these.

As they are dying they wail.

"*Kicheraboo*," they wail.

It means, "We are dying."

Their world during these seven weeks is the ship's hold, or orlop. The orlop is:

A confined cavity in the ship's maw well below its waterline.

As black and airless as the inside of a sarcophagus.

As hot as a forge.

As foetid as an open sewer.

A bisque of blood, mucus, pus, vomit, sweat, excrement, saliva, and urine that sloshes underfoot and spatters overhead with each heave of ship upon sea.

Overrun with cockroaches and bilge rats. Rats as big as beagles. Rats that bite. Rats that deposit feces on openmouthed, sleeping faces.

The orlop is multitiered. Five feet of vertical space separates one tier from another. This space is bissected by a shelf or subdeck that juts six feet from each side, allowing for a passageway or aisle down the middle.

The "cargo" reclines on the unhewn floorboards of the belly and on the unplaned planks of the shelves. They are shackled—eleven inches of iron chain attached to two iron cuffs—in pairs, left ankle to right ankle, left wrist to right wrist. Each is allowed a space five and one-half feet long by sixteen inches wide. Each is allowed twenty inches of head space. These dimensions necessitate that they lie like spoons, front to back, rather than on their backs. They lie along their right sides to lift the crush of their bodyweight from their hearts, to attain a measure of ease from the burden of themselves.

Before the ship reaches port children will have been sodomized, men will have been gelded, pregnant women will both have been raped and given birth while chained to corpses. As they are discovered, the corpses will have been gaffed from the orlop by crew members accompanied by an armed guard to fend off the biting and clawing of those still alive before being grapneled topside where one or more of their appendages—ear, finger, thumb, toe, nose, tongue, breast, penis—will have been detached and tagged as material proof that the number of slaves contracted for had indeed been purchased.

Each of these body parts will once have been a living, viable, blood-nourished piece of someone's mother.

Or father.

Or sister.

Or brother.

Or son.

Or daughter.

Or husband.

Or wife.

Or sweetheart.

Or lover.

To forestall putrefaction, the severed part will then have been slathered with ointment, trussed with herbs, and deposited in a barrel of pickle brine pigeonholed for the purpose.

The crew will then have wrestled the corpse overboard. Now chum.

The ship drops anchor.

Its cargo is offloaded.

At which point: What can they be thinking? Is it possible even to begin to imagine the nature of their thoughts as in all their nakedness they are manhandled ashore, strong-armed into this New World?

Their *Jong Sang Doo?*

The holocaust that awaits them?

Here's what I think they're thinking. I think they're thinking: "I am no man's dinner. Let any of those damn *Koomi* come near me, and I will not go quietly."

In 1808, the United States Congress, a governmental body dominated by wealthy, white, male, Southern slaveowners, passes legislation outlawing the Slave Trade. Their motivation is disclosed by one of their number when he observes that "every slave ship that arrives on our shores is to our nation what the Grecians' wooden horse was to Troy.

"To import slaves is to import enemies."

This awakening in the name of self-preservation occurs almost two hundred years after the handwriting already has been on the wall.

Some fifty years later, an old man and his band of young guerrillas will remind the world that what is scrawled upon that wall was and continues to be written in the blood of the Orlop.

One midnight at high tide, a ship bringing in a cargo of *Ibo* lands at Dunbar Creek. But the men refuse to be sold into slavery. Joining hands, they turn back toward the water chanting:

> *The water brought us,*
> *The water will take us away.*

They all drown.

—inspired by a folktale, traditional

We had some hardships to undergo. We lost our crops and then our cattle and so became very poor. Our barn was struck by lightning and burnt to the ground and then my wife gave birth to a daughter that died. She followed herself a few hours later. Those were days of some affliction.

—OWEN BROWN, his diary, entry on page 49

My mother died at the age of thirty-seven giving birth to the life my father had so casually sown inside her. There was talk that he should have known better, that he had been advised of the gravity of her condition, that he had thoughtlessly imperiled her life.

I learned this only later. We never spoke of it.

I was then but a boy of eight and she was everyone I adored in the world. My father was not the sort of man a young boy easily loves. Silent by nature, Owen Brown seldom spoke to his children. I did not dislike him as much as I liked to keep my distance from him.

He never suggested that the distance displeased him.

As a child I conceived of my mother and father so differently, they were so divorced in my mind, that I do not recall having ever regarded them as husband and wife. Whether they loved each other, who can say? They were not demonstrative in their feelings of affection.

I took her passing hard. Should I have been expected to take it otherwise? Yet it was expected of me. My father promised that were he to catch me whimpering or otherwise carrying on about "what's over and done and can't be done over," there'd be "hell to pay."

The true hell was he never caught me. How could he? I never whimpered, never whined, never wept.

I never mourned.

That *was the hell I paid.*

The price was my childhood.

Childhood is a lie of poetry.
—WM. GASS

When the end comes he is miles off, out killing time, seeking oblivion, whiling the day away deep in the winter woods. Seems lately once he's done his chores, that's all he does. Cuts the hell out. Shagtails it the hell away.

Truth is, he can't bear it any longer. Being around her. Watching her slip away. Seeing her slide downhill. Out of her head with the fever, keening hours on end like a creature gutstuck, and bleeding every day now, a little more each day, and the bedsheets so raddled with it they stink to heaven of rusted pipe and rotted fish and root cellar, like the basement of an old church been flooded out. Why, it's gotten so she scarce looks her rightful self, all sunk in and swoll up at once, the whole of her body shrunk to naught but string and bone save the feedbags of her breasts hefted with milk and the basket of her belly puffed up like a medicine ball with the baby.

His mother's bad-off is all he knows, the kind of bad-off so bad it scares him half to death to venture too near.

"Then pr-pr-pr-pray to G-G-God boy," his father keeps a-stammering at him. "Get on your knees and pr-pr-pr-pray to G-G-God to make you b-brave."

He's tried. Lord knows he's tried. Sunk to his knees, bowed his head, closed his eyes, steepled his hands. Thing is, the words won't

16

come. "Dear Lord." That's as much as he seems able to muster. "Dear Lord, Dear God, Dear Jesus. Amen."

It's as if all the praying's been spooked clean out of him.

He fetches home like always just before sundown and like always heads straight for her room. Knuckling the door twice softly (the way his father has so often admonished him), when he receives no answer he thumbflips the iron latch before shouldering it slowly open.

He'll swear later that he finds himself taking in each of the room's angles all at a fell swoop, that without panning his eyes stage left or right he registers the tableau vivant with the heightened acuity of a wide-angle-lensed camera.

His father is off at an oblique angle to his left sitting on the floor with his head bunkered in his hands and his knees foetaled to his chest and the small of his spine hitched to the wall as if pinned there by high winds. A mewling sound issues from his throat, but he does not glance up or speak or otherwise acknowledge his son's presence.

His mother looms dead ahead lying in bed faceup beneath a tattersall coverlet drawn to her chin. The coverlet, imbrued with blood, drapes flat to her midsection, and it is this fact more than the stupendous blood loss or the eggy whiteness of her skin that startles him.

"She looks all emptied out," he thinks to himself. "She looks scooped out clean as a cantaloupe." Her head is arched slightly back on her neck and her eyes and mouth are O'd open and rigid. Her mouth is as open as a seashell.

Her flesh is as white as ermine.

The baby, which he at first fails to recognize as a baby, is keen-angled to his right floating faceup in a beaten copper basin half filled with water atop a bird's-eye maple chiffonier arranged against the wall. The tiny body bobs slightly in the water, the surface of which is broken by the tip of its nose, the soft burl of its chin, and a gently humped, oblong area in the center of its forehead.

When he realizes it is a baby his first impulse is to race over and pluck it from the water, to rescue it from drowning. But this urge is immediately supplanted by another when it occurs to him with a certainty as sudden as it is perfect that the baby is as dead as his mother.

Standing in the threshold of the doorway he feels lightheaded and vaguely nauseous, but he does not burst into tears, or cry out, or so much as develop a lump in his throat, a display of stoicism which later will trouble him deeply.

All he can think is how wrong it is, her lying there like that, how *unbecoming.* All he can think is how her eyes should be closed and her mouth should be shut and her face should be covered over. How if he was any kind of proper Christian son he'd summon the nerve to snowshoe over and draw the coverlet across her face, he alone being the one to blame for all this, this *dreadsomeness* on account of his skylarking around the woods *enjoying* himself *a-lusting* after his own *self-gratification* when he ought to have been right here by her side doing his proper Christian duty.

If only he'd a-been here to hold her hand and wipe her brow and press the sponge soaked in ice water to her lips, she'd still be alive. He's as certain of it as he is his own name: had he been where God wanted him to be, where God *required* that he be in her hour of mortal need, she never would have left him alone and defenseless to face God knows what, even if he is a worthless sinner who must have committed some vile transgression, and likely a whole raft of them, and God's desperate angry with him, and this is His retribution, like when his father thrashes him, only this is worse because it's God getting in His licks and He doesn't just whip you bloody, He kills your mother.

"Dear Lord," he manages out loud as he yaws on his heels before lurching out the door, "forgive me all my wickedness."

Thirty-seven-year-old Ruth Mills Brown is buried with her un-named baby daughter in a wind-chapped, stump-scabbed field adjacent to the Brown family homestead in Hudson, Ohio, on

December 11, 1808. This still is frontier country and no preacher is available to perform the service which Owen Brown shoulders himself.

The inscription on her headstone reads:

"A Dutiful Child, A Sprightly Youth, A Loving Wife, A Tender Parent, A Kind Neighbor, An Exemplary Christian. Sweet is the Memory of the Just."

Her eight-year-old son John refuses in the teeth of his father's fury to attend the funeral. But that night, having first satisfied himself that his father, sister, and three brothers are asleep, he mouses from the cabin to go in search of her grave.

It is only the following morning when he visits the grave site on his way to the tannery that Owen Brown discovers the fresh-turned soilbed surfed wondrous-high with haw, holly, sanicle, and tansy, judas elder and mistle and oxeye and buckeye, pyracantha and poppy, bugloss and bull thistle, sedge and wood rush and knapweed and campion, chamomile, corn cockle, goldenrod, and yarrow, burdock and wren's flower and nettle and phlox. All of it, it is perfectly obvious, placed there lovingly. Arranged by some solicitous hand.

Unless, of course . . . could it be? That it fell while he slumbered? Fresh down from heaven? This celestial flowerdrift in the dead of the winter an offering from Our Father above?

A year later and it still feels as if the only tenderness he's ever known is gone fresh missing. A year later and he's more spectered by her death than on the day that she died. A year later and he's no closer to getting shed of the feelings powering through him than his father is to favoring him with a consoling word or an assuasive hand.

And now this.

Why'd he have to go and *marry* her? Marry *her*. A girl of eighteen. A girl twenty years his junior. And Mother scarce gone on to her reward. God A-mighty! How could he? His own father! How could he sully her memory so?

Miss Sally Root of Aurora, Ohio, has got to be the stupidest creature God ever set loose to walk upright on His good earth. And the plug-ugliest to boot. He won't call her Mother, he *won't*. She's *not* his mother. An interloper's all she is—Counterfeit! Imposter! Poacher! Sham!—nothing but the cross-eyed, pony-faced, toad-necked heifer his father lets cook and clean and companion his bed.

Wasn't him asked her here, and wasn't him asked to be mothered by her. He's made it as plain as he's able: She doesn't belong here. He doesn't need her here, doesn't want her here, won't have her here.

And if she won't clear out, she best stand clear.

Why can't she just leave him be? Why does she have to be always at him with the "darlin' Johnny" this, and the "doll baby" that, and "my brave little man" the other? All the sweet talk and sheep-eye and simper to win him over and lapdog him around. Why can't she just leave off and let a soul breathe?

If only she'd just leave off.

She won't, though. That's as clear as kerosene and as plain as porridge. She's single-minded that way. Like a bulldog. (She looks like a bulldog if you want his opinion.) A bulldog with a steak bone. And the bone is him.

"Might as well put all that spitefulness behind you, my darlin' Johnny-lad," she's fond of spanieling at him, "for sure I am your one and only blessed mother and so bounden to love you the same as my own true blood, 'til the death us do part."

The way he sees it, he's no choice, no choice atall. She won't stop, it's up to him to stop her. Fix it so she can't help but hate him, or make himself such a torment to love she reckons it's not worth the heartache. Maybe he'll even scare her off, send her packing, flush the nit from his hair once and for all.

He had it all mapped out once awhile back. If only it hadn't downpoured overnight, and the privy house roof leaked so the fuse didn't burn true, and the milk jug rigged with barn nails and gunpowder didn't blow, and the nails go grapeshotting, and Miss Sally Root and her bleeding, buck-toothed, cow-jawed heifer butt along with them.

Well, the jig's up, gal. What he's got in store for her this time is by-gum weatherproof.

Just jimmy three or four of these weeviled floor planks here, high up in the hayloft leading to the hen roost where she goes early most mornings to fetch eggs. Then birdnest the cracks and jackstraw the holes with a few armfuls of hay, like so, enough to mask it so the half-awake heifer won't notice in the shadows of the faintness of the first light. And—there, that ought to do it. That'll show her to get cuddlesome by him.

Because his ma may be gone, but Lord help them who'd deny him feeling afresh the chafe of her absence. Lord help them who'd deprive him of what little of her remains.

"Put the fear of God in her Lord," prays the little boy as he ladders down from the loft in the middle of the night before spidering across the barnyard back to bed. "Lay her out so bad it scares her off'n us forever."

———

Broke him.

Made him crack made him cry.

Dragooned him by an ear straightaway down to the barn. Stripped off his breeches. Hogtied his wrists. Calftied his ankles. Block-and-tackled him by his heels.

Dangling upside down like a drape of raw beef, a sling of red meat.

Terrified.

Triumphant.

Just like he planned: Plunged right through. Knocked her out cold. Hackled some teeth. Cleaved through a lip. Crimped shut an eye. Chamfered a cheek down to bare bone and gristle.

Clawed at her scalp like some critter'd took a chaw. Stove in a rib like a damn barrel stave.

Pa found her sprawled, face creamed with blood. Blood spattered heap a-slobbering the ground. Spitting out teeth like kernels of corn.

Wager she'll leave now, or least leave him be.
Nobody tangles with young Johnny Brown.
'Ceptin' Pa.
Now comes the sound of his switch swishing air.
The sound of old hickory swacking fresh flesh.
The sound of his childhood whaled clean away.

STEPMOTHER

Sally Root Brown

It's no secret the boy and me had our share of downs and ups, and by a damnsight, more of the former. Truth out though, reckon he hated his pa alike: hated me for trying so hard to be his ma, hated his pa for being the one let me. Reckon we was in good company all the same. Weren't like he carried no torch for the rest of the world neither.

In all my days I never seen a boy so balled up with hatefulness. Weren't anger neither. Anger's hot. This here was burr-cold. Anger's loud. This here was bier-quiet. Anger's—well, it's red somehow. This here was black as char.

I'd get to wondering sometimes where it could've sprang from, a hate like that, so bone deep, and the boy not ten year old. I swear, weren't natural.

I knowed the child missed his ma and all, but weren't like he was orphaned without a home or the kin to vet him through. I tried. His pa tried. I tried some more. After a while we quit trying. Far as he cared, the whole world'd forsook him and he aimed to nurse the grudge come hell or heaven's gate. Why, it got so you couldn't look the boy slantwise without his getting his hackles up. And go to touch him—hold his hand, smooth his hair, wipe his brow—why, he'd cut you a look so's to raise your gooseflesh. Personally, I'd a-sooner strolled bare-assed through a briar patch.

"Feed him some slack, Sal," Owen'd counsel when I'd get to fretting on it. "It's a mighty blow he's suffered. He'll come 'round."

'Course he never did.

Funny how I'm just now remembering. Never did hear that boy laugh. Ain't that a wonder? Not a cackle. Lord, now that's a shame. But that was him. That was Johnny Brown straight through and through. Not an ounce of merry to him. Steeliest child I ever known.

I'll say this last and go my way. Those people out in Kansas? The ones they say he kilt? Wouldn't surprise me none he done it.

Not saying it's so, but wouldn't surprise me so's to bat an eye.

FATHER

Owen Brown

The Good Book says spare the rod and spoilt the child.

I dunno. Maybe if I'd a-thumped him more . . .

Each morning at breakfast, as again that evening at supper, his father would repeat the same four, damnable words: "Mind your Bible, boy."

Owen Brown was a chronic, even a grotesque stammerer, but somehow he always managed "the four damnables," as Johnny came to think of them, with the abrupt finality of a hatchet swipe.

And so standing beside the table gripping the top rung of his ladderback chair as if all heaven hung in the balance, Johnny would recite from memory the passage of Scripture his father had assigned him but the day before.

His favorite—that is, his father's favorite—was taken from the twelfth chapter of Paul's Letter to the Hebrews.

> *For the Lord disciplines him whom He loves,*
> *And chastises every son whom He receives.*
> *It is for discipline that you have to endure.*
> *God is treating you as sons, for what son is there whom his father does not discipline. . . .*
> *He disciplines us for our good, that we may share His holiness.*
> *For the moment, all discipline seems painful rather than pleasant.*
> *Later it yields the peaceful fruit of righteousness to those who have been trained by it. . . .*
> *Therefore offer to God acceptable worship with reverence and awe, for our God is an all-consuming fire.*

If the boy faltered—if he forgot the words, or repeatedly tripped over them, or garbled them, or spoke them too haltingly or without enough conviction—he would be permitted a single opportunity to redeem himself.

If he fell short again, if his eyes wandered, or he tapped his foot or fingered his nose or fiddled with his hair, or if he stood too slouch-shouldered, if he betrayed the slightest hankering to wool-gather, the meal would without a word of reproach be withheld.

In this way he learned early on how to make do with less. It was a lesson that would later serve him well—in Kansas, then elsewhere—when he decided to become a guerrilla.

He liked to boast that he once went seven days without food or drink and not so much as a stomach pang.

True or not, one thing was gospel: John Brown had famine down to a regular art.

When John turns sixteen his father makes it known that he expects his able-bodied son to turn his labors full-time to the tannery, to toil alongside those like the twenty-year-old recently hired hand Jesse Grant who as of this Wednesday past beds down in the bunkhouse out back of the vats. Instead, besotted by his deepening personal relationship with Jehovah, God of wrath, revenge, and desolation, John enrolls in the Reverend Moses Halleck's Plainfield Ministerial Preparatory Academy in Plainfield, Massachusetts, hoping upon graduation to matriculate at Amherst Divinity School.

There he endures but a single torturous semester of Greek and Latin before transferring to the less demanding Morris Academy in Litchfield, Connecticut, where eight months later he awakens of a Sabbath morn to discover that he has been stricken with an eye ailment rendering him literally blind to all written text save Holy Scripture.

He believes this to be a sign from God.

His tutors believe it to be a sign that the boy is urgently in need of close vetting and prolonged rest.

Thirteen months after setting out, John Brown returns home.

Refusing to live with his family or enter the employ of his father, he exiles himself to Randolph Township in northwestern Pennsylvania where he clear-cuts twenty-five acres of forest, assembles an eighteen-vat tannery—the tannin from the oak bark, hemlock bark, and gallnuts dyes his hands the color of dead leaves—and constructs a two-story, double-room log cabin with glass windowpanes, a novelty so unheard of in those parts that his neighbors refer to it as "the house with eyeglasses on."

Enlisting a crew of fifteen to work the tannery, Jesse Grant apparently not among them, he hires the neighborhood widow Clara Lusk and her eighteen-year-old daughter Dianthe as live-in housekeepers and cooks.

"She was remarkably plain, pious, practical, and disdainful of all forms of vanity, humor and coquettishness," he writes of Dianthe later. "In short, she possessed all the qualities a man could desire in a woman."

(Jesse Grant, by the way, will work another year for Father Owen before leaving to pursue other interests, one of which will culminate in the birth of his first child, a son named Ulysses who some seventy years later will write in his *Memoirs*, "John Brown was a man of great purity of character and high moral and physical courage, but a fanatic and extremist in whatever he advocated.")

Following a brief and exceedingly cumbersome courtship, they wed. Upon which he proceeds to treat her precisely like a brood mare. He gets on her child after child. Seven in ten years. A son dies at age four. Another succumbs in infancy. It is too much for Dianthe. When her husband proves himself incapable of rallying her, she slides into madness—during the final year of her life she goes to bed each evening clad in her wedding dress—before dying as did his mother, in childbirth.

Like his father before him he delays barely nine months before remarrying a girl half his age. He later will describe the illiterate, sixteen-year-old Mary Anne Day as "large and wide-hipped, with ample bosoms and astonishing staying power."

That is, suspiciously like a heifer.

As of this writing evidence has yet to surface implicating any of John Brown's four sons in an attempt to nail bomb, booby trap, or otherwise do homicidal harm to their new stepmother.

Dianthe Lusk Brown

Mind how when we met we was little more'n children. He'd just a-rounded twenty and I weren't yet all the way haired over. So's most I can speak to is how he was *then*, the eleven years we lived man to wife.

I never knowed him when he was famous.

To take a fer instance, any so-called monomania he was took with in them days was on account of money, not slavery. That there was a man dreamt night and day of "striking it rich" and would yap hours on end 'bout "making a killing" and "grabbing the main chance" and "going for broke."

Money, that was the dear thing with him. Getting rich, getting rich quick, getting rich as humanly possible. It was all he talked about.

Didn't take long to reckon it was all he cared about.

Which ain't saying he weren't gung ho for abolition even then. His father Owen'd been raised such, and his son was such the same, and the Devil with them thought different. But he always made out how it was a question of theology, not politics. Way I recollect, he never once spoke out for acting up agin slavery, not by force of arms nor else such. Leastways not in the time we was together. Leastways not so's I heard.

Now, I do rightly recollect as how he raised a barn a brief spell after we come to Pennsylvania with a hidey-hole and trapdoor 'neath the haymow for a-stashing them run-off slaves, but that weren't nothing lots of folks in them parts didn't do the same. Besides, we never once had cause of it.

And I remember too his way of hectoring any fresh arrived thereabouts to "get on board the train for freedom"—to hook up with the old underground railroad—and if they shied off to swamp 'em with the handbills he'd a-troubled hisself to get up on the subject 'til they caved under or everafter steered clear.

And I surely do recall how partial he was to that there Mr. Garrison's *Liberator* newspaper, though it was Father Owen, not him owned the subscription.

But I reckon none of that's got spit to do with what you'd be itching most to know in light of all that business he got tangled up in later—first out there in Kansas, then at there Harper's Ferry—and which I weren't never no party to nohow on account of being dead then some twenty-aught years.

So: Was John Brown a violent man?

Well now, I'll not pretend he didn't whup his children more regular'n some—he weren't one to be overly stingy with the switch we used to say—but mostly they deserved it, and if that makes him violent, then many a parent's no better'n a brute and a bully.

No. Reckon I'd say no. Least not like some I known. He never kilt for sport nor pleasure. Nor never toted no gun nor rifle. Nor never took no buggy whip to the livestock, and only that once to me, and I won't say I didn't have it coming.

No, not violent then. Nor mean neither. Couldn't say mean. But hard? Now there's your huckleberry. Hardest man I ever knew. Hard to know, hard to love, harder still to live with. Not that he weren't capable of a gentlesome word or a tender touch, but such as that come to him less natural than any living creature I ever seen.

Behind his back people called him a tough nut, a cool customer, a hard case. And they was favoring him some.

I shared the man's bed everday for eleven years, and if the best of him was a dotish father and loyal husband, the rest of him was a natural-born sonofabitch whose hard, hard ways drove me mad afore they kilt me dead.

SON

John Brown, Jr.

Mother's death was explained to us by Father in religious terms. God was as much a member of that household as were ever any of us children, and we were told that Mother was with Him in heaven.

I accepted it because I was eleven years old and had no choice but to accept it. (Father wasn't the sort to field questions.)

But I didn't *believe* it.

Not then.

Not now.

She was dead, I was motherless, and the hell with heaven.

(Fearful of incurring his wrath, under the heading "Let sleeping dogs lie," never let on to Father the way I truly felt.)

John Brown, Jr.

Father kept a ledger in which he recorded a running tally of "debits" and "credits" respecting the behavior of each of us. "The Account Book of Transgressions," I believe he called it.

From time to time he would show it to us—usually of a Sunday morning—and if our debits too far outstripped our credits—"You see here the fearful footing up of debits," he would point out gravely—he would invite us to accompany him to the barn with the words, "I believe the time is come for a settlement."

There he would invite us to have a seat on the old chopping block he kept for the purpose before launching into a tearful and tormented harangue regarding the precise nature and extent of our sins. This diatribe I always felt more keenly than what I knew was to follow.

It happened that one Sunday I came up "bankrupt"—I was, as I recall, no more than ten or eleven at the time—so that to settle my account fully would have meant more lashes than he knew I could withstand without it doing sore injury. This seemed to upset Father greatly, for he dispensed with his lecture entirely, and after ordering me to strip off my shirt and "hug the stump," proceeded directly to lay on with the blue beech switch he reserved for such occasions.

I had "paid off" about a third of my "debt" when to my utter astonishment he abruptly left off, stripped off his *own* shirt, handed me the switch, and commanded that I trade places with him.

"Go ahead, lay on!" he said to me as he "hugged the stump" himself.

I dared not disobey him, but it felt to me so unnatural that at first I could not bring myself to strike with gusto.

"Harder!" he yelled.

But still I could not find the strength.

"Harder, I say! Harder! Harder! Harder! Harder!"

Which word he kept repeating until marblings of blood showed upon his back where the tip of the beech had bitten through his flesh and he had "paid off the balance of my account."

As I say, I was a mere boy and the lesson in which he had just instructed me—*how justice is done by inflicting punishment on the innocent in subrogation of the guilty*—was not one that I readily grasped.

I understand now that he was providing me my first practical illustration of the Doctrine of Christ's Atonement. I, of course, had played the role of Sinful Mankind. He the role of Christ.

It was a part he always did display a decided flair for.

Jason Brown

I was four years old and had been some weeks away to a neighbor's farm receiving close instruction in my three R's. The night before I was to return home I dreamed that by the corncrib I found a beautiful baby raccoon which I took for my pet. When I got home I told Father my dream as if it had actually happened. I don't know why. I wanted a pet so badly, perhaps by pretending I really had one I thought Father would understand the depth of my desire and so permit it. When Father asked to see it, I of course had nothing to show him.

"Then I am afraid you have told me a wicked lie," he said, and without a word of explanation stripped down my breeches, grasped me by the wrists, yanked me off the ground, and thrashed me well and roughshod.

I was only four. But it seems to me now as it seemed to me then:

He wasn't whipping me for lying.

He was whipping me for *dreaming*.

Oliver Brown

I remember him making us wash our hands seven, eight, nine times a day. No soap. Just water. Over and over again, him all the while a-hovering over us like an old Indian chief a-chanting, "Wash away the sin! Wash away the sin! Wash away the sin! Wash away the sin!"
  Did you know he took baths twice a day?
  Yup. God's truth.
  In ice.

Watson Brown

The trouble with Father was that he wanted his children to be as brave as tigers but still afraid of him.

Salmon Brown

Brave as *lions* and *scared to death* of him.

Unison

Whipped for not being man enough, whipped for standing up like a man.

Unison

Not enough to be just Father. Had to lord it over all. Had to *rule* the roost.

Unison

A king against whom there was no rising up.

Again, unison

He listened to himself and Himself alone.
Made more sense to argue with a fencepost.

He was born John Brown, no middle name, on May 9, 1800, at Torrington, Connecticut.

By age sixteen he had attained his full height, a quarter inch shy of five feet ten inches, above average by the reckoning of the times in which he lived.

He weighed 150 pounds soaking wet.

"Gaunt but thewy, withy but muscular," became the standard description.

Someone once commented that he was so spindly he seemed to exist at an oblique angle.

Others thought him "desiccated-looking," "rickety," "asthenic," even "phthisical."

He appeared ten years older than his chronological age.

His dark brown hair was coarse and bristly and sprouted straight up from his head, like stalagmites. It appeared to launch from his head like javelins.

His ears were as flappy and vulvate as orchids and appeared stuck on with chewing gum.

His eyebrows were bushy enough for a family of swallows to nest in.

His eyelids possessed the hooded downpitch of porch awnings.

His almond-shaped eyes were the color of a sky taking on storm.

His beaked nose angled from his face at a predatory slant.

His mouth was a slit downturned at the corners sandwiched between lips no thicker than baling wire.

He carried his jaw set like block ice above a chin out-thrust like the prow of a schooner.

People often likened his appearance to that of an eagle.

Others said hawk.

A few vulture.

He sounded like a vulture; his voice was redolent of ragged glass.

One of his sons thought he looked like a meat ax.

His head was small and triangular, and when he frowned it seemed to recede into his scrawny neck so that it resembled a drill bit.

He had no shoulders to speak of and even less of a backside.

His hands were mitts of callus as hard as cuticle, yet his fingers appeared as dainty and delicate as an old dowager's.

He wore a size seven boot.

There is an old Indian proverb, often erroneously attributed to the Irish, that says, "There are only three things that are real—God, human folly, and laughter. As the first two are beyond our comprehension, we must do all that we can with the third."

When John Brown heard this wisdom for the first time, he shook his head, pondered a second, and replied, "It is the *second* two that are beyond our comprehension.

"That is why I do all that I can with the first."

There is much about who he was and what he did that can be explained.

Clearly, much cannot.

At heart he was a shepherd. His flock once numbered 1,300 pure-blood Saxony and Merino, one of the finest in America. His fleeces won national competitions in New York City and Boston. His expert opinion was sought after and published in the *Ohio Cultivator* magazine and the *American Shepherd* digest. He knew how to cure foot rot (with spirits of turpentine, blue vitriol, and vinegar) and how to coax a balky ewe to nurse its lamb (by feeding it rowan hay, oil cake, and oats). Purely on a whim, he once taught one of his flock to crowhop on its hind legs from room to room throughout his house. Upon their deaths he arranged that they receive decent Christian burials.

He ate both tomatoes and cauliflowers whole, like apples, and sucked on lemon wedges as if they were a form of hard candy. When he ate corn-on-the-cob he held the cob on the vertical and proceeded top to bottom. He preferred green apples to red and devoured them core and all. He believed that eating ram's testicles boosted sexual potency and consumed them raw, like oysters, and smothered in chowchow and chutney. Each evening before retiring he consumed, as he preferred to think of it, an alembic of ginseng, camphorated spirits, chamomile tea, salts of tartar, powdered gum arabic, and brewer's yeast which on Sundays, and Sundays only, he chased with a jigger of Angostura Bitters. He slept with a sprig of fresh clove wedged between his gum and lower lip.

He scorned material wealth yet squandered most of his adult life in its headlong pursuit. Though he considered himself an infallible judge of human character and a businessman of acumen and ingenuity, he so mishandled each of his opportunities—twenty ventures in six states—that by the age of forty he found himself bankrupt, destitute, and embroiled in twenty-one lawsuits in which it was alleged he owed $60,000. He spent all but three of his fifty-nine years in obscurity and the lot in such desperate poverty that on more than one occasion his family was obliged to make chow mein of its household pets. He moved his wife and children ten times and thousands of miles while he sought a way out from under. He was convinced that the world had it in for him, that life held him back, that malevolent but unseen forces conspired actively to thwart him. While it is true that he experienced his share of bad luck, it is equally true that he courted poverty and hardship with the ardor a married man reserves for his mistress.

He sired twenty children by two wives. Eight lived out their natural lives. Three died violently. Nine died before the age of ten, four of dysentery within twelve days of one another, three of them so young they were buried head-to-toe in the same coffin. One experienced spells of insanity so severe he tried to castrate himself with a sheep snips. His first wife died in childbirth at the age of thirty-one.

. . .

He could not recall laughing heartily before the age of twelve. He was a hard man who counted on the world being hard. "This world is not the home of man," he wrote in a letter to his children late in life. "I'm nothing but a stranger in *this* world. I've got a home on high. Until I go there, I expect nothing but to endure hardship." He was a Calvinist of the Mystical New Light variety. He believed in predestination, providential interposition, innate depravity, and the Jehovah of the Old Testament. He found the notion of earthly delight preposterous. He was convinced that his own "first thoughts" were inspired by God, but he never claimed to hear voices or see visions. He not infrequently felt cataracted in "the rapture of the Lord." He considered himself divinely chosen.

When he was sixteen he studied briefly for the ministry. He received each word of the Bible as literally true and could cite nineteen separate verses in condemnation of the practice of slavery. Because the church he attended as a young man withheld the sacrament from Negroes, he refused to become a member of one as an adult. He thought the clergy "the Devil's own drummers and fifers," yet could quote passages verbatim from Jonathan Edwards's "The Eternity of Hell's Torments" and "Sinners in the Hands of an Angry God." His favorite hymns were from Watts: "Sin Like a Venomous Disease Infects Our Vital Blood," "Ah, Lovely Appearance of Death," and "Blow Ye Trumpet, Blow" which he sang to his children as he herded them off to bed each evening. He distributed religious leaflets of his own design and manufacture door-to-door in the dead of winter. He once let his brother-in-law freeze almost to death in a blizzard rather than admit him to his home on the Sabbath.

He distrusted pleasure, despised frivolity, disdained pretense. Displays of gaudiness left him bilious. He neither employed irony himself nor appreciated it in others. He did not use profanity. He did not drink liquor. He did not smoke, chew, or snuff tobacco. He did not dance or game or gamble or philander, or toy with the idea of philandering. He considered hobbies a waste of time. He did not daydream. He was not vain in the conventional sense, but when he turned forty he began washing his hair with beeswax, egg white, and coffee grounds because a relative had confided the practice delayed the onset of baldness. Soon he was giving himself oatmeal facials and polishing his fingernails with baking soda.

Each day at high noon he performed a series of three dozen somersets, the exact number required to complete a circle around his house. He once whitewashed all the tree trunks on his property, painted the branches red, yellow, and blue, then strung them with hundreds of glass bottles, like wind chimes. On long trips he carried a pair of his wife's unlaundered bloomers stuffed neatly into a boottop. At home, he kept a lock of his dead wife's hair in a half-filled saltcellar beneath his bed. He sometimes sat for hours in the doorway of his barn alternately firing beanbags and baseballs at rats before closing in to finish them off with a pitchfork.

He was an ascetic who beneath his shirt sometimes wore a surcingle of braided bramblebush sashed tightly about his torso. He filled the bottom of his boots with popcorn kernels to toughen the soles of his feet. He stared into the sun for hours on end because he believed it sharpened his night vision. He was riddled with energy and rarely slept more than four hours at a spell, yet could nod off in a driving rain or on horseback while ascending the side of a mountain. When circumstances required, he could sleep with one eye open.

. . .

He was reasonably healthy most of his life save for the recurrent bouts of ague that often left him bedridden for weeks. He wore a tuning fork in his hatband like a stickpin because he believed it repelled unseen miasmal vapors. Despite having weighed them on a butcher's scale, he was convinced that his right arm was several ounces heavier than his left due to "a pooling of the blood humors" and so kept it raised on end whenever possible to facilitate its drainage. A natural southpaw, he trained himself to eat, write, and shoot with his right hand. His hearing was so acute that he could detect the slither of a snake the way most people do the clop of a horse.

He had over time assembled a private library of some 300 volumes and was more widely read than most of his neighbors, yet he was capable of believing that coffee contained small amounts of arsenic, that stars were made partly of tinfoil, that the spirits of the dead gathered at predetermined forks in the road at the stroke of midnight. On occasion he could be found sitting with a Bible flopped open atop his head in the conviction that its verses would seep off the page into his brain through Scriptural osmosis. When he was feeling especially chipper, he wore his pants pockets inside out. He crammed his shirts, vests, and coats so full of news clippings that articles routinely spilled out leaving a paper trail wherever he went. When he read he moved his eyebrows the way most people move their lips.

His conversation was littered with Scriptural quotations and shopworn folk maxims, yet he was at a loss for small talk or idle chatter. "I have always been more afraid of holding forth at an evening party in the company of ladies and gentlemen," he once said in the the nasal twang native to the Ohio frontier on which he had grown up, "than of facing down a band of men with guns." He preferred to think of himself as a plain man who spoke plainly of plain matters, yet he was by nature wily, secretive, and teeming with guile.

Once having settled upon what he considered the moral course, he could be utterly unscrupulous in its pursuit.

He considered politics the last sanctuary of "trimmers, buffoons, scoundrels, and horse-apple merchants." The ballot he cast for John Quincy Adams in the 1824 presidential election was his first and last. He knew the Declaration of Independence by heart and kept a dog-eared copy hanging in a wormwood frame above his bed. He collected books pertaining to battle tactics and military history, yet refused to serve in his nation's armed forces and did not carry weapons until the final four years of his life.

He radiated a cold-blooded quality remarked upon by everyone with whom he came into close contact. People noticed an inexplicable nip in the air when he was nearby. He gave the reptilian impression of being cool to the touch. He took his nightly baths in a horse trough heaped with chunk ice. He could hold the palm of his hand in a candle flame for nine seconds without flinching. He could wake a napping dog with a steady gaze and shoo a cat from a room with a sharp glance. He liked to catch hornets with his hands and pop them into his mouth like peanuts before spitting them out in midflight. By the end of his life his reputation was so seldseen that had it been revealed he chewed glass after meals, decapitated poisonous snakes with his teeth, kept a Bengal tiger on a leash, and could ignite a pile of kindling with the snap of a finger, few would have disbelieved it.

Many found him needlessly cruel. Others thought him the most coldhearted man they had ever met. Some were positive he was irredeemably mad. Yet he could cradle a sick lamb in his arms all night long, go without sleep for days while he nursed a feverish wife, dandle a colicky child on his knee and coo baby talk until it fell asleep. Not even his worst enemies doubted his nerve. They were wiser than they knew; none but God Himself gave him a moment's pause.

He considered himself an ultraradical abolitionist and a guerrilla commissioned privately by God to wage a holy war against the enslavement of the Negro race in America and he regretted no act of violence he ever committed in that cause, though he regretted one in particular that he did not.

"I am a zealot," he once said. "I want to be a zealot. I intend to remain a zealot." In that solitary regard he was a singular success, and had they not hung him by the neck before the fireworks began, he would have hoorayed the commencement of the Civil War and gleefully toasted the unspeakable butchery that followed as the retribution of a just and angry God.

anhedonia, *n.* 1. the inability to feel pleasure

It later became fashionable to dismiss him as insane.

Personally I don't believe it.

Personally I think he was anhedonic.

Or maybe the anhedonia is what drove him insane.

Or maybe not.

Maybe if you can't feel a thing in the first place, you don't know what it is you're missing, so you don't miss its not being there.

Or maybe you do.

Maybe you miss it terribly. Maybe you miss it with all the ache of a phantom limb.

I don't know.

What I do know is, he sure was one for the books.

Faith of Our Fathers
(Edited Transcripts)

To set the slaves afloat at once would, I really believe, be productive of much inconvenience and mischief. (**George Washington**)

As much as I deplore slavery, I see that prudence forbids its abolition. I deny that the general government ought to set them free. (**Patrick Henry**)

The bill for freeing the Negroes I hope will sleep for a time. We have cause enough of jealousy, discord, and division. (**John Adams**)

Their manumission is incompatible with the felicity of our country. (**Patrick Henry**)

I have all my life shuddered and still shudder at the consequences that may be drawn from immediate abolition. (**John Adams**)

If emancipation is left to force itself onward, human nature must shudder at the prospect. (**Thomas Jefferson**)

Under the Constitution the slaveowner is safe. It would be madness for the federal government to abolish slavery. No sane person would ever propose so irresponsible and calamitous a course to commit mayhem on his fellow citizens. (**James Madison**)

NAT

Had:
brass
balls,
big as
cotton
bolls.

Strapped them on,
and went

a-spreeing.

"Slavery contains the seeds of its own destruction," concluded John Brown, once he had studied the matter to his satisfaction. "Its continued existence results only from the exercise of brute force by the owner, coupled with the consent or submission of the slave. When the moment arrives that the owner is prevented from exercising brute force, *or* that the slave refuses to submit, the institution will crumble."

That moment arrived for Nat Turner at 2 A.M., August 22, 1831.

"I knew then," remarked John Brown later, "that the power of God had at last been loosed upon this sinful nation."

Nat Turner claimed that he acted as he did owing to visions and voices and heavenly signs.

He was mistaken.

Nat Turner acted as he did because he was a slave and his victims were slaveowners. Because he was oppressed and they were his oppressors. Because he was emasculated and they were his emasculators.

Nat Turner acted, because for all of his thirty-one years on this earth he had been what the South Carolina Supreme Court within months of his "insurrection" called: "One doomed in his own person and posterity to live without knowledge and without the capacity to make anything of his own, and to toil that another may reap the fruits."

For thirty-one years he had lived deprived of the right to:

marry
rear a family
own property
earn a living
learn a trade
receive an education
bear arms
use the courts
speak freely
worship
vote
travel
assemble
receive medical attention
receive or give gifts
leave a will
make a contract
know his African heritage
purchase his freedom or that of his descendants
ensure the inviolability of his physical person

For thirty-one years he had been nothing but:
property
chattel
merchandise
a personal belonging
a capital investment
a financial asset
an economic imperative
a piece of inventory
a commodity
man-meat
human dung
a thing

"Slavery is nothing else but the state of war continued between a conqueror and a captive," wrote John Locke, whom Nat Turner did not know from John Donne, but who we know inspired Thomas Jefferson's authorship of the Declaration of Independence, which we know contains the words "all men are created equal."

Nat Turner apparently felt so keenly Locke's "state of war" (if not Jefferson's state of equality) that he actually did what people do in wartime. He engaged in mortal combat. He killed the enemy.

In his case—after having first issued the order "Kill everything white!"—fifty-seven of the enemy: nine white men, fifteen white women, and thirty-three white children.

In his case, having first armed himself and his disciples with the adzes, axes, knives, and swords, pitchforks, pikes, and sickles of their victims.

In his case, in the middle of the night, while they slept, or more often, having first rousted them from their beds.

Forty hours of frenzy later, it was over. His sixty followers were apprehended to a man. Eight were murdered on the spot. Three were lynched. Forty-eight separate trials were conducted. Eighteen resulted in the death sentence. Twelve in permanent sale out of state.

In the four days following the "insurrection" (or "the niggra rebellion," as it was called down South), between one hundred and two hundred slaves living in Southampton County, Virginia—the number apparently was considered too inconsequential to document precisely—were indiscriminately killed.

A similar number were tortured.

Despite the $1,100 bounty on his head, Nat Turner eluded authorities for two months.

At his trial on charges of "making insurrection and plotting to take away the lives of divers free white persons," the flabbergasted judge appeared unable to conceive of what dark impulse possibly could have inspired him.

"For the life of me, I do not understand it boy," remarked the Honorable Jeremiah Cobb, Esq., before passing sentence. "I daresay I will go to my grave not understanding it. A bright boy like yourself. You can only have been led astray by some inexplicable fanaticism or mental derangement.

"Do you not find yourself mistaken now?"

And so this thirty-one-year-old slave whose African mother had in his infancy attempted to drown him like a puppy to prevent his growing up in bondage, this prematurely bald, knock-kneed, Bible-thumping desperado whom a Virginia official had the day before called "the most dangerous man in America," offered for the benefit of Judge Jeremiah Cobb a word or two of clarification.

"Was not Christ crucified?" answered Nat Turner.

In western Pennsylvania, John Brown, then tending to a wife tumbling rapidly into mental derangement herself, understood all too clearly what Jeremiah Cobb apparently understood not at all: that at high noon on November 11, 1831, even as Nat Turner thrashed between heaven and earth at the wrong end of a hempen rope fastened by a clove hitch to the limb of a pecan tree outside the Southampton County Courthouse, his executioner, Southampton County Deputy Sheriff Edward Butts, was delivering to Nat Turner's owner, twelve-year-old Putnam Moore, a drawstring coin purse containing $375.86, the sum awarded by the court in compensation for his having suffered "an egregious, if unavoidable deprivation of property."

That—the unleavened obscenity of that—was what John Brown understood that the judge, and those of the judge's ilk, did not.

That, and that so long as he, John Brown, drew breath, such a sin *never* could be allowed to go unpunished.

Southern trees bear a strange fruit,
blood on the leaves and blood at the root;
black body swinging in the southern breeze,
strange fruit hanging from the poplar trees.

Pastoral scene of the gallant South,
the bulging eyes and the twisted mouth;
scent of magnolia sweet and fresh,
and the sudden smell of burning flesh.

Here is the fruit for the crows to pluck,
for the rain to gather, for the wind to suck;
for the sun to rot, for a tree to drop,
here is a strange and bitter cup.

(Lewis Allan,
Strange Fruit)

I have not slept without anxiety in three months. Our nights are spent listening to noises.

    —a Virginia slaveowner, anonymous, in the wake of Nat Turner's execution (subsequent to which Nat's head was sawed off and impaled on a fence pole at the intersection of Barrow and Jerusalem Roads, known thereafter as "Blackhead Signpost," and his torso and nether parts delivered up to Dr. Hendley Graves for dissection, only to have souvenir coin purses fabricated from their flesh instead)

Never do to be too slack with niggras.

—a Virginia slavebreaker

They will love you the better for their whipping whether they deserve it or not. Besides, by this manly course you will show your spunk.

—*Maxims for Young Farmers and Overseers*

Now, when correction and chastisement is given you, you either deserve it or you do not, but whether you do or you do not, it is your duty, and God Almighty requires, that you bear it patiently.

Suppose you are quite innocent of what is laid to your charge and suffer wrongfully. Is it not possible that you have done some other bad which was never discovered and that Almighty God who saw you doing it would not let you escape without punishment?

And ought you not in such a case to give glory to Him and be thankful that He would rather punish you in this life than destroy your soul in the next?

—REV. WILLIAM MEADE, Bishop, Episcopal Church of Virginia, *A Sermon to the Slaves*

So de preacher is apreachin' 'bout the goodness in gittin' whupped, same as always, an' de slaves is sittin' dere sleepin' an' fannin' deyselves wid oak branches, when Uncle Silas git up in de front pew an' halt dat preacher so:

"Is us slaves gonna be free in heaven?"

De preacher he stop an' look at Uncle Silas like he wanna kill him 'cause no one 'spose to say nothin' 'ceptin' "Amen" whilst he preachin'.

"I say is God gonna free us slaves when we gits to heaven, or ain't He?"

Dat preacher pull out his kerchief an' wipe de sweat off his face and say, "Jesus says, 'Come unto me ye who are free from sin and I will give salvation.' "

"Gonna give us freedom 'long *wif* salvation?" Uncle Silas ask.

"The Lord gives out and the Lord takes away," say de preacher, "and he that is without sin will have life everlasting." And he go on ahead preachin' fast-like without payin' no mind to Uncle Silas.

But Uncle Silas, he don' sit down, but jus' stand dere for de res' of de service jus' a-gazin' an' a-gawkin' at dat dere preacher like he still waitin' on his answer.

An' when dat service done an' dat preacher long gone, Uncle Silas he still standin' dere waitin' 'til all de slaves left out de door, and den he turn 'round slow-like an' walk outta dat dere church and from dat day to dis, he never been back.

—inspired by a slave remembrance, anonymous

FAITH OF OUR FATHERS
(Edited Transcripts)

Slavery in this country I have seen hanging over it like a black cloud for half a century. I have been so horrified with this phenomenon that I constantly said in former times to the Southern gentlemen, "I cannot comprehend the object. I must leave it to you. I will vote for forcing no measure against your judgments." (**John Adams**)

When slaves who are happy and contented with their present masters are tampered with and seduced to leave them; when masters are taken unawares by these practices; when conduct of this kind begets discontent on one side and resentment on the other; and when a master loses his property for want of means to defend it; it introduces more evils than it can cure. (**George Washington**)

I shall frankly declare that I do not like even to think, much less to talk of slavery. (**George Washington**)

At the time of Nat Turner's insurrection, there were in the Commonwealth of Virginia three crimes for which a white person could be sentenced to death.

For a slave there were seventy-one.

However, with the market value of prime field hands hovering between $1,100 and $1,600 (this in an age when a day's wage seldom approached $1), and most others at $500 and up, the courts were exceedingly chary about meting out the death penalty in any but the most heinous cases.

Slaveowners therefore took it upon themselves to devise their own system of alternative sentencing or "corrections," which quickly became the cornerstone of the milieu of coercion, terror, and vigilantism in which all slaves daily moved.

BULLWHIP DAYS

THE WHIP was commonly a stout, flexible stalk of willow or beech about three and a half feet long, wrapped taut with a tapering rawhide plait attached with a soft but dry buckskin cracker about three-eighths of an inch wide and ten or twelve inches long.

Variations included:

A three-foot-long elastic strap of untanned oxhide one inch thick at the butt end tapering to a V at the striking end.

A leather strop eighteen inches long and two and a half inches wide attached to a foot-long helve.

A rope of nine braids each strung intermittently with knots, attached to a small wooden handle (also known as a cat-o'-nine-tails).

A long-handled wooden paddle studded with protruding metal bolts, screws, crockets, cleats, or spurs.

When applied to the flesh of the human back—the preferred number of lashes was thirty-nine as derived from Hebraic Law—the object was to slice open grooves and rip up divots in the skin (accompanied by the appropriate flying arabesque of flesh and blood) that weeks later appeared as a ridged mass of roughage, scar tissue running neck to waist, as if the skin of the back had been chopped up and left to heal in a carapace of weals, a vast cicatrix.

WHIPPING was fine as far as it went, but too often—in the particularly chronic, recalcitrant, or incorrigible cases—simple prudence dictated other, more innovative measures.

CURRYCOMBING (or **CATCLAWING**), for instance, was the practice of stripping the slave naked, tying it to a post, and scraping its backflesh raw with the comb's wire teeth or bristles (or the cat's severed claws) before giving it a vigorous rubdown with stalks of dry hay in advance of salting the wounds with brine, alcohol, turpentine, kerosene, coal oil, lye, or quicklime, or hot lard, wax, paraffin, or tar.

In **HOGSHEADING,** the slave was stripped naked and stuffed inside an empty barrel into which nails had been randomly driven on all sides before its being rolled downhill.

FLECKING was the practice of stripping the slave naked, tying it to a post, and employing red-hot tongs or pincers to tweeze bits of flesh from various body parts.

TOBACCO-ING was the practice of stripping the slave naked, tying its wrists and ankles to a spit, and rotating it slowly over a bed of burning tobacco leaves.

In **HOISTING,** the slave was stripped naked and its arms tied snugly behind its back before its being hoisted by the wrists off the ground, dislocating the shoulders.

In **COBBING,** the slave was stripped naked and the soles and heels of its feet bludgeoned with a metal spar or hardwood board.

THE STAKEOUT involved stripping the slave naked, spreadeagling it face down with with its hands and feet fastened to stakes in the ground, then whipping it before abandoning it overnight to the elements.

THE NIGGER BOX was a three-foot-square wooden cell roofed with tin into which the naked slave was stuffed after having been gagged with cotton batting and left to broil in the sun.

NIGGER DOGGING or SETTING THE DOGS was the practice of stripping the slave naked and chaining it in place inside a ring of "biting" dogs whose leashes were intermittently played out to allow them to draw blood.

THE PILLORY involved stripping the slave naked and locking its head to a wooden yoke to which its ears were nailed for a minimum of one hour.

THE IRONS were some arrangement of wrist cuffs or manacles, leg cuffs or fetters, neck collars or yokes, balls-and-chains or shackles, metal-studded face masks, and leashes, worn by the naked slave, often for weeks at a time.

MAIMINGS or MUTILATIONS included extracting healthy teeth with a pliers or digging them out with an awl; severing ears, noses, fingers, and toes with a dull or rusty knife; gouging out eyes with a spoon, spatula, or thumb.

COERCED SEX.

In those cases where the spirit if not the body remained unbroken, the slave was BRANDED with an *R*—for "runaway" or "rogue"—on its right cheek or in the center of its forehead, before being HOUGHED or HAMSTRUNG, a life-crippling procedure in which the main tendon of the thigh muscle behind the knee was severed.

Alternatives to hamstringing included AMPUTATION of feet, CASTRATION, and CLITORIDECTOMY.

It was THE SELL OFF, however, for which the slave reserved a distinct and abject horror: that a loved one should be sold to a different or distant master never to be seen or heard from again.

We do not know how many of the "corrections" Nat Turner may have undergone himself, though he likely witnessed firsthand or heard of the ongoing occurrence of most of them.

We do know this: that he was married to a slave girl named Cherry, that she bore him two children, and that sometime prior to his insurrection, all three were *sold off*.

THE SLAVEOWNER'S LAMENT

1. THE BIBLE CONDONES IT
In Leviticus 25:44–45, Ephesians 6:5, Colossians 3:22, and 1 Peter 2:18–20, where we read, "Slaves, be submissive to your masters with all respect, not only when they are kind and gentle, but even when they are *perverse*."

2. A ROBUST ECONOMY RELIES UPON IT
Without it, the cotton raised in the South—the same cotton that the North purchases to manufacture the textiles the sale of which creates most of the country's wealth—would be left to rot in the fields.

3. CHRISTIANITY PRESCRIBES IT
It bestows upon an ignorant, heathen people the comforts of Christian civilization, the benefits of Christian enlightenment, and the blessings of Christian salvation.

4. THEIR WELL-BEING DICTATES IT
It protects them from experiencing the asperities of a freedom they are ill-equipped to withstand.

5. OUR WELL-BEING DICTATES IT
It prevents the bloody revenge they would be certain to exact were they permitted to indulge the savagery that is their nature.

6. HISTORY AFFIRMS IT
It has been employed throughout recorded time in the building of most of the world's great civilizations.

7. BIOLOGY PREDICTS IT
That they so uniformly submit proves that they are by nature physically, intellectually, and temperamentally suited to it.

8. THE GREATER GOOD ENCOURAGES IT
It provides that the few will suffer that the many might prosper.

9. RACIAL SOLIDARITY IS BOLSTERED BY IT
It unites whites of otherwise diverse means and outlook in their common superiority over blacks.

10. PATRIOTISM IS FORTIFIED BY IT
It makes whites better appreciate by comparison the freedom afforded them by their government.

11. SOCIETY BENEFITS BY IT
It nurtures in the property owner the skills of command and authority and sharpens his sense of responsibility toward the less fortunate.

12. THE CONSTITUTION OF THE UNITED STATES ENDORSES IT
In: Article 1, section 2—counting a portion of the slave population in each state to assess taxes and apportion congressional representation.

Article 1, section 8—empowering Congress to aid the states in the suppression of slave insurrections.

Article 1, section 9—forbidding congressional interference in the international slave trade until 1808.

And article 4, section 2—providing for the "retrieval" and return of fugitive slaves to their owners.

---

*To forestall the Union's stillbirth—to write an end to the threatened walkout of the Southern Slavocracy at the Constitutional Convention—the framers assented to making slavery a private property right protected by the highest law of the land. Thus did they conceive an America born and bred to slavery. A home of the brave perhaps. Hardly a land of the free. As a result—**because the slaves were exclusively Negroes**—they midwifed a nation enfeebled by a racialism so ingrained, a "Negrophobia" so organic, that the ensuing two hundred years, far from effecting its demise, has witnessed only its metastasis.*

This pathology I believe to be God's curse on the nation's soul for having so long countenanced the sin of slavery, and while the lifting of that curse may alone be God's affair, collecting the wages of the sin I took to be mine.

*If God is just, as I know Him to be, there is reserved a special corner of hell for more than a few of our Constitutional Fathers, for theirs was the **original** sin.*

An Apologia for Mass Brutality: 325 Words

The institution of slavery is a principal cause of civilization.

It is as much the order of nature that men should enslave each other as that animals should prey upon each other.

The African slave trade has given the boon of civilization to millions who would otherwise never have enjoyed it.

It is true that the slave is driven to his labor by stripes. Such punishment would be degrading to a free man. It is not degrading to a slave.

Odium has been cast upon our legislation because it forbids education of slaves, but what injury is done them by this? A knowledge of reading, writing, and arithmetic is important to the free laborer, but of what use would they be to the slave? Would you benefit a horse or ox by giving them a cultivated understanding, or fine feelings?

The law has not provided for making the marriages of slaves indissoluble. It may be said then that the chastity of slave women is not protected by the law. It is true that the passions of the men of the superior caste are tempted by and find gratification in the easy chastity of the female slave. But she is not a less useful member of society thereby. Her offspring is not a burden, but an asset to her owner. It is provided for, brought up to usefulness, and its condition actually raised somewhat above that of its mother.

I am asked, how can an institution be tolerable by which a large class of society is cut off from improvement and knowledge, to whom blows are not degrading, theft no more than a fault, falsehood and the want of chastity almost venial, and in which a husband or parent looks with comparative indifference on that which to a freeman would be dishonorable and abhorrent?

I answer, why not, if it produce the greatest aggregate good? Sin and ignorance are evil only because they lead to misery.

—a South Carolina legislator

AN APOLOGIA FOR MASS BRUTALITY:
NINETY-EIGHT WORDS

Don't like it much, but wouldn't do no good to free 'em neither. They's monstrous lazy and they'd jus' hang around with nobody to take keer of 'em, not doin' nuthin' but jus' naturally lazin' 'round stealin' and pilferin'. No man could live, you see, whar they was. Not if they was free he couldn't.

'Sposin' you had a family of children. How would you like to have a niggra feelin' he's jus' as good as a white man?

What I mean to say is, how'd you like it to have a niggra steppin' up to your darter?

—an Alabama dirt farmer

An Apologia for Mass Brutality: Nineteen Words

Slavery is a great evil from which it is impossible to escape without the introduction of evil infinitely greater.

—President James Buchanan

An Apologia for Mass Brutality:
Enough Said

They's niggras.
—the South

I have heard you have abolitionists here. We have a few in Illinois as well, and the other day we shot one.

—ABRAHAM LINCOLN (before an audience in Worcester, Massachusetts)

This affair is destined to jolt the Yankee conscience like the shock of an earthquake.

—JOHN QUINCY ADAMS

ABOLITIONIST EDITOR
SLAIN BY MOB!

Illinois' Elijah Lovejoy
Killed in Pro-Slave Rampage!

Rioters remain at large.
No arrests imminent.

Graphic's correspondent
Reports from scene.

ALTON, ILL.—Elijah P. Lovejoy, Presbyterian clergyman and crusading editor of the *Alton Observer*, was gunned down in a hail of rifle fire here Wednesday evening defending his paper's printing press against armed rioters who later hurled it by torchlight into the Mississippi River.

Authorities have yet to bring charges in connection with the rampage wreaked by a mob estimated to have numbered "in the hundreds."

"We presently are discussing the advisability of launching an investigation into the matter," said a law enforcement spokesman. "Our desire is to see justice done, but justice in a case like this may well rest in the eye of the beholder, and at the moment we are finding eyewitnesses extraordinarily hard to come by."

Lovejoy, 35, had been editor of the *Observer* —the state's foremost anti-slavery publication —for little more than a year. He had recently established the Illinois headquarters of the American Anti-slavery Society here.

Yesterday's incident marked the fourth time in as many months that he had been the target of mob violence. On each of those occasions the paper's printing press had been destroyed. On at least two subsequent occasions his home was ransacked and he and his wife threatened by armed intruders.

No arrests have been made in connection with any of those incidents.

Although he had written and spoken extensively in support of non-violence, Lovejoy, who recently had called for the "summary execution of all mobites," purportedly was seen discharging a pistol at a rioter trying to set fire to the building containing the printing press when he was slain.

Yesterday's incident comes on the heels of a speech delivered by Lovejoy at a public rally in Alton four days earlier.

"You may hang me, you may burn me at the stake, you may tar and feather me and throw me into the Mississippi, as you so often have threatened," Lovejoy reportedly declared, "but you cannot persuade me to deny my Master by forsaking His righteous cause.

"God has determined that I maintain my

ground here, and so I will. Why should I flee? Is this not a free state? Why should I be silent? Is it not within the law to make free speech?

"No, the contest has commenced here, and here let it end. Before God, before you all, I pledge myself to continue it—if need be, to my death.

"If I fall, my grave shall be in Alton."

The state's largest city is a riverport whose economy is largely dependent on downriver trade with its southern neighbors. Several of its civic leaders recently had voiced concern that Lovejoy's "inflammatory rhetoric" was fueling an image of the town as an "abolitionist hotbed" that could prompt its pro-slave trading partners to boycott its business.

The son of a Presbyterian minister and a graduate of Princeton Theological Seminary, Lovejoy was a native of Maine. Before founding the *Observer* he had edited newspapers in St. Louis, Mo., where two years ago his office was destroyed by a mob protesting his coverage of the lynching and immolation of a Negro man.

According to his wife, Celia, it was that affair which spurred their move to Alton, 25 miles upriver, while strengthening her husband's resolve never again to yield in the face of gang violence.

"I wanted to leave and start up again somewhere else," sobbed the grieving widow yesterday. "I begged him that I couldn't stand it anymore. But Elijah said he was fighting the Lord's fight, and if he fell martryed in battle it was for a purpose Our Heavenly Father must foresee."

In his November 3rd speech Lovejoy had declared: "There is no escaping the mob. I realize now that though the names and faces may change from town to town and state to state, the mob is everywhere, and that it is bound to hound and harry and persecute me, and those who think like me, wherever we may go."

—*New York Graphic*
November 8, 1837

At first the news so unnerves him that when the words at last splinter forth, he does not recognize them as his own.

"This earth—

no place—

fit—

call home."

They strike him as the splayed and fragmentary utterances of a stroke victim.

Or the played-out gasp of a dying man.

Suddenly the world, at best never an overly hospitable or even-keeled place (in his estimation), seems to have wrenched free of its axis completely and gone wholesaling straight to hell.

"Sweet—

Jesus!"

He senses himself in imminent danger of cartwheeling off the rim of the universe. He senses history tipping over.

"Now—

murdering—

US!"

He feels fatigued and oddly fractured, and even more ridiculous. Only months before, he had written his brother Frederick:

Dear Brother,

For years I have been trying to devise a way to do something practical for our poor fellow men who are held in bondage & after much thought have decided to get a kind of model school a-going here for blacks. If the young blacks of our country could become enlighten'd it would surely operate on slavery as gunpowder confin'd in rock. Educate the slave & the slaveholder must be driven to set about

72

the work of emancipation immediately or suffer himself to "reap the whirlwind."
I have pray'd much o'er the matter & believe it to be the course Our Heavenly
Father intends that I should follow.

Remembering these words, the rims of his ears redden as they habitually do when he is overcome with self-disgust.

A man lies dead as scrap iron having sacrificed himself willingly on the altar of the Lord, and *he* dreams of playing schoolmarm to a passel of ignorant black'uns.

He feels himself pathetic and pitiable in the eyes of God. He feels himself . . . superfluous. It is an emotion that frightens him like no other because he knows it is the one—the only one—capable of making him despair.

That evening, after the four babes, Sarah, Watson, Salmon, and Charles, have been put down, he rallies the rest of the family around the hearthfire in the kitchen and each a chair at the table.

(And none of the six a clue what's got into him *this* time.)

On the tabletop before each, a Bible lies flopped open to a line of Scripture bracketed hysterically in ochre ink.

"Mother," he says to Mary, stationed as always at the foot end of the table, "you will kindly begin."

When she hesitates, appearing at a loss, he adds patiently, "Just there. You'll see 'tis marked."

Looking imploringly from her husband to the page, from the page to her husband, he responds only by closing his eyes, bowing his head, and lacing his fingers in prayer.

"But . . . but . . . John," she stammers, sheepishly clearing her throat, "you know well I cannot read it. I han't the . . ."

"Ezekiel, chapter 21, verse 3!" he brimstones. "Thus saith the Lord: Behold, I am against you and will draw forth my sword out of its sheath." His eyes remain closed.

"Now—John Junior!"

"And will cut off from you both righteous and wicked," reads the boy tremulously.

"Ruth!"

"Because I will cut off from you both righteous and wicked."

"Jason!"

"Therefore my sword shall go out of its sheath against all flesh from south to north."

"Owen!"

"And all flesh shall know that I, the Lord, have drawn my sword out of its sheath."

"Frederick!"

"It shall not be sheathed again."

The fire hawks and splutters.

The silence hangs and hefts.

The eyes grow wide with waiting.

"It shall not be sheathed again," he fulminates at length, swacking his Bible shut with such ferocity that the mortified family starts in its seats as if jolted concurrently by the selfsame current. "His mighty sword from this day forward shall *not* be sheathed again."

Only now does he open his eyes before fishing himself to his feet, raising his right hand well above his head, and placing his left palm atop the brutalized Bible.

"I, John Brown," he says bloodlessly, "do hereby solemnly pledge my determination, in secrecy before God and my family, to dedicate my life henceforth to do all in my power to carry forth the eternal war on slavery—the mother of all abominations and the sum of all villainies—neither by word nor by deed, but by force of arms alone, certain in the knowledge that the cost of liberty is less than the price of repression, and that without the shedding of blood there can be no remission of sin.

"This I swear in the name of my Father in heaven, who is the Father of the slave, and in the name of Christ, who is my Master, and who is the Master of the slave, and in the name of the Holy Spirit, which gives me strength and comfort, and which gives strength and comfort to the slave. So help me God."

Clasping both hands behind his back, he proceeds methodically left to right around the table, halting in succession behind each chair where he stoops forward at the waist to whisper briefly in the ear of its occupant.

What he whispers is a verse of Scripture—Luke 11:23—that he

has employed on countless occasions in the past, but never quite so artfully (he is calculating) as at this moment.

It goes, "He who is not with me is against me."

After resuming his place at the head of the table, he surveys the table much in the manner of a king his castle before exclaiming with manufactured brightness, "Now, which of my dear family will pledge alongside its loving father?

"And which"—he feels it happening, cannot help himself even so, something about moments like these—"will dare to"—his upper lip has begun to curl, proceeds to curl, is curled—"go against him?"

His sneer fans ear to ear.

How many Negroes, slave or free, did you know at that time?

At the time of the Lovejoy affair? On a personal basis I knew comparatively few.

How many, say on a last name basis, give or take?

I would not venture a number. As many as I was able to help ferry north on the Underground. A dozen. Maybe more.

And on a more permanent, intimate footing, say in the neighborhood where you then resided? In Franklin or in Hudson, Ohio? In the whole of the Western Reserve?

None that I recall specifically. Not then.

Had you, at that time, ever stepped foot on so-called slave soil? Had you ever visited the South?

I had not.

Not so much as overnight?

In the spring of 1840 I was hired by Oberlin College to survey two thousand acres of Virginia land donated to it by the New York abolitionist Gerrit Smith. I then spent several weeks of overnights. That was the first I had been south of the Mason-Dixon.

Is it safe to say, then, that you had never spoken with, made the acquaintance of, or however briefly shared the company of a single slaveholder? Up to that time.

Providentially, it is.

I am curious. How is it that you became interested in the so-called Negro problem?

There is no Negro problem, so-called or otherwise. The problem is with those who would enslave him. If you mean to ask how I came to abolitionism, that is a more complicated matter. I imagine part of it was owing to my being reared to it. My father was outspoken on the subject, and I can recall as a boy his telling me the story of how when he was a small child one of his neighbors owned a slave from Guinea, and how this young slave, whose name was Sam, used to carry my father on his back and sing him the songs of his native land while he worked the fields, and how—these are his words—"I fell in love with him." I recall too his instruction to me as I was growing up: "We are abolitionist. We are not loved by many. You need make no confession for being one." I never have.

Did you know Elijah Lovejoy?

I knew of him. I did not know him personally.

Had you ever visited or passed through Alton, Illinois?

I had never visited Illinois. I had occasion to do so later, during my Kanzas excursions.

The Lovejoy killing occurred November 7, 1837. How long after that date did you secretly pledge to use armed force to end slavery?

I couldn't say exactly. As long as it took for the news of the murder to reach my ears in Franklin.

The instant you became aware of the Lovejoy killing, in that instant you made your pledge?

More or less. At first I was too dumbstruck. It was later that day. Late that evening actually.

So, having never known a slave, having never met a slaveholder, having never set foot on slave soil much less a slave plantation, within hours of your hearing about the killing of a white man you had never met, in a distant place you had never visited, you swore a sacred oath to commit the rest of your life to the violent overthrow of Negro slavery. Do I have it about right?

More or less. I would take exception only to your use of the word white.

Pardon?

You said "white" man, the killing of a "white" man. I should have reacted no differently had the color of Lovejoy's skin been black. Skin color, as always, was irrelevant.

The fact that Lovejoy was white, and that you likewise are white, bore not atall on your decision to make your vow of violence?

It was utterly beside the point.

Which was?

Why, that when an innocent man, a man of God, a man who preaches non-violence, is murdered in cold blood in a free state for no reason other than his possessing the temerity to inform the public of the truth about slavery, then non-violence is become but a philosopher's conceit.

You say the truth about slavery. You mean *your* truth, don't you?

If you like. And [the eyes roll heavenward] *God's.*

So you presume the ability to read God's mind?

I presume the ability to read Scripture.

And in this instance—and it might be better if you could refrain from quoting passages verbatim—when you read Scripture, it told you what, exactly?

Exactly? It told me that in the Old Testament alone there are six hundred passages that speak explicitly of individuals or nations attacking, destroying, or killing others. It told me that another one thousand passages refer to God's bloody vengeance, his punishments by death and destruction, and his threats of annihilation. It told me that in yet another one hundred passages God expressly gives the command to kill a person or persons. It told me that no other human activity—be it sex, sport, commerce, politics, religion, or family—is mentioned as often as is violence. It also told me [the voice lowers] *that well over seventy passages in the Old Testament pertain specifically to self-inflicted violence.*

Self-inflicted violence?

Self-mortification. [A certain glittering enters his eyes.] *Flagellation.*

Yes, well, I'm sure. But even if your figures are correct—and I confess that I lack the scholarship to refute them—you do little but quantify.

You asked that I refrain from quoting passages verbatim.

[An exasperated sigh and a concessionary wave of the hand.]

A single verse then, and let it suffice for the rest. Leviticus, chapter 19, verse 16. "Thou shalt not stand idly by the blood of thy neighbor; I am the Lord."

And you resolved not to stand idly by the blood of Elijah Lovejoy.

I did not resolve. I was commanded.

Commanded? But how commanded? By whom?

From on high. By the Lord Jehovah.

God spoke to you? He personally ordered you to avenge Lovejoy's killing?

*You ask two separate questions. To the first I answer, God speaks to all who would hear Him. To the second, clearly He did not order me personally to avenge Lovejoy's killing. He ordered me to ascend the stair, to take the next step, to raise the stakes, to up the ante, to go **farther**. He ordered me to take up arms.*

And what were your intentions regarding the form this armed conflict would take?

I could not say. In those days I had no definite plan. My intentions were not specific. I had yet to think it through to that extent. I imagine I was content for the moment to let the course of events dictate my course of action.

A course of action composed of *inaction*?

I'm sorry. I'm afraid I don't . . .

The question is why, once having pledged your life to—I quote your own words here—"henceforth do all in my power to carry forth the eternal war on slavery by force of arms alone"—why, once having made a vow of such apparent urgency, you proceeded to do exactly (the voice rises) nothing?

Ah, yes. Well. That was a particularly difficult period for me on certain other fronts respecting certain other concerns. Certain events beyond my control—the president's vendetta against the federal bank, the government's introduction of the Specie Circular, the Grand Panic of 1837, the depression in England, the unbearable tightening of credit—certain, uh, evils conspired at that time that I hadn't anticipated, and were unavoidable, and couldn't be dodged, and that looking back I wrongly judged to be more, well, pressing. It was an error of judgment on my part. I was then still overlymuch in the ways of earthly vanity and worldly comfort.

Could you be more specific? Or at least less vague?

[A conspicuous clearing of the throat.] *I was going bankrupt. I **went*** *bankrupt. All my investments, my business concerns, my land holdings—I had speculated quite heavily in real estate, once held title to four farms and sundry industrial lots—my very home and personal possessions, everything I had worked for and built up over twenty-five years lay under the hammer.*

I see. And so the war on slavery was put on the backburner as it were, while you attended to more, shall we say, mundane matters.

God helps those who help themselves. I had a wife and eleven children to feed.

Of course. One final question. Do you believe that the Negro is fully the equal of the white man?

Save for the apparent differences in outward appearance, I do. In heart, in mind, in soul and spirit, without condition, without qualification, without exception, emphatically yes.

Would you agree that, so far as the white people in this country are concerned, North and South alike, you are in this opinion—this apparent "color blindness"—distinctly a minority of one?

I would agree that one with God is always a majority.

Are you ashamed, sir, of being white?

Did not the Lord make me in His image? How then could I be ashamed? No, I am ashamed of those of my race who would enslave those who are not. Such as they are beyond the pale of humanity. They are not fit to live. They have forfeited the right.

Says you.

Says Jehovah God. And yes, says John Brown.

FAITH OF OUR FATHERS
(Edited Transcripts)

We hold these truths to be self-evident, that all men are created equal. (**Thomas Jefferson**)

I advance it as a suspicion that the blacks are inferior to the whites in the endowments both of body and mind. (**Thomas Jefferson**)

They are as far inferior to the rest of mankind as the mule is to the horse, and as made to carry burdens. (**Thomas Jefferson**)

Their inferiority is not the effect of their condition, but is produced by nature. (**Thomas Jefferson**)

Prejudices which proceed principally from the difference in colour must be considered as permanent and insuperable. (**James Madison**)

The two races equally free cannot live in the same government. Nature, habit, opinion have drawn indelible lines of distinction between them. (**Thomas Jefferson**)

The amalgamation of whites with blacks produces a degradation to which no lover of his country, no lover of excellence in the human character, can innocently consent. (**Thomas Jefferson**)

DAUGHTER

Ruth Brown

When I was a little girl, Father would sometimes perch me on his knee and tell me the stories of his childhood.

He told me about how he and his family had wagoneered out from Connecticut to Ohio when he was five, and how the woods was then teeming with Indians and rattlers, and how he befriended an Indian boy from the Delaway tribe who gave him a yellow marble which was the first he'd ever seen, and how he prized it for a charm, but then lost it through a hole in his breeches and cried for months after.

And how once he nabbed a baby squirrel, but tore off its tail and got bit, but still managed to hold on though his hand bled right terrible, and in time tamed him so's to eat from his hand, and named him Bobtail, only to lose him to one of the hunting dogs his father kept.

And how his father favored him then with a little ewe lamb which doted on him until it was two-thirds the way grown when it fell sick of a winter's night, and though he put it in warm water, and rubbed it, and wrapped it in a warm blanket, and held it in his lap, and fed it warm milk from a teaspoon all through the wee hours, it died the next morning.

Though most of his stories saddened me—he didn't seem to have happy ones or ones about friends or schoolmates or neighbors, about *people*—I loved hearing them in the way that all children love hearing about how their parents were once as young and wonder-struck as themselves.

But as I grew older, he stopped telling me those stories and started in with his abolition talk. That's when I first heard the name Elijah Lovejoy and began to understand how much Father hated slavery.

Of course I grew to hate slavery too, we all did. But Father's hatred was violent and *personal* in a way that ours—even John Junior's—never was, for as much as he hated slavery, he seemed to hate the slave*owners* more. His talk upon the subject had about it such a quality of vindictiveness that I would try to slip away whenever he started up, for I could scarcely bear to watch as his eyes went to agate and his jaw set in crag ice, or to listen while his voice volleyed the words forth like shellbursts.

At moments like those he became another person. Not my father at all, the one of marbles and squirrels and ewe lambs, but some stranger fleeing his past, blinded by hate, utterly beyond the reach of a human touch or voice or kindness.

The sort of man, I had no difficulty believing, who was capable of absolutely anything.

Only once, once only did I dare ask him about it.

"Daddy," I began uncharacteristically, for I seldom called him that, though he never seemed put out when I took the liberty, "what is it that sorrows you? What do you want to do?"

I expected either to be shooed away or have the Bible spouted at me, for rare were the times when he would reply to a question such as that without citing the authority of his Scriptures. So I was taken aback when he answered, unblinking and stern-visaged as ever, but without the least hint of rancor, "Daughter Ruth, I want what any decent, God-fearing man wants. I want to see accorded to our fellow men the respect and consideration intended them by their Creator. I want to purge this land of slavery.

"I so intend, and so will do."

And then he paused and drew me so near, our cheeks nigh well grazed.

"Ruthie," he all but whispered, a rough tenderness glittering his eyes, "it is what men do to each other that sorrows me. 'Tis this sinful world that they would happily call their home."

It was only at that moment that I finally, fully understood. It is said that each of us has our own cross to bear. But Father had taken the suffering of the whole world for his own.

And it was slowly driving him mad.

September 28, 1842
United States Bankruptcy Court
Akron, Ohio
Presiding Judge Geo. B. De Peyster, federal assignee for settlement
of the estate of John Brown

Possessions granted:
  10 dining plates
  1 set (10 ea.) cups and saucers
  1 set (10) teaspoons
  1 pepper mill
  1 cider barrel
  1 cast-iron washtub
  1 sadiron

Provisions granted:
  1 bushel dried crab apples
  20 bushels corn
  15 gallons cider vinegar
  1 bushel snap beans
  150 pounds salt pork

Tools and implements granted:
  1 mattock
  1 maul

1 adz
1 peg awl
1 auger
1 gimlet
1 hand rasp
2 claw hatchets
2 beaming knives
2 roping knives
1 draw knife
1 harrow
1 ploughshare
1 cradle scythe
1 jack plane
1 log chain
1 cant hook
1 frow
1 plumb bob
1 trestle frame
1 grindstone
1 sheep snips

Other articles and necessaries granted:
2 mares
2 hogs (shoats)
19 hens
7 sheep (pledged to H. Oviatt)
2 cows (one Devon, one Holstein)
1 dray
4 cords bark
1 ton hay

Miscellaneous granted:
11 Bibles and Testaments
1 book *(The Beauties of the Bible)*
1 leather whip (wood helve)

At this time:

Could not afford postage to mail a letter.
Could not afford leather for shoes.
Children left school to work for whatever pittance.
Wife took in other folks' laundry.
Survived on lard and suet sandwiches.
Killed dogs to tide them over. (Mary boiled them up with
chives and carrot tops. Reminded him some of rock hen.
Wouldn't touch cat.)
Wrote to Frederick:

*Inst'd of adhering to the doctrine of pay as you go, I believed nothing
could be done w/o capital, that a poor man must use his credit to
borrow. This pernicious notion was the shoal on which I foundered.
In consequence, my life now is that of a toad kept under a harrow,
& lately I must confess to being so wrought with the desire to die
that my imagination follows those of my family who have gone to
their reward, & I would almost rejoice to be permitted to make them
a personal & lasting visit.*

*Still, notw'standing that God has seen fit to tax me most sore,
before Him I bow my head in submission & hold my peace in the
faith that tomor'w may bring a brighter dawn. Indeed, my growing
conviction is to promote **my** happiness by doing what I can to render
that of **others** more so.*

*New watchwords: Remember them that are in bonds as bound
with them.*

*P.S. Dear Fred'k—Never forget—Buy thee what is unnecessary
and ere long thou wilt have to sell what is.*

Without the money to post it, stowed the letter 'neath some
socks begging darning at the bottom of a drawer, slipping
his mind 'til now.

SECOND WIFE

Mary Day Brown

He just couldn't fathom it after all we'd gone through, going under the hammer and all, that the Lord'd do us that way again.

Reckon it just goes to show how when a soul's brought so low he can't feature worse, that's when he's drug all the lower.

You never seen a man so chopfallen as on the day he reeled out of that courtroom. And who to blame him? Forty-two years old and all come a cropper. His life a shipwreck. His good name tarred. Obliged to go a-begging hat in the hand to his father. A failure to all he knew and knew him.

Forty-two years old and still a-waiting on his rightful start in life.

Not that he blamed *himself,* you understand. He *never* done that. It was always the politicians or the banks or Andy Jackson or the lawyers. All the same, you best believe it knocked him down a peg or two.

And then when the pestilence come so soon afterwards and carried off those poor young'uns all at a fell swoop, well, that like to have knocked him to his knees.

Didn't, of course. Being John Brown, weren't near that much bend in him.

Charles Brown
September 11
Age six
(Cool-headed Chas, Father's favorite)

Austin Brown
September 21
Age one
(Baby Auts)

Peter Brown
September 22
Age three
(Petey-bird)

Sarah Brown
September 23
Age nine
(Sweet, sweet Sarah, sweet on Pa)

He built the coffin's belly wide,
He laid them in it side by side.

He nailed the lid
as mother cried,

Then buried them snug.

And turned aside.

To John Brown, Jr.

Dear Son:

God has seen fit to pay us a visit since last you saw us, and four of our number now sleep in the dust.

Dust to dust. Ashes to ashes.

Charles, Sarah, Peter, and little Austin now slumber together in a single grave.

(We felt toward each a mite partial.)

*Once more we smart under the **whip** of our Heavenly Father.*

This has been a bitter cup and we have drunk the dregs.

The Lord chastises us often and sore. I expect nothing but to endure hardness.

Blessed be His name forever. He does right. Thanks be unto Him. He reigneth forever and ever. Though He slay me, yet I cleave unto Him. His will be done.

Your mother mourns copiously. I feel the loss but very little. I am numbed and dead becalmed.

Why? Did I not love my children?

Nothing is ever given that in time is not likewise taken away. Nothing lasts but faith.

Can it work miracles?

Because my attachments to this world have been so strong, He cuts me loose one cord at a time, snatching from my hands all that He has placed there.

Son, it is a great mistake to think more of this world than of the next.

Life is a bloody perch, not a crystal stair. The well-paved order of existence is a pernicious fiction.

Life is a stormy sea o'er whose waters I have sailed for almost half a century.
God only knows how it all will end.
Black blackened waters.
Rising risen waters.
Praise Jehovah Lord.

P.S. [appended weeks afterward, having in the meantime mis-placed the foregoing] *I feel quite unconscious of any feeling of greediness, or of a desire to become rich. Getting a little money and property together is really a mean mark to be firing at throughout life. Wearing robes of splendor in **this** world is absolute vanity. My motive for exerting myself is to benefit my fellow man, not to gain more for myself.*

I want to reach Higher than this world.

*I often feel considerable regret that my manner is not more affectionate around those I really love. But I want **your** face to shine, though my own be black as bark. Had I a proper sense of my habitual neglect of you, and the rest of my family, and their Eternal interests, I should positively go crazy.*

Amelia Brown
October 30, 1846
Age one
(His darling "Kitty-cat")

He receives word while away on business in Springfield, Massachusetts, of the death of his youngest daughter in Akron, three weeks before.

His mind sprockets back to the day that he departed: Sitting his big-assed roan, delving into his surtout to fish out the little calico kitten—this gesture so unlike him—his daughter's eyes beaming big as all outdoors as he fetches it out, she hoisting herself up in her mother's arms flapping her hands like bird's wings squealing "Kitty! Kitty!" as he bends to gentle the animal into her outstretched arms before riding off down the rutty lane, and she naturally too taken with her first kitty-cat to trouble herself to coo or wave or blow kisses to the likes of such as him.

And as he'd clopped off he'd caught himself smiling, because unknowingly the child had touched a part of him that hadn't been touched in so long, he'd all but given it up for lost.

"Leave it to Amelia," he'd thought to himself then. "Leave it to my little Kitty-cat."

The laundry vat brim-full with water and lye had only just been brought to a rolling boil when Amelia, catching sight of her kitten swiping dust motes in the sun-

beams splashed upon the nearby hearth, had wrenched free of her sister Ruth's grasp and plunged arms outstretched headfirst into the scalding washboiler, submerging fully.

His bellow of pain and outrage stuns the vestibule of the boardinghouse where he has taken rooms. He feels himself stepping through bottom. He feels himself trepanned to his knees.

Why Amelia? Why his *children*? He has never asked why before, but he is asking now.

Oh God, when does it stop? Where does it end? When they are taken from me all, every one? After I have been struck down myself?

He demands to know. Then immediately recoils at his presumption. It is not for him to know. Knowing belongs to the Lord alone. It is for him only to forbear.

"Forgive me, Lord," he begins to apologize, only to discover that this time it is not in him.

Unhorsed by grief, the God-shout fills his mouth as like Cain he wails, "My punishments are more than I can bear!"

The establishment's proprietor rushes to his side thinking to offer him a brandy, but he is John Brown, and even now he waves the liquor off.

He is John Brown, and all he can think to say is, "If you wish to be of some use sir, you will go straightaway and fetch me a Bible."

The family lives in Springfield now, luxuriating as he describes it, in "the most comfortable arrangement of our worldly concerns that we have ever had."

For this he can thank—as he does daily in his prayers—God and Colonel Simon Perkins, a wealthy sheep rancher from Akron, Ohio, who, infatuated with his moral zeal no less than his technical wizardry as a shepherd, has taken him on as partner in his wool-raising business.

At the offices of Perkins & Brown, he and John Jr., now twenty-six, work twelve hour days, six days a week, offloading, warehousing, sorting, grading, pricing, and selling wool to the textile industry in behalf of a consortium of woolgrowers from eight states. (Hard work has never been the issue with him. Even at his age he can work as hard as any and harder than most. The issue is rather what he has to show for it. That the slaveowner should prosper by sin while he lives empaupered in the Lord has always been a torment to him.)

They hire as their warehouse porter a well-spoken, fugitive slave from Maryland named Thomas Thomas. Not yet a full-fledged "conductor," Thomas is active on Springfield's underground railroad lying on the Connecticut Valley Line running northward through Vermont and New Hampshire into Canada. He is also an intimate of another well-spoken fugitive slave from Maryland just then concluding a lecture tour of New England. ("His stirring oratory depicting his heart-rending personal experience living beneath the lash of the most monstrous and peculiar institution of our age cannot fail to touch the conscience and fire the soul of every God-fearing citizen of our fair Republic," reads the handbill.)

John Brown takes it into his head to invite the orator into his home.

"Y'r cause is no less my own than it is that of our Our Lord," he writes him. "Let us now be about His work, you & I. I have it in mind soon to commence some *action*. I speak confidentially, for it is with me as it was with the Psalmist: 'More in number than the hairs of my head are those who hate me w/o cause—Mighty are those who would destroy me, those who attack me with their lies.' "

This invitation he entrusts to Thomas Thomas before lending him his horse and Godspeeding him eastward.

Last word has Frederick Douglass about to depart Boston for his home in Rochester, New York.

Frederick Augustus Washington Bailey Douglass arrives by phaeton at 31 Franklin Street, an unpainted frame house of frayed clapboard and ragged shingle situated on a squalid back alley tucked deep in the belly of a low-rent neighborhood of wheelwrights, smithies, and day laborers.

Even before he alights he is thinking to himself that he must have mistaken the address, for the sagging, yardless structure before him more closely resembles a dog kennel than the home of the man represented to him by Thomas Thomas as "a prosperous and highly regarded wool merchant."

"It was apparent to me that he must be living far and away beneath his means," Douglass comments later, "for he lived in a state of such perfect destitution that it clearly was of his deliberate choosing, as if by making some ostentatious display of monkish austerity—of showy humility, as it were—he might catch the approving eye of the Almighty.

"Which is to say, his *notion* of the Almighty."

Douglass, too self-engrossed ever to concern himself with more than first impressions, is wrong as usual. Their relationship will last fully a dozen years, and about John Brown he will remain until the end utterly clueless. Brown lives shabbily not because he wishes to impress God—he has other, more flamboyant ways of doing that—but because he is husbanding what he might to bankroll what lately he has taken to calling "the Enterprise." (Not that Brown comprehends Douglass appreciably better; from the outset each will sadly misjudge the nature of the other's character.)

The interior of the home, as Douglass discovers directly, is drearier still. The walls are unpainted and bereft of adornment, the floors are rough-hewn and raw, the windows want drapes or curtains, and the few sticks of unupholstered furniture are artlessly constructed of unplaned jack pine.

The house smells overpoweringly of camphor, lye, quicklime, naptha, and borax. (Which given the alternative is just as well.)

Later, after a meal of mutton stew—heavy on the stew, light on the mutton—Douglass fobs his timepiece from the pocket of his step-collared brocaded weskit as Mary and the children clear the table in advance of attacking the dishes.

It is just past 8 P.M.

He is the most famous Negro in America (Douglass would argue the most famous in the world and could offer a credible case, save that as the illegitimate child of a black woman sired by a white rapist, he is more precisely mulatto, a shade of difference that in 1847 amounts admittedly to no difference at all), and yet as they talk he senses himself at risk of being "mastered."

"He was unquestionably the master of his house," he later writes of John Brown on that November evening, "and of all those who entered there, and I knew that he should become my own were I to stay much longer."

Mastered.

Even Douglass. (*Especially* Douglass. But that is another story.)

They face each other across the kitchen table. No satin-lapeled smoking jackets. No porcelain cups of demitasse. No inlaid silver serving tray heaped with canapés. No crystal snifters ambered with cognac. No filigreed dispensers of snuff or twenty-five-cent panatelas. No winking, elbow-to-the-ribs, off-color references to the weaker sex. Straight talk, served straight up.

The first words spoken by either of them are, "Mr. Douglass, I mean to emancipate your race."

To which Douglass, brought up understandably short, decides on the spur of the moment not to quip:

"And I intend to sprout fins and swim each of the Seven Seas."

Instead, as he writes later, "Hating slavery as I did, I was ready to welcome *any* new mode of attack upon it."

Stroking his chin pensively, he says (in all gravity), "Hmmmmmmnnnnnn. How?"

The reply to his question is characteristic of the man proferring it —sotto voce and behind-the-hand—and what with the clink of glasses and clatter of dishes issuing from the opposite end of the room, Douglass cannot for the life of him get a fix on what he is being told.

"The . . . what?" He shifts uncomfortably in his chair. "I couldn't . . . it sounded like 'The summer rain passed this way.' What is it, some sort of secret code or password or something?"

John Brown shakes his head, glances furtively right to left around the room, hunches forward across the table, and says cryptically, "The Subterranean Passageway."

It means as little to Douglass as it seems to mean everything to John Brown.

Douglass gives a mental shrug: white folks.

"Ah," says Douglass, nodding his head knowingly. "The Subterranean Passageway."

He hopes it is enough to humor him. He hopes this strange, secretive man, whose antique presence inspires in him at once such confidence and such dread, will condescend to explain himself, to trust him enough to reveal whatever dark stratagem lies back of his words. One means, the Subterranean Passageway. Could anything sound more sinister?

"Indeed the Subterranean Passageway," repeats Brown. "The *Grand Stampede* down the Subterranean Passageway."

"Aha," offers Douglass, feeling increasingly foolish. "The Grand Stampede."

"What you need to understand about me, Mr. Douglass," says Brown, abruptly switching horses, "is that I am at heart a business-man. Supply and demand, profit and loss, assets and liabilities, dol-lars and cents. These are my stock in trade. And it is with these that I intend to emancipate your people.

"The issue here is one of risk and investment. How to render the

100

slaveowner's investment so fraught with risk that not only will he be loathe to invest further, but will actively seek to divest himself of that particular species of property. In other words, how to so meddle with slavery as to make it unprofitable, or lacking that, more trouble to maintain than to abandon.

"It is my experience that a man will avoid laying out good money for a horse if he knows for a certainty that that horse will bolt the moment he turns his back—particularly where that horse costs him some $1,500 up front.

"You see my approach."

Douglass suspects that he may have caught a glimmer, and in truth is disappointed. From this particular man he had expected something, well, *else*.

"But we have the Underground," he protests.

"The Underground is all well and good, sir. Some $200,000-worth escaped this year alone. I am as aware of the figures as yourself. But those are fled at random and of their own volition one, two, half a dozen at a time. It pinches, no doubt, but it does not bite. Much less"—he pantomimes a man wringing out a dishrag—"throttle."

"No sir, what I have in mind is an Enterprise that is a tad more, how should I put it?"—Douglass detects a glint enter his eye, or perhaps he only imagines it; no matter—"dynamic. A touch more *reckless.*"

Douglass, far from a reckless man himself, feels for a moment oddly elated.

"Here then." Producing from the breast pocket of his coat what appears a tangle of wadded paper, he uncrumples it with neither flounce nor flourish across the tabletop where it lies in several impossibly tattered pieces. The more westerly of these—those comprising everything from the Mississippi River to the Pacific Ocean—he sweeps off the table onto the floor like so many offending bread crumbs.

"Here is what I propose." Prompted by a coffee-stir of Brown's forefinger, Douglass scooches his chair with an intolerable scraping to the opposite side of the table until the two men are sitting at such close quarters that their shoulders—Douglass's as broad as an easel, Brown's as narrow as a coatrack—appear almost to nuzzle. "Oh yes," remarks Brown as if only that instant remembering, "two things further.

"First, I have characterized myself as a businessman, and so I am. But while I am a businessman foremost, I am scarce a businessman only, and so you must understand that while I would be slow to welcome it, neither am I bashful about commercing in such bloodshed as may be required to achieve our end.

"Second, and this I must insist upon, everything said inside these walls must remain inside these walls. So long as we understand one another upon these points, we may proceed in the same spirit of collegiality that I am hopeful will mark each of our future relations."

Douglass—who appears as stricken as a man who has just been informed that his drink is laced with weed killer—can only nod. It is as if his mind has gone to pasture; thoughts gallop like headless horses hither and yon as he listens half in a daze to Brown outline his "Enterprise": "Cadres of armed guerrillas . . . south down through Virginia . . . free-float Appalachias . . . descend at co-ordinated intervals . . . strip slaves off plantations . . . retreat into mountains . . . arm liberated slaves . . . away north on the Underground . . .

"God has given the brawn of these hills to the cause of freedom," says Brown, drumming the part-map with his knuckles. "They were placed there by Him in the distant past expressly that I should use them to liberate the Negro race in the present."

Douglass is aghast. Heaven-sent or not—he is himself far less *gnostic* about these things than Brown—such an "Enterprise" strikes him as sheer lunacy. Not only does it invite bloodshed, it is a logistic horror. Food, clothing, arms, munitions, horses, fodder, provender, harness. How are they to be raised? How collected, transported, delivered, distributed, stockpiled? Where is it all to come from, where precisely to go?

And yet, if such an operation *can* be carried off, he is confident—God knows why—that this *particular* man must be the one to manage it.

Still, even if the logistics can be answered for, the potential for violence is frightening. Personally he finds violence abhorrent. Professionally he has passionately preached against it because he considers it both morally repugnant and politically self-defeating. Like most of the abolitionist community, he features himself a Garrisonian: he believes that the sheer weight of moral argument must over time persuade the slaveowners to free their slaves.

"I think it imprudent," he ventures.

"Imprudent? Really?" Brown appears more surprised than offended. "Well then, would to God that there was more imprudence in these United States.

"I believe I know what discomfits you, Frederick, if I may call you Frederick. It is unfortunate that we who wish to lay the foundations of kindness cannot ourselves be kind, but we haven't the luxury. War is no gentleman, and slavery *is* a state of war, the slaves are prisoners of that war, and they delude themselves who believe that it will end by employing any method—prayer, pamphlet, protest, petition, or ballot—short of the methods of war. Anything less amounts to trying to lasso a locomotive with cobwebs.

"No, the slaves must be armed, and I intend to arm them. God helps those who help themselves, but those he helps first are those with the better weapons."

"You do not trust God then," says Douglass, "that the meek shall inherit the earth."

"Oh, but I do. I trust God. And I keep my powder dry."

"And if they, the slaves I mean, prefer to remain where they are, or choose to flee on the Underground rather than join you in the mountains?"

"Then that is their choice, though once armed as men, I have faith they will perform their duty as men."

"You believe it to be the *duty* of the slaves to free themselves *and* their fellows?"

"I believe it to be their duty to do everything in their power to alleviate their condition and that of their fellow sufferers."

"Or die trying."

"That is correct. Or die trying."

"I think you expect too much."

He shakes his head emphatically. "With God, all things are possible. Besides, it is not a question of what I expect, or what is possible, or even of what may befall us. It is a question of what is required, of what must happen, of what must be done."

Pivoting in his chair so that he faces Douglass head-on, he grips him by both shoulders and looks him squarely in the eye.

"And you better than I know too well what that is."

Douglass cants his head even as he rucks his brow. Once again he is at a loss. Mindlessly he slips his watch from his vest pocket and glances at the time. It is well past 3 A.M.

"No?" says John Brown. "Why, God's will, Frederick. God's will is what must be done. And God's will I mean to do."

FREDERICK DOUGLASS

I am tempted to say he was the blackest white man I ever knew,
save that I knew too well he was beyond all that—color, race, black,
white.

But those err who call him nigger-lover.
He wasn't interested in freeing Negroes.
He was interested in freeing slaves.
Not a nigger-lover; a freedom fighter!
I never approved of his methods.

JOHN BROWN

*He was then the most eminent black man in the country and accordingly well-
connected. Knowing this, I calculated that he could be of some positive use to me.
In this I was to be positively disappointed.*

They would accuse me later of being possessed of a Redeemer complex, a Moses fixation, as if that were something to disavow or be ashamed of.

The truth is, I never thought of it in those terms. At the time I had my hands full just trying to salvage my own few from the wilderness.

I know how the notion took hold, of course, for I had written Douglass in the autumn of 1850:

The Lord Our God shall raise for us a Deliverer in the very best possible time. Who shall say that he is not walking upright among us even now?

But I was not referring to myself. And if hypothetically I was, what of it?

I didn't notice anyone else—mind you, not a solitary soul—queuing up for the job.

Perhaps we will revisit this thought later.

The Timbucto Mission furnishes him the opportunity both to mold a colony of Negroes in his own image and to recruit, drill, and arm prospective Enterprise men.

It is a combination too seductive to pass up. For now, the Grand Stampede down the Subterranean Passageway will hold.

The mission is a Negro farming settlement and fugitive slave sanctuary high in the Adirondack Mountains of upstate New York, the brainchild of philanthropist Gerrit Smith who has donated seventeen thousand acres for the purpose.

There, where winters can last six months out of twelve and temperatures free-fall past thirty-below, the first wave of settlers—a dozen families, most of them runagate—eke out a living on forty-acre parcels spread across a raw, barren, rock-strewn plateau tucked into an amphitheater of soaring mountains named Buck, Baldhead, Bullhead, and Catamount; Nob, Saddleback, Noble, and Whiteface.

Harsh, desolate, all but inaccessible—John Brown is utterly captivated. He sees not a howling, impossibly hostile wilderness, but an earthly paradise—pristine, impregnable, and consecrated to the greater glory of God.

"I feel more alive here," he writes Mary back in Springfield, "more at home, at peace, at one with myself, & closer to God than anyplace I have ever been.

"Everything you see reminds you of Omnipotence."

He pays Smith $244 for 244 acres at the foot of Lake Placid, assuring him, "I will look after these poor, despised people in all ways, teach them by example and precept, and be a kind of father to them. I can do no less."

Leasing a nearby farm while he lays in his own, he fetches Mary and the children from Springfield, hires fugitive slave Cyrus Jefferson to pitch in with the farm, distributes ten barrels of flour and salt pork among the settlers, and preaches a Sabbath-day sermon upon the subject "Whither the Christian Soldier Marching as to War?"

Then, vowing to return at the first opportunity, he asks his family to remember him in their prayers, swings up astride his mount, and hightails it back to work at Perkins & Brown.

Ruth Brown

When we were living in Springfield our house was sparsely furnished, the parlor not at all. Mother and I often told Father how we wished that eventually it too might be furnished, and with this he took no issue.

But one day, not long after he had made up his mind that we were to go to Timbucto, he called us to him and said: "I want to plan a little with you. I find that we have been able to lay a little by this month, and I wish to know whether we might use it to furnish the parlor, or to buy food and clothing for those Negroes who may need it at Timbucto."

Naturally we said, "Save it for the Negroes," and this pleased him so that he gave each of us a hug, a thing he seldom did.

Timbucto was a place of neither ease nor comfort, and at first I did not like it there. It was cold beyond knowing, and the skies were too often downcast and muttersome, and it was hard to find the purchase to grow things upon the rocks. But I met my husband there, and we were lending our soul and spirit to a cause I knew to be just, and in time I became reconciled to it as my home.

Father moved us around so very much you see, owing to his flitting from job to job the way he did, and this constant uprooting I believe to be especially hard on a child. Not that I was a child any longer by the time that he moved us to the mountains, but I felt sorely for my brothers and sisters.

I have often wondered whether his perpetual migrations didn't stem from his being uncomfortable in his own skin, for he moved about *so* much that it was almost as if he were searching for the right fit—trying on one self here, slipping into another there—before settling on one that he could live with.

In any event, and despite everything, I think Father was a godly man.

I know that after he was executed he was praised for a saint by many great and famous men. (And derided as a lunatic by a fair number more.) But they did not know him. Or knew him not enough. Father was not a saint. He was not even saintly.

You have heard the saying "touched by genius"? That was Father. Only it wasn't genius he was touched by. It was faith. Or the genius *of* faith.

I did not envy him that, for the sort of faith he kept, the nature of the genius he possessed—or that possessed him—seemed to goad him to things that brought him only sorrow.

Not for him the faith of saints.

For him the faith of martyrs.

Ellen Brown
April 30, 1849
Age eleven months
(His "little chick")

He was pacing the floor holding her in his arms when the fever took her.

He closed her eyes, folded her hands, and returned her to her cradle.

He did not cry, believing he had no tears left in him.

In the middle of the night, having failed to dream her back to life, he awoke sobbing.

History-as-received . . .

The country was unraveling.

Everybody knew it. Everybody *sensed* it. North. South. The country was coming apart at the seams.

Wishing to delay the inevitable, Congress took a stitch in the fabric. It legislated the Great Compromise of 1850.

It pleased no one, displeased most, enraged a good many.

That is the nature of compromise.

But *this?* "An Act to Amend, and Supplementary to the Act entitled, an Act respecting Fugitives from Justice and Persons escaping from the Service of their Masters."

In other words, the Fugitive Slave Act.

Aka the Negro Kidnapping Law.

Aka the Man-Stealing Measure.

Aka the Bloodhound Bill.

Overnight it became utterly legal for a self-described slaveowner —or more often, his hired bounty hunter—to pluck at will from any free state, any Negro, anytime, anywhere, and abscond to any slave state without a thought for due process.

Under the law, the identity and alleged fugitive status of that Negro need not be corroborated or verified beyond the affadavit of the slavehunter.

Under the law, that Negro was invested with no legal right to challenge, dispute, or appeal his apprehension and extradition.

Under the law, the final disposition of that extradition lay with an *un*salaried, federally appointed commissioner compensated ten dollars for each extradition, five dollars for each manumission.

Under the law, that commissioner could draft any citizen into the ranks of a slavehunting posse, or impose a thousand-dollar fine if refused.

Under the law, any citizen "obstructing the arrest of, attempting the rescue of, aiding in the escape of, or harboring and concealing" an alleged fugitive, could be fined one thousand dollars and sentenced to six months in prison.

Frederick Douglass, who abhorred violence, remarked of the law: "The only way to make it a dead letter is to make a half-dozen dead kidnappers. Let it be put into operation, and the streets will run with blood. Every colored man should sleep with a loaded revolver under his head. It is not only justice, but wisdom to shoot down slavehunters. Such as they have divested themselves of the right to live."

John Brown wrote of the law (to Mary): "I believe this bill will be the means of making more abolitionists than all the lectures given upon the subject in the last ten years. Thus do I see God's hand actively at work in this apparent wickedness. Praise Him for it. For myself, you may rest certain that I will not take this evil lying upon my back."

Nor did he.

———

Jam-packing several pairs of saddlebags, he lights out for Timbucto to admonish each of its homesteaders "not to be taken alive should any attempt be made to drag you back in Southern chains, and I pray only that they may venture it, for they will not be found wanting a warm and lively welcome."

Then, going to the saddlebags, he withdraws holsters, gun belts, pistols, and stack after stack of cartridges.

"Wear them at all times," he says. "Make quick use of them where necessary. Liberty before life."

Reminding his own family to "stand toe to toe and shoulder to shoulder with our neighbors, even need you resort to hot water," he shagtails it back to Springfield to arouse the Lord's host.

FAITH OF OUR FATHERS
(Edited Transcripts)

I consider expatriation of the Negroes to governments of their own colour greatly preferrable to the mixture of colour here. To this I have a great aversion. (**Thomas Jefferson**)

Owing to probably unalterable prejudices, including the contempt known to be entertained for their peculiar features, freed Negroes ought to be permanently removed beyond the region occupied by, or alloted to the white population. (**James Madison**)

No satisfying plan has yet been devised for taking out the stain. If an asylum could be found in Africa, that would be the appropriate destination for the unhappy race among us, for the Negroes are everywhere regarded as a nuisance. (**James Madison**)

The two races cannot co-exist both being free and equal. The great sine qua non, therefore, is some external asylum for the coloured race. (**James Madison**)

Why should we in the sight of superior beings darken America's people? Why increase the sons of Africa by planting them in America where we have so fair an opportunity, by excluding all blacks and tawnys, of increasing the lovely white? (**Benjamin Franklin**)

This unfortunate difference of colour, and perhaps of intellectual faculty, is a powerful obstacle to the emancipation of these people. Among the Romans, emancipation required but one effort. The slave when made free might mix with, without staining the blood of, his master. But with us a second is necessary unknown to history. When freed he must be removed beyond the reach of mixture. **(Thomas Jefferson)**

You shall not give up to his master
a slave who has escaped
from his master to you.

Rather he shall dwell with you
in your midst in the place of his choosing
where it pleases him best.

You shall not oppress
him.

—Deuteronomy 23:15–16

From the portmanteau discovered under an upstairs bed in the Kennedy farm-house across from Harper's Ferry afterward . . .

WORDS OF ADVICE
(The Manifesto)

Adopted January 15, 1851, at Springfield, Massachusetts,
the Credo as written and recommended by John Brown

"Union Is Strength"
(The Motto)

Nothing so charms the American people as personal bravery.

To my colored friends: Should one of your number be arrested, you must collect together as quickly as possible so as to outnumber your adversaries and effect a rescue.

Let no able-bodied man appear on the ground unequipped or with his weapons exposed.

Let the first blow be the signal for all to engage, and when engaged, make clean work of your enemy.

The point is to create such confusion and *terror* that your enemies will be slow to attack.

Be firm, determined, and cool. Do not be driven to desperation.

If assailed, retreat to the houses of your most prominent and influential white friends. Take your wives and children to gain sympathetic entry. Once admitted, the suspicion of being connected with you will fasten upon them and compel them to make common cause with you whether they would otherwise do so or not.

And now:

A lasso might be applied to a slavecatcher with good effect.

Hold on to your weapons. Never leave them, part with them, or have them far away from you.

Stand by one another while a drop of blood remains.

Be hanged if you must, but tell no tales out of school. Make no confession.

Union is strength. Strength in Union.

AGREEMENT

As citizens of the United States of America, *trusting in a just and merciful God whose spirit and all-powerful aid we humbly implore,* we will ever be true to the flag of our beloved country, always acting under it.

We invite to join with us every colored person whose heart is engaged in the performance of our business, whether male or female, young or old.

We will provide ourselves with suitable *implements* and will aid those who do not possess the means if any such are disposed to join us.

Liberty before life.

———

The marks or signatures of forty-four Negro men and women were attached to the bottom of the document. None were ever obliged to lift a finger in rescue or self-defense.

Slavehunters uniformly swung well wide of Springfield.

Perhaps we could take a moment to review.

As you wish.

In '37, Lovejoy is killed and you vow the violent overthrow of slavery.

Correct.

But you do not violently overthrow slavery.

Not at that time, no.

Ten years later, in '47, you meet for the first time with Frederick Douglass and reveal to him your plan to run slaves off Virginia plantations.

Not exactly, but close enough.

But you do not run slaves off Virginia plantations.

Correct.

Four years later, in '51, you organize a Negro self-defense league in Springfield, Massachusetts, advocating armed resistence to the Fugitive Slave Law.

Correct. The Springfield Branch of the United States League of Gileadites. Also known as the Secret Forty-Four.

But you do not engage in such armed resistance.

The opportunity never presented itself.

So, over a period of fifteen years, you preach, plan, and prepare for the violent overthrow of slavery, yet neither engage in a single act of violence nor liberate a single slave.

Discounting my intermittent work with the Underground Railroad, that is so. But I never ceased extolling the virtues of righteous violence.

Righteous violence?

Godly violence. Violence prescribed by divine law and Holy Writ. Violence pleasing in the sight of the Lord.

The point is, you talk, write, meet, organize, you even arm, but over fifteen years you do not—not once—act.

Fifteen years may seem an eternity to we mortals. To God it is as the blink of an eye. The time was not propitious. And for such as I intended, timing was everything.

Were you in the habit of carrying a weapon?

For a brief period after the passage of the Man-stealing Law, I carried a revolver, or kept one within armslength. I did not habitually carry arms until I went to Kanzas. Thereafter I was obliged to wear on my person any number of weapons, twenty-four hours a day. Before Kanzas, I had never in my life fired a shot, drawn a knife, or so much as thrown a punch in anger.

And between times?

Between times?

Between '51 in Springfield, and your going out to Kansas in '55. What, if anything, were you doing toward the violent overthrow of slavery during that period?

I couldn't say.

Couldn't, or wouldn't?

That time has always been lost to me. I have endeavored to resurrect it on numerous occasions, but it remains beyond my remembering. My recollection of that period is of faces and voices and images that seem to me disconnected and fleeting. Shadows in fog. Echoes under water. Night smoke. My wife used to call them my sleepwalking years.

You might try Mesmerism.

When the Lord determines that I am ready, I shall remember. For now, I am content to leave well enough alone. You will forgive me, but on this subject I am useless to you. Is there anything further?

Not at the moment. Later perhaps.

Very well.

When *Uncle Tom's Cabin* is published in March of 1852 it becomes a runaway best-seller literally overnight. Three hundred thousand copies are sold in the United States, another two hundred thousand in England. Phenomenal, unprecedented numbers. It also evokes an outcry throughout the South, and unleashes a torrent of abuse, including death threats, directed against its internationally acclaimed author.

Although he will never bestir himself to read the book—he holds fiction in low regard; it smacks to him overmuch of "idle fancy"—by the time he is introduced to Harriet Beecher Stowe at an abolitionist fund-raiser in Boston, John Brown is well aware of the controversy it has provoked.

And continues to engender.

———

Gentling her discreetly aside, he lowers his voice.

"Do they persist in their threats?"

"Oh, to be sure," she replies. "Scarcely a week goes by that some missive does not arrive on my doorstep from one of our fire-eating Southern *gentlemen* quite all *aflame* with the most dire and dreadful sentiments. It really is most upsetting."

"You take precautions, then."

"Precautions?"

"Forgive me, madam, but you are a marked woman. It is only prudent that you should arm yourself."

She recoils in alarm. *"Arm* myself? But what can you mean?"

"I mean that I know perfectly well what these jackals are capable of." Reaching inside his coat flap, he withdraws from his vest pocket a sparrow-sized, ivory-handled derringer, concealing it in the palm of his hand. "As it happens, I have here just the thing."

Enfolding her hand in the both of his, he presses the pistol into her palm. "I fancy that you should have it," he whispers, "and should the occasion arise, enjoin you most heartily to employ it. Consider it a gift, in appreciation of," he hesitates, "of your *novel* efforts in the service of the Lord."

The look on her face is one of undisguised horror as she snatches her hand away.

"Rest easy, madam," he thinks to reassure her. "It is not loaded."

"But," she is in full retreat, shaking her head in disbelief as she backpedals across floor, "I cannot . . . I would never . . . how could you possibly? . . . you will excuse me, sir."

He can only watch in bewilderment as she hikes her skirts above her shoe tops, turns high heel, and hurries away.

"So she fancies her pen mightier than their sword," he thinks to himself in exasperation, catching a glimpse of the back of her head as she disappears through a side door. "Unfortunately, madam, God does not protect the pure at heart. Them he crowns with martyrdom. He protects those with the better weapons.

"I will pray for you, madam, but I fear that you sadly mistake your enemy."

Late that evening he sighs resignedly, harrows an oily hand through oilier hair, thumbs the snaggles from his eyes, and flicks closed the cover on the ledger book one last time. Then, dousing the lamp at his elbow, he hoists himself creaking from the chair at his desk and trudges to bed in the dark having finally accepted that Perkins & Brown is gone belly up.

He does not blame himself—the bottom has long since dropped out of the domestic wool market owing to the blowing of economic breezes he can neither control nor comprehend—but in the morning certain unalterable facts remain unaltered.

He is fifty-two years old.

He is out of work.

He is virtually penniless.

He has a wife and four young children to provide for.

The wool growers, middlemen, and manufacturers who once so esteemed him, have made him the target of so many of their lawsuits, to keep them straight he's taken to carrying their names on a scrap of paper inside his billfold:

The Henry Warren Suit of Troy, New York.

The Burlington Mills Company Suit of Boston.

The Pickersgill Company Suit of New York City.

The Patterson and Ewing Suit of Pittsburgh.

Et cetera.

His creditors are clamoring for their money:

The Cabot Bank alleges that Perkins & Brown owes it $57,000.

The Burlington Mills Company alleges it is owed $60,000.

Et cetera.

Writing Mary, he describes himself as "no longer so stout." In fact, he suffers from chronic dizziness, shortness of breath, thumping headaches, transitory numbness in his arms and legs, flaking skin, and bleeding gums.

His short-term memory has begun to fail him.

His eyesight is blurred.

His scalp is patchworked with impetigo.

His hair has gone from brown to gray in the span of a fortnight.

His rosacea is in full flower.

He is losing weight at an alarming rate.

He incessantly fantasizes not only his own death, but the deaths of those he sees in the street.

Friends, associates, and acquaintances have begun to make it known that they pity him.

In truth, he has begun to feel much the same.

He suspects an acute riboflavin deficiency.

He moves the family from Timbucto back to Akron where they occupy a far-flung farm on the Perkins estate while the older boys find work shepherding the colonel's flocks.

For three years he maunders the northeast—Troy, Utica, Burlington, New York City, Boston, Pittsburgh—going from attorney's office to attorney's office, courtroom to courtroom, retaining lawyers, supplying depositions, answering writs, responding to summonses, tracking down witnesses, attending pretrial hearings, giving sworn testimony, existing hand to mouth and pillar to post.

He is in New York City when word arrives that son Frederick, now twenty-four, has taken to tenting overnight in the fields where he can be heard engaged in animated conversation with the sheep —when not indulging his newly acquired taste for timothy.

WIFE

Mary Day Brown

Evenso, I never become so desperate as to think, "Whatever will become of us?" The older boys was working steady, so worse on worse, we'd always get by one way t'other.

But I worried for him. I'd never seen him so castdown. Wouldn't hardly talk. Wouldn't work a stitch. When I'd ask, he'd say he couldn't. Just that. "Not now," he'd say, not looking up. "Can't."

He'd take long naps, or sit and stare for hours. Not a budge. Rigid. Like the *rigor'd* set in. Not happy, not sad. Listless. Like he was bogged down, stuck in place. Or in time maybe. Suspended, froze in time. Three years' worth. Three years' worth of froze plumb stiff.

You want my opinion, weren't them lawsuits had him world-wearied. Weren't the money neither. Weren't the *present* atall. The future, that's what gnawed at him.

Nothing seemed possible no more. He'd lost track of himself. What he aimed to do. Who he aimed to be.

The truth? I reckoned him for a goner. Clear around the bend and clean up over the hill. I figured him for gone to run with the wolves and howl at the moon.

I hadn't counted on Kanzas.

Or the grit of old John Brown.

As I was saying, my memory of those days is gone so dark it's like they never happened.

Mary considered it a blessing, said it was God gave me permission to forget.

I reckon I closed down is what it was. Went walkabout. Noctambulant. Dozed off awhile. At least that's much in the fashion of how I recollect it. The way you would a dream you'd dreamed the night before. All flinders and wisps and susurrations. And none of it adding up to jack-squat.

Except this dream lasted most of three years.

It wasn't until John Junior's letter that I really came out of it. That I actually woke up. That I finally snapped to.

That I was resurrected.

That I ascended unto Kanzas.

That spring the United States Congress passed the Kansas-Nebraska Act, legislation which dissenting Senator Charles Sumner of Massachusetts clairvoyantly characterized as "putting freedom and slavery face to face and bidding them grapple."

Indeed, slavery, throughout Kansas for the past thirty-five years as frowned upon a crime as horse theft, acquired overnight the cachet of a cause célèbre subject to the onetime, simple majority, up-and-down, ad hoc vote of all then resident on Kansas soil.

Touted as Popular Sovereignty by some, derided as Squatter Sovereignty by others, where the Compromise of 1850 had sutured the national fabric, the Kansas-Nebraska Act of 1854 rent it wide enough for a herd of rogue elephants to stampede through, as indeed by the thousands they did, five of John Brown's sons among them.

A race race for Kansas.

A recipe for carnage.

Little did they know, even less did they comprehend: when they sowed the Kansas-Nebraska Act, they reaped John Brown.

And made of poor Kansas the whirlwind.

From John Brown, Jr.

May 20, 24, & 26
Brown's Station, near Osawatomie, Kanzas Territory
Dear Father:

As I write I am seated in one of our canvas-duck tents upon a bedstead of hatcheted poles thatched with sagebrush. Our situation is 30 miles s. of Lawrence, 10 miles n.w. of Osawatomie at the head of a ravine putting into North Middle Creek, a right smart tributary of the Osage River. We have made five claims of 40 acres each, each with living water, timber for firewood, & stone enough to make good walls. What is peculiar is that all the stone hereabouts is flat, or nearly so. The prairie rolls away, the bluestem vast as all Creation in every direction. On the whole, it is the greatest country for a poor man to make money in that ever I saw.

If only we can succeed in making this a free state, then a great & glorious work will have been done mankind, but at present 100s & 1000s of the most desperate & murderous men armed to the teeth with revolvers, Bowie knives, shotguns, rifles, howitzer & cannon—& well-supplied with whiskey—are arrayed throughout the territory under the pay of slaveholders, while the friends of freedom are half-armed at best, wholly disorganized & exhibit naught but the most abject & cowardly spirit. Not only Missouri, but every slaveholding state from Virginia to Texas is pouring in men & money to fasten slavery upon this land by means fair or foul, including driving from the territory every anti-slavery man they can flush out.

To remedy this will require the immediate & thorough arming & organizing into military companies of the whole of the anti-slavery population here.

At present we—Owen, Salmon, Frederick, Jason & myself—share among us:

1 revolver

1 small Bowie knife

1 middling rifle

1 poor rifle (our old squirrel gun; its stock attached by metal clips & baling wire)

1 pocket pistol (single shot)

1 hatchet

2 slingshots

We require for us each:

1 Colt large-sized revolver (six-shooter)

1 Allen & Thurbers large-sized revolver

1 real Minie rifle

1 heavy Bowie knife (12-inch blade minimum)

With these, we could fairly compete even against cannon, as the real Minie rifle—as you well know—has a killing range almost equal to cannon & is more easily handled.

Now, we realize you have been feeling poorly of late, but we implore you to *rouse yourself* & raise for us these arms. We need them more than we do bread.

All we should be wanting then is some *stalwart* to lead us off in the matter.

P.S. Perhaps you could raise the money to pay for the arms & munitions from Gerrit Smith in the form of a loan we pledge to refund him later from the *free* soil of Kanzas.

In any event, by hook or by hangnail, we must have them at once.

If we begin the matter now, Kanzas may yet have a chance for freedom.

You may send the arms to St. Louis, Mo., c/o Walker & Chick, c/o B. Slater, #19, Levee St.

P.P.S. Word has just arrived of a talk given some days previous at a public rally in St. Joseph, Mo., by one of the bully-boy chieftains, one B. F. Stringfellow. Here is his speech as we have it:

"Mark every scoundrel among you that is the least tainted with abolitionism and exterminate him. Neither give nor take quarter from the g'damned rascals. The time has come to disregard all such law as may impinge on your lives and your property. Enter every election district in Kanzas and vote at the point of the Bowie knife and revolver. War to the knife, knife to the hilt!"

Father, for the love of God, *arise!*

Revisiting this thought now:

It would be said later that I was possessed of a Redeemer complex, that I was hell-bent on single-handedly delivering the Negro race from the jaws of American slavery.

Allow me to make a confession. When I went out to Kanzas, I did indeed have redemption on my mind.

But not of Negro lives.

Of my mislaid own.

(My investment in upholding the status quo, my stake in contributing to a system that had actively sought my ruin: nil.)

Mary Day Brown

He told me over and over, told me 'til I wearied of the hearing, when it come time to give up his all agin slavery, that'd be the time for our parting.

And no tears shed for what can't be helped.

" 'Tis my bounden and sacred duty," he'd say, "and naught must hold me aground. Neither wife nor kith nor kin, nor health nor happy home. When the Lord makes known His own time, then I'm all for Him and no other."

So when he went on to Kanzas, I knew to say nary a word.

"Wife," he said, "you must try to understand, they will never take me alive."

"Then husband," said I, "you best see to it you give better'n you get."

He lights out for Kansas, his prairie schooner so laden with weapons that his horse balks at doing more than eight miles a day.

Take the claymores.

A few days earlier he had made a modest little speech at the Akron Bandshell in the course of which he had read John Junior's letter in advance of making his pitch outright for arms and munitions—not that he had expected to barnstorm much of a haul.

But the crowd had been larger than he had anticipated, and it had applauded him extravagantly, and in the end he had been obliged to postpone his departure while the rifles, shotguns, revolvers, pistols, dirk knives, powder, shot, lead, boots, shoes, shoepacks, clothing, bedrolls, and blankets—this *manna*, as it were—had come raining down from the heavens above, and praise God for every blade and barrel of it.

Even the mayor had anted up. He owned, he had said, some few "odds and ends of military paraphernalia" to which he was gladly welcome, though he doubted they'd interest him much being they weren't the sort of accoutrements considered these days "to be on the cutting edge, so to speak"—and well, truth was, folks generally considered them more antiques than anything else, their being such *throwbacks*, you might say—so he'd understand if he found them too outdated or impractical for his purposes, but he might as well have a look and judge for himself, nothing ventured nothing gained.

And so off to the storm cellar of Mayor General Lucius V. Bierce, hurricane lamp held high battling the fust and the cobwebs, each step of the gangway emptying toward the bank of shelves lining the far wall, the bottommost bowed beneath the weight of a pair of coffin-length footlockers, their lids fairly duned with dust.

"Truth be told, I haven't given them a thought in years," the mayor had said, doing his best to kid-glove the lids aside. "There now."

Shoveling the lamp back to the mayor, he had dropped to his haunches then, captivated at once by the workmanship evinced in the wooden racks fitted with brass latches bradded to the caisson's baize-lined inner walls.

"But—how many are they?" he had asked wonderingly, half mesmerized and not a little aroused by the high gleam of so many yards of tempered steel so close at hand, so beguiled in fact that you might have thought he was assaying the contents of a Grecian cist or appraising the priceless antiquities of some archaeological dig.

"An even dozen," the mayor had said. "Last I looked anyway."

"But how ever did you come by them?"

Slipping one of the implements from its niche, he had hoisted it confidently by its handle—its hilt, he could not help noticing, emblazoned with an American Spread Eagle grasping a writhing serpent in its talons—remarking upon its superlative heft, enviable balance, and razored edges.

Scotch Highlander claymores. Honest-to-God *broadswords*!

"I've had them a considerable while," the mayor had said. "Fifteen years, give or take. Used them against the Brits in the Patriot's War up to Canada. Headed a company of volunteers. Nothing came of it of course, save a good butt-kicking. Ours, by Jove."

"So here they've lain ever since?"

"Oh, they're in working condition. You can rest easy on that score. Fearsome-looking devils, aren't they?"

"Fearsome," he had repeated thoughtfully, reluctantly replacing the sword in its reliquary. "I reckon that's one word for it."

"So, I don't suppose you can use them then. Too unwieldy, I'd wager."

"Unwieldy? Well, no match for Colt's revolver, that's a fact."

When he had hesitated, the mayor had interjected, "Thought as much. No obligation, you understand."

"But then I suspect it's an unwieldly business I'm bound for. No, they'll do. I reckon they'll do and then some."

"Really?" The mayor had appeared almost as relieved as he did gratified. "You're quite certain? Well then, by all means, consider them yours."

"I am in your debt, sir," he had said then, "with no method of repaying you save to affirm upon my sacred word that they shall be employed in the *execution* of God's work, and God's work alone."

History-as-received . . .

He arrives in Kansas ill-prepared for the Hydra he encounters there: a brace of dueling governments—one Pro Slave, one Free Soil—each claiming legitimacy, neither fit to govern a tea party much less an unsettled territory of 126,000 square miles.

The former—composed chiefly of neighboring Missourians whose interest in seeing Kansans vote in favor of slavery stems from a desire both to safeguard their own multimillion-dollar investment in chattels back home and to extend the opportunity for similar investment westward—has recently authored a territorial constitution which reads in part:

Those professing anti-slave sentiment are barred from serving as jurors or holding political office.

The dissemination of anti-slave speech or literature is punishable by five years at hard labor.

Any attempt to agitate, incite, or organize the slave population is a capital crime punishable by death.

Declares its principal author, "So far as the rights of property are concerned, I acknowledge no difference between a free-soiler and an abolitionist."

Its counterpart—composed chiefly of New England émigrés whose interest in seeing Kansans vote against slavery stems from a desire both to check the westward extension of slavocracy and to gain a foothold for free white labor and commerce in the West—has recently authored a territorial constitution which reads in part:

The best interests of Kansas require a population of free white men.

We are in favor of stringent laws excluding all Negroes, bond or free, from the territory.

We denounce any attempt to interfere with slavery where it exists outside the territory, and concede the right of slave-owners to hold and recover their slaves without obstruction from us.

We are not abolitionists and have no truck with abolitionists.

Declares its principal author, "So far as the rights of property are concerned, I know of no difference between a Negro and a mule."

———

The murders commence the third week following his arrival:
   Sam Collins is gunned down by five men in late October.
   Charlie Dow is backshot a month later.
   The unarmed Tom Barber is killed during the second week in December.
   Reese Brown is chopped to death by a hatchet-wielding, Missouri bully-boy border gang known as the Kickapoo Rangers on January

15, 1856, his filleted and frozen remains dumped at the feet of his wife and small children outside their cabin door.

That winter is fiendish. Temperatures rarely exceed twenty below zero. Winds rarely subside to twenty miles an hour. A procession of blizzards and ice storms clamps an eighteen-inch lid of ice on the creeks and a three-foot mantle of snow on the ground. Bread can be sliced only after being thawed by the fire. Water freezes in its tumblers before it can be consumed. People, the Browns included, take to their beds at midday like hibernating animals.

For the moment, Kansas stills.

In Washington, President Franklin Pierce calls a special session of Congress to publicly announce his support for the Pro Slave legislature and constitution while denouncing its Free State counterparts as "treasonable insurrection." Then, warning that resistance to Pro Slave authorities will not be tolerated, he places the federal troops garrisoned at Forts Riley and Leavenworth at the disposal of the Pro Slave government.

Come April, as the weather lifts and the adder's-tongue sprouts, all hell busts loose.

To the Hon. Joshua Giddings,
United States Congressman, Ohio:

A number of federal soldiers are now quartered in this vicinity for the purpose of enforcing the hellish enactments of the so-called Kanzas Legislature which is as bogus a body of men as ever collected in one place for the purpose of molesting the rights & liberties of innocent civilians. The next move on the part of the President & his Pro Slave masters must be to **make** *the people here submit, & when they do not, to arrest them for so-called treason.*

I ask in the name of our venerated forefathers, I ask in the name of Almighty God, will Congress suffer us to be driven to **dire extremities** *to defend ourselves?*

I might cheer the prospect.

From the Hon. Joshua Giddings,
United States Congressman, Ohio:

Mr. Brown, sir. The President will never dare to employ the troops of the United States to shoot down the citizens of Kansas. The death of the first man will light the fire of Civil War in these formerly United States.

To Mary Day Brown:

All things considered, I have no desire to have the slave power cease from its acts of aggression against us. Indeed, I might wish them increased tenfold & exported abroad. There are some seventeen thousand slaves working the hemp & tobacco farms in the half-dozen Missouri counties bordering this territory who, furnished suitable **utensils** *& the proper* **lead,** *might be persuaded to raise a hand in the matter.*

MID-APRIL

St. Anthony Hedgpeth: horsewhipped, stomped, tar-and-cottoned, stoned.

Johnnie Stewart: carotid artery slit.

Davis Hoyt: backshot, face scored with muriatic acid.

Jonathan Jones: caught, hogtied, tortured, headshot.

LATE APRIL

Over the winter he has let flower his beard; it flows like white froth from his face. "My burning bush," he calls it. As in "I am that I am." He looked, an associate will say later, the spitting image of an Old Testament prophet.

The effect is scarcely unintentional.

Beneath an ankle-length white linen duster he is armed. We know this because when he addresses the First Free Soil Settler's Safety Committee Meeting at Osawatomie, he wears the duster's front flaps open and batwinged aside looped behind the handles of the loaded Navy Colt six-shooter revolvers that roost prominently aslant each hip. A pair of bandoliers crisscrosses his chest. A Bowie knife juts from a boot top.

Beard, Bandoliers, Bowie knife: he fairly *bristles.*

At the moment, he is fixing to go public. He teeters this day on the brink of notoriety.

Let's listen in.

"I am an abolitionist dyed in the wool come to Kanzas for the sole purpose of promoting the killing outright of American slavery, and I would rather see the Union dissolved and the nation at Civil War than submit to the bogus men and their godforsaken laws a second longer.

"I cipher it seven innocents murdered and not so much as a voice to answer or a soul to pay. So then, you can protest, publish, petition, pray, whine, wheedle, weep, and wait—or you can fight. For myself, I have been charged by God to break the jaws of the wicked, and that much I aim to do.

"I aim to do that much.

"At least."

The committee is abuzz. This is medicine harsher than they are accustomed to. This is, as one will describe it later, "rifle-ball words shot from a rifle-ball tongue."

"We know you, Brown," they fleer. "Cozy saying yer for the niggers when it ain't yer home they're bound for. Well, it's our'n, all of our'n, and we say this: We say that dog won't hunt. We say niggers don't go around here, not now and not a-never.

"So why'nt you just leave us be, huh? Whyn't you just take yer damn insurrection talk and mosey back on home?"

"But I deny it, sir," he answers. "I deny that I am an insurrectionist. I say that it is Kanzas that is in a state of insurrection, and that *I* sir, *I* am law. *I* am government. *I* am right. *I* am justice. *I* am religion. I say that I am the bringer of God's will to a Godless land.

"I am here to create difficulty, gentlemen, and I suggest that you accustom yourselves to the fact. Samson slew the thirty citizens of Ascalon. Gideon fought the Midianites. I wreak havoc upon slavekeepers. That is what I do, gentlemen, and that and that alone is why I have come.

"They have sowed the wind. Now let them reap the whirlwind. I think it high time to let a little blood."

John Brown, Jr.

Well, he came through for us, he ferried out the weapons—which, I might make mention, he unloaded from the back of his wagon as if they comprised the very Covenant itself—and that alone made him most of a hero in our eyes. (It is a wondrous fine thing to realize that one's father is truly brave, brave to the point of fearlessness, braver even than oneself. Indeed, infinitely braver than oneself.) Still, by the time he arrived, certain events had transpired, certain circumstances arisen that rendered his arsenal rather less . . . essential.

I had in the meantime been elected to the Free State Legislature, had helped author the Free State Charter, was even then working actively within the Free State Party whose Negro Exclusion policy I had against my better judgment publicly embraced. Had, in other words, become much the politician.

Well, I thought he would combust. No son of mine, et cetera. He had come to kill off the specter of slavery in Kanzas, he thundered, and I could stand with him, stand aside, or stand in the way and reap hard buffets—and the Devil with political reality.

"It is not *my* reality," he huffed. "It is not *God's.*"

And of course he was right. It was not his, and it was not God's, but it *was* everyone else's. The fact was, the Free State population would sooner have seen the territory go slave than allow a single free Negro to live amongst them.

Those folks didn't care shucks for abolishing slavery. They cared that Negroes be kept out of their communities and off their streets, out of their neighborhoods and off their land; they cared about clearing their acres and laying in their farms and building up their towns and being free to attend to their business without, as one of them told me, "having to rub shoulders every whipstitch with a bunch of stinking Africans."

Not that they wouldn't defend themselves against bully-boys like the Kickapoo Rangers, but only if push came to shove, only in self-defense, and never against the federal troops.

You see my predicament. There I was, doing my damnedest as the duly elected representative of the vox populi to put their interests above all else, as befit my office, and here comes Father breathing fire and spitting venom, preaching abolition and spouting insurrection and citing Scripture to boot.

Father wanted slavery killed yesterday.

I wanted Kanzas free for tomorrow.

Lord knows there was room enough there to wrangle, and to my everlasting sorrow, once he charged fighting mad onto that godless savannah, wrangle's nigh all we did.

I had no stomach for his brand of moral ruthlessness.

Without so much as a volley fired in self-defense, the Free State capital at Lawrence falls to eight hundred mounted Kickapoo Rangers who storm the town beneath a pair of flying bedsheets reading:

The supremacy of the White race!	and	Let yankees trembel and abolishunists fall Suthern Rites to one and all!

Free State legislators are arrested, Free State newspaper offices are destroyed, the Free State Hotel is torched, a dry goods store is looted, the home of the Free State congressional representative is razed. The indictments on charges of high treason of each of the named members of the Free State Legislature are read aloud in the middle of Main Street.

John Brown, Jr., is high on the list.

HIGH NOON

It is high noon the third Thursday in May on the floor of the United States Senate. Senator Charles Sumner (R-Mass.), deliverer three days earlier of the anti-slavery speech "The Crime Against Kansas," is sunk in thought writing purposefully at his desk when Congressman Preston Brooks (D-S.C.) approaches from the rear, shillelagh in hand.

The shillelagh is the genuine Maylasian article: a meaty length of gutta-percha as knobby as the scutes along the back of an alligator.

"Mr. Sumner," says Brooks closing fast over Sumner's right shoulder, "I have read your speech twice over carefully." Half awares, Sumner birdcocks his head, glancing up from his desk squinting as if directly into the sun. Brooks does not register. "It is a libel, sir," says Brooks, bearing down-in, "a libel on the South."

The shillelagh arcs up and sledges down.

Sumner's head roostertails blood as he thrusts his arms above his head to ward off God knows what.

The shillelagh arcs up and sledges down.

Arcs up, sledges down.

Arcs up, sledges down.

Each blow bounces off the top of Sumner's skull with a crunch like the crack-of-the-bat.

Sumner struggles to gain his feet—to fight, to flee, to get out from under the bludgeoning, to live—but he is six foot three, lanky and long-limbed, and he finds himself entangled in chairlegs and desktop.

The shillelagh arcs up and sledges down.

Arcs up, sledges down, arcs up, sledges down, arcs up, sledges down.

Sumner's head is cowled with blood. He feels himself blacking out, fights it long enough to wrench the desk free of its floor rivets and reel lurching to his feet blinded by blood.

The shillelagh arcs up and sledges down.

The shillelagh arcs up and sledges down.

The shillelagh arcs up and sledges down.

The shillelagh snaps clean in two.

Sumner crumples to the floor like a suit of clothes slid from a hanger, his head emptying itself into the aisle like a leaky wineskin, the blood pooling to a pillow beneath his head.

Brooks is breathing heavily, his face highly flushed, when he remarks, "Kansas is none of yours, sir."

The day after I arrived in Kanzas I awoke with a ringing in my ears, odd high-pitched dissonances that did not cease until the morning after we had concluded the business upon the Pottawatomie.

It was—I believed then and believe now—the wailing of the millions of my enslaved black brethren whose tribulations none but God could know.

The business done, I awoke thereafter fresh as morning mint.

Come on over here.
Now, look up the barrel of my shotgun.
Go on. Take your time. Have yourself a good long look.

So, see any of your slaves?

   —inspired by Michael S. Harper, "History as Cap'n Brown"

The essential American soul is hard, isolate, stoic, and a killer

—D. H. LAWRENCE

Real wickedness is rare. Certainly it does not rest in the tawdry murder of millions. . . . It rests rather on the pale brow of every saviour who to save us all from death first kills.

—WM. GASS

there is always a time to make right
what is wrong,
there is always a time
for retribution

—SUSAN GRIFFIN, "I Like to Think of Harriet Tubman,"
Like the Iris of an Eye

BUSHWHACK

By the light of a cuticle moon the old man slowpokes the Kansas savannah hip-wading cross-country through the Swamp of the Swan.

His head is canted beneath an extravagantly brimmed straw hat angled low to his forehead and chinstrapped to the eave of his jaw against the damp blow of a risen wind. He wears the shawl collar of his ankle-length linen duster turned up to his ears.

Visored by the hand-width of downbent brim, his face appears adumbered. It is too dark to discern its expression, yet one can easily imagine something gelid yet exalted, something gladiatorial; the unflinching fixity of the duelist.

The night is come alive; yip of coyote, jatter of cricket; the sky above his head is webbed with bats. So close are they, so number-less, he imagines his face being brushed by the wash of their wings.

"The wings of angels," he thinks to himself.

The thought comforts him.

The orbiting of the bats describes a black halo above his head.

Seven silhouettes trail hard on his heels, broadswords hitched to their hips. With each stride the blades strobe moonlight.

(Can it be but an hour gone-past that the old man, clad in an outpour of sparks, spraddled a stool in the bed of Townsley's wagon parked on the prairie in the middle of nowhere chewing lemon rind to lemon pulp as he set those same blades to skreeing on the grind-stone?)

Four of the silhouettes belong to his sons: Owen, Salmon, Freder-ick, and Oliver.

Oliver is sixteen.

Another is that of his son-in-law Henry Thompson, Ruth's hus-band. The others are neighbors: the Yid grocer, Teddie Weiner, and Black Jack Townsley, who reeks perpetually of shellac—he is a housepainter by trade and has for some months now been dying incrementally of lead poisoning—and who better than the others knows the lay of this land.

Save Weiner, all are Christians: they know well how to hate.

Today is Saturday; judging by the stars, the old man reckons it the cusp of twelve.

He has not slept in twenty-four hours, he is deeply unrested, yet he has never felt more awake in his life, more alive to his surround-ings.

He slows when he hears the rainsplash, flips a palm upward feel-ing for the force of its slant, feels nothing. Only then does he under-stand—most of the company is relieving itself back there in the brush and the bushes.

A touch of the jangles, probably.

"Should be up ahead a piece," he gruffs to himself, more than mildly put out at their dalliance.

The creek is called by an Indian name, the Pottawatomie, and come Sunday—which is to say, sometime in the next few minutes— with a hand from the death squad presently hosing down the Kansas steppe, he aims to sweep it like a Biblical torrent.

("But Father," Oliver had remarked earlier, "those are not slave-owners on that creek."

"They are slave *worshipers*," the old man had replied, "and for what I have in mind, they will serve so much the better. Do not trouble yourself. All this was decreed to happen long before a man among us was born.")

Once they have regrouped, he addresses them in the darkness. "Time to cross the Rubicon," he says bloodlessly. "God awaits His sea of corpses.

"Doyle's first."

Oliver is staring at his father when for a moment and a moment only, the moonlight spangles his face and the son thinks to himself not for the first time how much he resembles a vulture, a great, sombreroed, broadsword-wielding vulture, and how grateful he is that *he* is not the Doyles.

"God help them," he thinks with a shudder, wishing the business over and done. "God help us all."

James, Billy, and Drury Doyle are Clinch Mountain Tennesseeans, father and sons who once made their living training and selling Russian wolfhounds to the slavehunting trade. (Though the bloodhound is the more widely employed, it is the opinion of the Doyles that the wolfhound, while clearly less efficient at tracking and treeing its quarry, is more adept at bringing it down.)

After being roused from their beds at pistol point, the three of them are gunbarreled from their cabin by the old man and herded barefoot in their nightshirts onto the California Road where Frederick, Townsley, and Weiner hand each of them a prairie grass torch in advance of cattleprodding them down the lane at sword point.

The entourage has proceeded no more than one hundred yards when Father Doyle remarks, "Who ye be and what ye want?"

"It matters not who I am," replies the old man, reining up short. "You are prisoners of the Northern Army, and I want nothing but that you hold your tongue and hie yourself down the road 'neath your feet."

"What fer?" pipes up Drury, raising his torch on high and rubbernecking the darkened highway. "What's out there?"

"Couldn't say," says the old man. "Could be heaven, may be hell. Reckon you'll find out soon enough."

"You ain't a-comin?" asks Billy.

When the old man shakes his head, Billy says, "Then we ain't a-goin."

Training his pistol on Billy's midsection, the old man cocks the hammer by the web of his thumb. "Beat it. Go on. Take a hike," he says grimly, pointing the barrel at each of them in succession before aiming suddenly sidewise and high in advance of releasing the spur.

The shot powders the night to fractions.

"Runaway! Now! All you Doyles!"

Drury and his father cover forty yards on the dead hurtle before meeting up with Owen, Salmon, and Oliver standing musketeered across the middle of the road, their swords gripped like bayonets out-thrust at armslength before them.

So intent are father and son on getting away, so hell-bent on outrunning their imaginary pursuers, that they collide head-on with the roadblock, impaling themselves to the hilt on the blades.

Billy lags some distance behind. When he registers what has happened he tosses aside his torch, shears off the road, and crashes into the underbrush where he pitches headfirst into a coulee, becoming as entangled in the sage, cocklebur, and bramblebush as a toddler in a snirkle of barbed wire.

Oliver tracks him down no more than twenty yards from the shoulder of the road overturned and upended, sprawled on the ground like a crustacean on its carapace.

Billy Doyle is barely twenty.

Oliver, who is almost seventeen, decapitates him with his broadsword. (It takes him four ineptly applied swaps.)

When Salmon arrives a short while later he lops off Billy's arms, the right at the shoulder, the left above the elbow, a single exemplary whop per limb. Salmon, like his headless amputee, is twenty years old.

Allen Wilkinson resides on the creek roughly half a mile south. He is a member of the Pro Slave Legislature, the "bogus" legislature so-called by the old man, and the lone settler on the creek who can read and write.

A few days earlier he had ballpeened a manifest to the door of a neighborhood dramshop:

> **As chairman of the Vigilance Committee I call upon all loyal citizens to observe and report all persons as shall by the expression of abolition sentiments produce disturbance to the quiet of citizens or danger to their domestic relations. Abolitionists take heed! Get off the creek in 30 days or have your throats cut—man, woman, and child!**

An overweight, pudding-soft man with a bonnet of lawless red hair and a piratical black eyepatch, when he is not impersonating the politician—he owes his election to the customary bully-boy ballot-stuffing—he greatly relishes cuffing around his wife, Louisa Jane, whose nickname is Powderpuff.

The old man corkscrews Wilkinson from bed by an earlobe (not bothering this time even to unbelt his pistol).

"What do you intend with him?" croaks Powderpuff, who is down with the rubella. "I am feeling mighty poorly and need someone to stay with me."

Wilkinson stands trembling next to his bed, naked but for his stockinged feet, cupping both hands to his crotch.

"You have neighbors," says the old man.

"I do," she answers, "but they are not here and I am not well enough to fetch them. One of your men must stay with me."

"I cannot spare a single one," says the old man.

"Then let Allen stay the night. He can bring one of the neighbors in the morning and you can come for him after. I will see to it that he remains here."

"Not on your life," says the old man, shaking his head. "I believe you will recover all the same. I am sorry you are off your feed. I myself suffer with the ague from time to time. You might try tincture of lime and saltpeter."

Outside, as they jostle him down the road leading away from the cabin, Henry Thompson batswoops up behind Powderpuff Louisa Jane Wilkinson's husband, fishooks his broadsword around his neck from behind, and wings its blade exuberantly aslant his thropple.

Allen Wilkinson's hands fly from his crotch to his throat as he plunges to his knees and pitches forward on his face.

Teddie Weiner watches contemptuously as Wilkinson jerks and thrashes in the middle of the road, his calcitrate and naked body disgorging life.

The color of his skin makes Weiner think of the belly of a fish. It could be argued that it more closely resembles shortening or parsnips.

It is only when he hears the gurgling that the kike becomes furious. Growling an epithet in German, he draws his broadsword and cleaves in two the back of Wilkinson's skull.

When the blade strikes occipital bone, it shivers in his hand.

Dutch Henry Sherman is a Prussian-immigrant saloonkeeper who with his less enterprising, alcohol-addled brother, Will, runs Dutch Henry's Crossing, the squalid cluster of log cabins and sod houses that landmark the creek's fording place.

The Shermans, both of whom stand six feet, four inches, are nearly as fond of rustling Free Soil cattle as they are of ravishing native women, particularly those off the neighboring Pottawatomie Indian Reservation. (Wilkinson, it should be stated, never cast a vote without which it was first approved by Dutch Henry; the Shermans run Wilkinson like a stalking-horse.)

Rumpusing through the window of one of the cabins, Owen and the old man find Dutch Will, also known as Blotto Will, abed.

"What's it?" slurs Will, awakened by the ruction. "Who's there?"

"Where is your brother?" demands the old man as Will fumbles the coal oil lantern on the endtable beside his bed. "Where is Dutch Henry?"

"Ain't a-saying." His breath is a stew of liquor. "Who be asking?"

"The Northern Army is upon you. Resist and you shall be killed. Do you surrender?"

"You have the drop on me." As the lamplight flares, the whiskified Dutch Will finds himself nose to nose with the barrel of the old man's sidearm. "Reckon I must."

"Then where is your brother?"

"Out after cattle. Out on the plains."

"Do you have weapons here?"

"Not much. A pair of rifles. The Bowie there." Still fuddled with sleep, he nods blearily to an enormous knife hanging sheathed in its belt from the antler rack on the wall.

"See to it," the old man generals Owen. "Sherman, come with me."

"But—my boots."

"You'll not be needing any of that."

Prodding him at gunpoint from the cabin, the old man finds Weiner and Henry Thompson wardening outside the door. Together they rustle Dutch Will down to the creek bank where he stands pie-eyed and yawing like a gyroscope.

"Get in," sighs the old man, waving his handiron halfheartedly toward the water.

"In?" asks the diplopic Will, uncomprehending.

"Go on." The old man sounds abstracted and world-wearied. Or bored stiff. "Get on down there. Wade in."

"Wade? But . . ."

"We don't have time for this," says the old man, glancing reproachfully from Weiner to Thompson and back to Dutch Will.

When Will topples into the creek it is much in the manner of a poleaxed lamb, his gross anatomy flopping ignominiously down the mud embankment where for the briefest instant it flippers about the shallows like a beached mackerel.

"Du vergut dis," growls Weiner, using the face of his brain-glopped blade to hockeystick the bodyless head down the bank where it jounces to a stop in the crook of its arm.

Henry Thompson hurdles into the creek and hacks off the no longer Blotto Will's left hand with a single swap, raising a flowerburst of reddened water.

It is the sockdolager. The business is done. The old man stands on the creek bank, his head cocked like a terrier as he interrogates the lifeless body cradling its severed head.

Only then does he appear to take in how it has come to posture upside down and winking, one eye swocked open, the other squinched shut.

"Gather up the others," he tells Weiner and Thompson, his voice sounding not so much emotionless as wrung of all emotion. "Tell them they must wash their weapons in this creek, that they must wash their hands. Tell them they must wash this night from each of their persons."

Waiting until they have scuttled off downcreek, he strips off his clothes, fishes a ball of tallow soap from the pocket of his duster, and enters the blood-taintured waters below.

It takes precisely four days for the Pro Slave Territorial Court to swear out the first-degree murder warrant authorizing the launching by United States marshals, federal soldiers, local militia, and Kickapoo Rangers of the most elaborate manhunt in Kansas history.

In the meantime the old man receives word from home for the

first time in months. "We are middling well," writes Mary. "Our little cow is farrow. Old Spot came in on the 4 of this month & gave a nice mess of milk. Ruth has got a dreadful cross baby. Our boy Watson complains a little with worms. We try to stay out of debt & so have no money to get leather for shoes. I make what we want from cloth. We have made 64 pounds of sugar, 3 gallons of molasses, & a little vinegar. It was a very poor year for making sugar."

As the world comes crashing down around his head, he goes to ground, losing himself deep in the interior of the bush country.

"They fear most what they cannot see," he says, and makes himself invisible.

Those men were not killed in retaliation, or self-defense, or because an emergency existed in that neighborhood. They were not killed because of what they had done. They were killed because of what they believed. They were sacrificed as examples. They were offerings to God.

Matters had become intolerable. I wished matters brought to a head. I wished to create a new set of circumstances, to reverse the momentum.

I acted to head off history.

Those killings were calculated to strike terror and provoke reaction and achieve shock value. Thus their nature: the victims—none of them slaveowners—dragged from their beds on the Sabbath in the dead of the night—I had not forgotten the lesson of old Nat Turner—dispatched with broadswords, their corpses mutilated and abandoned.

I believed then and believe now, that however savage, it was a righteous act and accomplished good. It succeeded in getting the ball rolling in favor of God and against the godless. I feel no regret about it. Had circumstances warranted it, I would not have hesitated to execute a good many more in precisely the same manner. Millions were then being held in bondage. The moral arithmetic was entirely on our side.

To label it murder is to confuse petty legalism with divine decree. It requires neither defense nor justification by me and I offer none. Posterity has since vindicated every act of mine to prevent slavery from being extended into Kanzas, and no blood was ever shed by my hands save in self-defense or by the grace of God.

"I have not come to bring peace," said Christ to his disciples, *"but a sword."*

"I will devastate the land so that your enemies who settle in it shall be astonished at it," said Almighty God, *"and I will unsheath the sword after you, and your land shall be a desolation."*

I am content to let the Lord Jehovah stand my judge.

Hold on just a second. Did any of those men die by your own hand?

I approved of their deaths, which were a service to God and decreed by Him through all eternity.

That does not answer. Did you kill any of them yourself?

Having as much as committed murder in their hearts, according to Scripture they deserved to die. I acted in obedience to the will of God. The Lord Jehovah directed me what to do.

You refuse to answer direcuy then.

God smote them dead through His agent on earth, which agent I was. He used me as an instrument in His hands to kill those men, and had I lived awhile longer, I believe He would have used me as an instrument to kill a great many more.

I take it then that you did in fact slay them with your own hands.

I was present at their deaths. Their deaths were my idea. The manner of their deaths was of my making. Their deaths were deserved. I approved them. I arranged them. The swords that slew them were sharpened upon my stone. I accept that their blood is on my hands.

I remind you that confession is good for the soul.

And I you that every lie is a truth somewhere in time.

You balk then at confessing your crime.

Not at all. Indeed, I confess now that I was prepared to do whatever was necessary, up to and including killing the enemy. Kanzas was in a state of war. I operated under the rules of that war. I took that war very much to heart.

Those who were not there cannot conceive of what it was like. Certain measures became necessary and certain steps were taken.

That night on the Pottawatomie I stood low before the Lord and did His bidding.

I would do it all again. I would do it again in a heartbeat.

John Brown, Jr.

When I heard what Father had done I could scarce credit my ears. I fear I came quite unglued, for public sentiment ran so high against him that, though I had had no hand in the business myself, I was judged guilty by association and had no choice but to resign my captaincy in the militia, give over my office in the Legislature, and take asylum in the thickets where I was directly hunted down, arrested, tried, and imprisoned. Father's action produced a shock upon my mind from which I fear I never fully recovered. Even now I cannot brood upon it without feeling embittered. In one night he had blasted my future forever.

Jason Brown

What Father did was a wicked, uncalled-for, unforgivable crime. I did not approve of it then, and approve of it the less so now. Receiving the news of his atrocities was such a terrible shock to my feelings that I believed I must lose my mind. "If these be the things that make war honorable," I remember thinking to myself, "then please God deliver me from its honors."

Owen Brown

What Father did was the work the rest wished done but deemed too dirty to do themselves. He did their dirty work, and none dare judge him for it.

Salmon Brown

What Father did saved the day. It resulted in good for the Free State cause, especially for the settlers along the creek. It was often said after the killings that a single Free State man could put the fear of God into an entire company of Pro Slave. Father single-handedly turned the tide.

Frederick Brown

Those men had murder in their hearts. They required regulating, and regulating's what they got. They had a sort of trial. They were found guilty. They were executed. How and by whom is unimportant.

Oliver Brown

By his act Father covered himself in glory. He made himself dreadful. Thereafter his name carried all the weight of an army armed to the teeth with banners flying. Overnight he became the most feared man in Kanzas.

NEIGHBORS

Charles Robinson

He was the only man at that time who comprehended the situation and saw the absolute necessity of striking a blow—and had the nerve to strike it. Of course, none of us had any use for his abolitionism.

James Hanway

We were all shocked at first and not a little frightened at the prospect of reprisals, and I won't gainsay that many condemned him loud and long, but I did not know a Free State settler but what in time regarded his actions as the most fortunate event in the history of Kansas. He saved the lives of the Free State men on that creek and they looked upon him as their Deliverer—no mean feat in light of his abolitionist sentiments, which they roundly considered wholly obnoxious.

George Crawford

I confess I protested against it. We were settlers. He was not. He could strike a blow and leave. The retaliatory blow would fall on us. "When a snake bites me I don't go a-hunting for that particular snake," I recall one of their bully-boys telling me, "I kill the first snake I come to."

No, the only thing born of his violence was more of the same. He brought it on the whole territory: a freefall into slaughter.

That said, he never flinched. "Stay away from me and my family," I warned him after. "You are a marked man."

"I intend to *be* a marked man," came his reply.

He had a pair on him the size of a bull elephant. I reckon that counts for something.

Samuel Adair

Everafter the Pro Slavery men stood in terror, for they knew not when their end would come. Or where. Or how. The idea of him, the mere notion that he existed and was out there someplace, an unseen presence armed and watching, made him a power. The Pro Slavery crowd had been discharging its guns at us all along. Now, in a single night, it had had its barrels turned back upon itself. It was a tragic and bloody act, but oh, how it made us take heart.

Clad in a cassinette nightshirt out at the elbows, a rabbit's fur chapka tugged down past his ears, and a pair of weevil-gnawed moccasins worn through at the toes, he appears much the bedraggled half-wit, but lolled tailorwise atop his swaybacked paint in the middle of Main Street polishing off the last of his gingersnaps, the dust-talced, squint-eyed old veteran is listening fully mindful.

This time of day in the pro-slave capital of Topeka the sun is so unblinking, you'd swear it could see right through you and out the other side; the old man can feel it chewing at the back of his neck. Crescents of perspiration canoe his upper lip; the sweat forms rafts across the front of his nightshirt.

"I say he's a murdering cutthroat," fanfares the ostrich-plumed young champion of slavery for the benefit of the pre-lunch throng congregating in the bakeoven air outside Morrison's Cafe & Groggery. "I say he's a mangy cur who never dared to fight fair, but skulked and backshot and bushwhacked in the dark. And I say if I could but catch sight of him this fine day, I would shoot Old Brown down for the pile of cowflop he is."

"That is all very well," says the grizzled veteran, scissoring down from his mount and slippering forward through the parboiled crowd, raising the white-caliche alkali dust like ground fog in his wake, "and brave as brass to boot.

"So here," he quickdraws a pair of revolvers from beneath his nightshirt and thrusts them handles first at the dumbstruck speechifier. "As you are unlikely ever again to chance upon the opportunity, I suggest you make good your claim upon the spot.

"Go ahead, son. You know what they say. No time like the present. The sun's at your back and you've got him dead to rights. Make the play. Go to work. Take the pistols and blaze away. Send Old Brown to his Maker.

"You'll be a dandy if you do."

Mouth agape, the young fop looks as if he's about to bust out crying. "A piece of friendly advice though. Best shut that yap of yours first. Keep on blathering thataway, and it's like to queer your aim."

The young hotspur looks as if he's about to make water. "Shucks, mister," he finally scuffs together, "I was just funnin'. Them was just words. I couldn't shoot you."

Returning the pistols to their hideouts, the older man breasts up chest to chest with the younger.

"No, you couldn't, son," he says simply. "You surely couldn't.

"Would've been an entertainment, though, to see you try."

Kickapoo Ranger bully-boys torch Brown's Station while the old man watches powerless from the bullrushes. The family has vacated the premises but moments before; they watch transfixed as the flames of their hard-had home scarve the distant sky broadcasting their dispossession.

"God sees it," says the old man, blinking back the tears. "God sees it all."

He lives at large now, one "with the serpents of the rocks and the wild beasts of the wilderness," as he writes Mary when he contrives the opportunity; he lives "like the David of old."

He is wanted dead or alive, a fugitive from justice, a chevied beast with a price on its head.

He keeps his head down.

He self-suffices.

He lives off the land. Green corn and unbolted oatmeal. Unboiled creek water and sorrel pie. He sleeps in the saddle in the belly of the bush.

He hawkeyes the horizon and bloodhounds the terrain, tea-leaving the scat and the spoor of animals, olfactoring the aromas of the air for the salient tales they may tell.

He forages the heavens, computes the circuitry of the stars, calibrates the configuration of the clouds, calculates the phases of the moon, ciphers the spectacle of the sun—the intentions pentimentoed in each of its sunset colors.

His beard snowfalls past his sternum.

His toes protrude from his heel-worn boots.

His body shakes with ague.

His eyes are chromed with fever.

He clays his body with creek mud to quell the itch of insects.

He lives like a cornered animal—knived, revolvered, cutlassed, and carbined—twenty-four hours a day.

Bandoliers X his chest.

He recently has come into possession of one of the newfangled Sharp's, a lightweight, superbly balanced, breech-loading carbine capable of firing with accuracy ten shots a minute at distances exceeding three hundred yards. His boasts a globe sight. The double click of its hammer cocking, the oiled metal slide of the breech block are the most melodic sounds he can imagine.

He gathers about him a dozen Sharp's-armed horsemen. He calls them the Free State Kansas Mounted Regular Volunteers. (Two are *John E. Cook* and *William H. Leeman*: remember them.) He nominates himself their captain.

He becomes a guerrilla.

His cardinal rules are:

1. Hurry up the fight and press close quarters.
2. Take more care to die well than to live long.
3. Avoid at all costs resting to death.

He sleeps sitting upright in the saddle, loaded Sharps idled across his lap, back braced by the trunk of a tree. "Look at him," one of his men marvels. "He looks more awake asleep than most do awake."

He draws up a "Covenant of Enlistment." No smoking, no drinking, no cursing, no philandering. (About profanity he remarks, "I will not tolerate it. It is not only wrong but foolish. If there is a God, what is to be gained by taking His name in vain? And if there is not, why ask His curse on anything?")

He prescribes prayer twice daily and Grace before all meals.

He tells his Covenanteers: "Never molest women or children. Never take property that is useless to Free State people. Never destroy property wantonly. Any horses and cattle taken are to be held as the common property of all."

He tells his Covenanteers: "I would rather have smallpox, yellow fever, and cholera all together in my camp than a single man without principles. Give me men of good principles, God-fearing men who respect the Lord Jehovah, men like yourself, and with my holy dozen I will oppose any one hundred of these Ranger infidels."

The Holy Dozen rustles cattle, confiscates horses, requisitions provisions, appropriates property, captures arms and munitions, takes prisoners, fights skirmishes.

The Holy Dozen makes holy war.

Kansas bleeds.

They win a handful of minor affrays against long odds which he describes as "giving the elephant another tug." These scrimmages are covered by correspondents employed by magazines and newspapers in the East.

When in the summer of 1856 Acting Governor Dan Woodson declares the entire territory "in a state of open insurrection and rebellion," the old man remarks, "Out of chaos comes cleansing."

In a scuffle near the settlement of Osawatomie he is badly bruised in the small of the back by spent grapeshot. "If all the bullets that have ever been aimed at me had hit," he joshes good-naturedly, "I should have been as full of holes as a riddle."

He is widely reported scalped, castrate, and "stiffened with death."

When he emerges essentially intact, the press dubs him Osawatomie Brown; overnight, he is become a celebrity.

Salmon, Oliver, and Henry Thompson decide that they have had their fill and leave the territory. John Junior languishes in a Pro Slave jail having earlier been arrested on charges of high treason. Owen and Frederick stand stoutly by their father.

When Governor John White Geary assumes office he dismantles the Pro Slave militia and employs the federal troops in the eviction of the Kickapoo Rangers from the territory.

Racked by malaria and dysentery, the old man secretly prepares to exit Kansas with his sons. Lying beneath a sea of alpaca blankets on a false-bottomed wagon bed, he tells his Covenanteers who have gathered to bid him farewell, "As I have but a short time remaining on this earth and but one death to die, I prefer to die fighting for this cause: that there be *no* peace in this land until slavery is finished.

"Now I will give them something else to do than to extend slave territory. I will carry the war unto darkest Africa. I will Kanzify all the South. I will unleash the beast of freedom that it may havoc in their midst.

"Enough of bleeding Kanzas. The time is now to make a bloody spot elsewhere."

Frederick Brown
August 30, 1856
Age twenty-six
(Wild-hearted Fred)

Roughly 8 A.M.

About a mile west of Osawatomie.

Frederick Brown stands clutching the leads of his horse in the middle of the road that hugs the ridgeline balconying the town.

Three horsemen crest the ridge at an easy canter, draw close.

"Hallo boy," says the one out front, reining up his sorrel.

His name is Martin White, he is a minister, and in his spare time he pilots for the Kickapoo Rangers.

"Hallo back," says Fred half smiling. His brow pleats. "Hey, don't I know you?"

"I know *you*!" roars White. "You are part of that damned Brown rabble! You are my enemy!"

The Sharps leaves a hole in Fred's chest the size of several thumbs.

Dismounting, White walks over and shoots the recumbent Fred in the back of the head through the mouth, spraying his brains to leftovers. Then, kneeling beside the body, he tugs off his boots and tries them on.

They don't fit worth a damn.

From the crown of the hill they can see the cabin in the distance.

One of them fishes a field glass from his saddlebag.

"Yep, it's him all right, murdering polecat."

He hands the scope to the old man who grunts in recognition. The Reverend Martin White is sitting in a church pew reading a book in the shade of a tree.

"What say, Cap'n? We go down?"

"We will not hurt one hair of his head," says Osawatomie Brown. "I will not go one inch to take his life. It would be taken as an act of revenge. It would appear personal.

"I act from principle, not passion."

Sabers left snug in their scabbards, the horsemen pass by.

Kanzas I always considered much of an abortion.

Despite my diligence, the fighting never amounted to more than a neighborhood brawl. The larger war I had prayed might result, the **national** *war, never materialized.*

Kanzas was like a prairie fire that, absent the winds to fan it, just up and burned itself out.

———

When I came out of Kanzas I had a plan, and each of my thoughts, words, and deeds would from that time forward be directed toward the implementation of that plan.

Much of that comportment I found personally distasteful.

I apologize for none of it.

I was poor, time was short, and the plan required financing.

I could not afford the luxury of splitting moral hairs or observing ethical niceties.

I tried my best to keep the deceit, dissembling, and duplicity to a minimum.

I fear my best too often fell far short.

Knowing from his days at Perkins & Brown that the real bullion lies coffered along the seaboard, he catches the first train East, debarks at Hartford, Connecticut, opens an account at the Cashier State Bank, and places an order at Caledonia Printer's & Publications, Ltd. for a single gross of circulars that read:

TO THE FRIENDS OF FREEDOM

This is to introduce the undersigned, a friend whose means already were dangerously depleted when he first went out to Kanzas to undergo untold hardship for the Cause of Liberty, and whose resources are now completely exhausted. No less anxious to continue his effort to sustain that Cause in which he figured with some success, if at constant peril to his life under the title "Osawatomie Brown," he is reduced to making this earnest appeal to the Friends of Freedom.

I implore all honest Lovers of Liberty and Human Rights to hold up my hands by contributions of *pecuniary aid.* Same may be sent in drafts to W. H. D. Callender, Cashier State Bank, Hartford, Ct.

Will either gentlemen or ladies, or both, who love the Cause, volunteer to take up the business? I need not mention that every citizen of this Republic is under moral obligation to sustain the Cause for the neglect of which he or she will be held accountable by God.

It is with no little sacrifice of personal feeling that I appear in this manner before the public.

John Brown.

He travels the East Coast abolitionist salon circuit, circulars strewn like confetti in his wake: Boston, New York City, Albany, Springfield, back to Hartford, New Haven, Concord, back to Boston.

He leaves holstered and unbrandished the envelope containing his letter of reference and introduction vouchsafed him by Ohio Governor Salmon P. Chase; with this crowd his celebrity is entre enough.

He meets with what the newspapers later will label "the Secret Six," but to which he refers derisively as "the Claque of Humanitarians" or "the Men without Fists."

Theodore Parker.
Samuel Gridley Howe.
George Luther Stearns.
Thomas Wentworth Higginson.
Gerrit Smith.
Franklin Sanborn.

They are some of the wealthiest, most learned men in the country. They are America's anointed, her fair-haired favorites, her illuminati, cognoscenti, and glitterati, snowballed into one. Smith is the nation's largest landowner and leading philanthropist—at his death he will have underwritten charitable contributions in excess of eight million dollars. Stearns is a multimillionaire industrialist. Four of the six are Harvard graduates. Sanborn is the protégé of Ralph Waldo Emerson. Parker, a Unitarian preacher whose personal library boasts twelve thousand volumes, is fluent in twenty languages, including Icelandic.

Rich, brilliant, refined, they are to a man ardent abolitionists.

And unregenerate racists.

"The African race is greatly inferior to the Caucasian in intellectual power and in the instinct for liberty," Parker has written, "even though the African man has the largest organs of generation in the world, and the African woman the most exotic heat."

"Destruction of slavery will remove artifical protections and allow fair play to natural laws which will eventuate in the disappearance of the colored population from the continent before the more vigorous white," Howe has written. "Abolitionism thus becomes a sacred duty since it promotes the purification and elevation of the national blood."

Aiming to curry their favor that he might tap their resources, the old man stages for his audience the performance of his life.

Taking deliberate care with his costume—black patent leather cravat of the sort worn by the United States Marines; caped, gray military surtout; visored fur cap; calf-high cowhide topboots; six-shooters jutting from the waistband—he expertly exploits what he knows instinctively makes them tick. He works the holy con. He pushes both their buttons:

Nostalgie de la boue—the vicarious thrill experienced by the sophisticated from romanticizing the primitive and exotic

and

Noblesse oblige—the sense of self-righteousness experienced by the privileged from acting charitably toward the underprivileged

He's got them coming and going.

Armed with props and visual aids—a fire-chewed Bible plucked from the ashes of Brown's Station, the blood-encrusted shackles worn by John Junior in prison, the enormous, gilt-mounted Bowie knife lifted from the Kickapoo Ranger Captain Henry Clay Pate at the Battle of Blackjack—he delivers his lines with a thespian's aplomb:

It was just after daylight. I had less than a dozen men, the enemy over eighty. Pate and his crew were lurking in a ravine with plenty of brush for cover. I advanced on their flank and pressed to close quarter. The sun was well up and the grass was dry and I remember thinking how it would look well spattered with blood. Suddenly one of the ruffians stands up flying a white kerchief from a rifle barrel. This is where he reaches down and hoists the gleaming blade from the top of his boot. *Look here.* **This** *was Pate's.*

AND

I once saw a swollen and blackened body in the middle of a road with its head and heart shot out, this after the body had lain on the ground for some eighteen hours worked at by blowflies and maggots. That body had been left to rot in the sun by the bully-boys who had made of it nothing but carrion and who had a perfect right to be hanged. This is where he pauses at some length, apparently to wipe a tear from his eye. *That body belonged to my son.*

AND

I am a wanted man in Kanzas and have been reliably informed of the possibility of some of Uncle Sam's hounds being on my track even as we speak. This is where he swings a furtive glance left, then right, in advance of lowering his voice as if complice in an intimacy. *They shall never take me. I will resist any process whatsoever served upon me with irons* **in** *rather than* **upon** *my hands, for I claim there is no law there, only law-***breaking***.*

They believe—both because he leads them to believe and because they wish to believe so desperately—that he means to raise funds to mount a reconstituted defense of Kansas. He suggests the creation of a "Secret Service composed of border patrols, vigilance squadrons, mounted regulators, and home-guard companies stocked with men who fear God too much to fear anything human." He predicts that the Pro Slave faction will attack in force come spring.

Let them inquire too long or probe too deeply, however, and he bridles. "I will not be interrogated," he declares sharply. "I do not

179

expose my intentions. No one knows them but myself. I serve from secret, no questions asked.

"If you wish to know what I am about, do not examine me too closely. Rather consider the work in which I am engaged. There you will discover all that need concern you. You know my history. You know of my activities in Kanzas. I am no adventurer. Support me because you support the cause that I embody. Take me as you take God. Take me on faith alone. I have no purpose but to serve the cause of liberty."

Bronson Alcott, father of Louisa May, and a "Claque" spear-carrier, comments, "I have spoken with him on several occasions, but he leaves much in the dark concerning his destinations and designs for the future. Still, our best people contribute in aid of his plan even without knowledge of particulars, such confidence does he inspire."

Ralph Waldo Emerson, who invites him to spend the night, later describes him as "artless goodness and sublime courage."

Henry David Thoreau, who invites him to dinner, later describes him as "a transcendentalist saint and an angel of light."

There is more going on here than a shared commitment to the Cause. There is the near sexual allure that the Fist-in-the-flesh possesses for the Men without Fists.

"I think him the manliest man I have ever seen," remarks one.

In the end, they all but bulldoze one another over scrambling to assume the Missionary Position:

The Massachusetts State Kansas Aid Committee, chaired by Stearns, votes him custody of a dozen trunks of clothing, two hundred Sharp's carbines, four thousand ball cartridges, thirty-one thousand percussion caps, various sabers, one brass cannon, and one thousand dollars.

The National Kansas Aid Committee, of which Howe is a member, votes him supplies for one hundred men and five thousand dollars for "defensive measures in Kansas."

He collects on the fly well over one thousand dollars in private donations.

Stearns spends thirteen hundred dollars out of pocket to buy him two hundred Navy Colt revolvers, then pledges to deposit seven thousand dollars in his Hartford bank account.

The lot is arranged in darkest secrecy and strictest confidence.

The old man intends not a farthing of it for Kansas.

Thanking them profusely, he makes for Collinsville in Connecticut where he has it from a well-informed source that there lives a forgemaster whose work is well worth the visit.

FRIEND

Mrs. Judge Thomas Russell

When he came to Boston that first time, he stayed with the judge and me the better part of a week, almost the entire time barricaded in his room declining to receive a single visitor, the help included.

However it happened one evening that the two of us were sitting to ourselves in the parlor when suddenly he drew from a boot top a long, evil-looking knife. Well, you can imagine the start it gave me. The judge did not keep weapons, we had children in the house you understand, and, well, I wasn't accustomed to knife play in my parlor. One means, just imagine.

Not that that was an end to it, for he directly drew from his other boot two smaller, though no less wicked-looking knives, and then from an inside coat pocket a large pistol, and then from the pocket of his weskit yet a smaller one.

Here I must say he looked at me rather doubtfully, for I believe he had yet a third concealed upon his person which he also would have removed had it not been inappropriate in my presence to resort to the indelicate measures necessary to get at it.

In any event, he proceeded then to draw each and all of the charges from the guns, after which he arose and solemnly deposited them in the palms of my hands filling them both with cartridges while I sat mouth agape, paralyzed with fear.

"Now, don't be awkward," he cautioned. "Keep steady, or they will all fire off. You hold in your hands there the lives of twelve men deserving of death."

Returning to his seat, he then blew into each end of each of the gun barrels, examined meticulously each of their locks, ran a thumb along each of the knife blades, and having retrieved the munitions from me, one by one reloaded the firearms.

"You haven't had this in your parlor before, have you?" he asked.

When I answered no, he darkened and said, "I shall never be taken alive you know, though it would be a shame and a pity to stain so fine a carpet as this.

"Now let me remind you once again that should you hear a noise in the night, be quick to put the baby under the pillow."

Whether he seriously wished to assure himself of the condition of his defenses, or was more interested in amusing himself with the effect it had on me, I never have satisfied myself.

I believe he was a great man; and by far, by far the queerest I ever knew.

During a reception arranged for his benefit at the Exeter Street manse of Theodore Parker in Boston, the old man had found himself embroiled in a heated exchange with William Lloyd Garrison, the abolitionist editor he once had so admired.

"Where there is no life, sir," the bespectacled Garrison had declared in response to the old man's increasingly fervent argument espousing violent intervention with the peculiar institution, "there is no freedom!"

"But I am stunned, sir," the old man had retorted. "Did not my master Jesus Christ come down from heaven and sacrifice Himself to free the human race? Should I, a mere worm not worthy to crawl under His feet, then refuse to sacrifice myself?

"No sir! If by going up to heaven I can effect the going down of slavery, Lord take me now!"

It had been just then that one of Parker's liveried servitors, entirely by coincidence and wholly oblivious to the tension of the moment, had approached the two men with a gleaming platter ornamentally arrayed with canapés of the sort often referred to colloquially as pigs-in-a-blanket.

As it happened, Garrison's favorite.

"Ah, what have we here?" the Quakerish editor had remarked, eyes widening as he helped himself to a toothpicked pair.

The old man could only shake his head and sigh. "I am sorry," he had said, declining, "but I fear I have long since forgotten what it means to eat for pleasure."

WILLIAM LLOYD GARRISON

I never could get at his theology. For him there seemed to be but a single wrong, and that was slavery. On anything else he refused to express himself. There was no question that he believed in God, but his attitude seemed to be, if anything stand in the way of getting rid of slavery, one might properly break all the Decalogue to mow it down.

You might say I respected him, but did not admire him.

I liked him even less.

JOHN BROWN

William Lloyd Garrison was an old woman. History is deaf and implacable; history is made by men's actions, not their sentiments. He thought he could jaw slavery to death. Well, by the time I met him he'd been jawing nigh a quarter of a century.

Appeared to me slavery was as full of sap as ever.

Before departing Boston he troubles himself to pay his respects on the still bedridden Charles Sumner.

"Ah, come in, Mr. Brown, come in," says Sumner, peering at him over the half-rims of his reading glasses before motioning him on with the flop of a limp wrist.

" 'He has shown strength with his arm, He has scattered the proud in the imagination of their hearts, He has put down the mighty from their thrones, and exalted those of *low* degree.' " His voice, once that of a cannoneer's, is as weak and runny as a librarian's.

"Ah," says the old man, standing by the foot end of the bed. "Luke. Chapter 1, verses 51 and 52. A particular favorite of mine."

"Why does that not surprise me?" says Sumner, unhooking his spectacles from behind his ears and dabbling at his nose with a handkerchief. The cartilage there has been slow to mend; he is plagued by chronic sniffles. "So, I had been informed that you were in our fair city. You must forgive my having left you unattended until now, but I fear I am not up to that sort of thing just yet. The receptions and banquets and so forth.

"But here. I forget myself. Have a seat."

"Not atall, Senator," says the old man. "I won't be staying but a moment. I intended merely to wish you a speedy recovery and be on my way." He pauses. "You know I am no politican. For the vast lot I would not fetch a bucket were they to ignite before my eyes."

"A helpful image," says Sumner chuckling softly, wincing for the trouble. "Not atall unpleasant, I must say."

"And *I* say this, sir. *I* say the Cause cannot spare you. Your voice. Your fire. Especially now. You must hasten back."

"I will try, Mr. Brown. I will try as my best allows."

"No sir. Do not try. Do!"

The old man is halfway out the door when something stops him and he wings back around. "Your frock, sir. The one you were wearing that day?"

So summarily does Sumner respond, it is as if he had anticipated the request from the outset. "Absolutely. Just there. In the wardrobe. Feel free."

The coat, once a fine black bombazine, hangs from its rack browned with blood. How much blood is shocking; from collar to waist-button the coat is so stiffened with it, it appears less cloth than cardboard.

For a long moment the old man is silent. ("I felt," he will say later, "as if I were in the presence of a holy relic.") Then, eyes glistening, he does something so peculiar that Sumner will take each nuance of it to his grave: he steps forward, buries his face deep in the garment's folds, and inhales with all the lust of a lover filling his lungs of a sweet-clovered morn.

The forgemaster's name is Charlie Blair.

"They say, Mr. Blair," says the old man, "that in these parts you are the man for a decent edge tool."

" 'Tis only my specialty," answers the aproned Blair from behind the counter. "And it is Chas to you sir. No Mistering about the shops, if you please."

"Ah, Chas is it? Then Chas, if I might inquire, what would you charge to make five hundred or one thousand pikes?"

"What sort of pike would that be then?"

"Say a Bowie blade or the like, eight or nine inches in length, double-edged of a tempered cast steel fastened by ferrules of a strong but malleable iron to the tip of a stout shaft or ash handle pole about six foot long, not dissimilar to the sort peculiar to the common hay fork."

"Well sir, something along them lines—I reckon I could make you five hundred such pieces at a dollar and a quarter a piece, or one thousand pieces at a dollar a piece."

"I believe it a fair price Chas, and would be glad to pay it for the one thousand. Shall we say five hundred dollars now and five hundred dollars on delivery?"

"Suits me," says Blair, repairing to his backroom. "I will go now and draw up the contract."

"Give a slave a pike," thinks the old man to himself, "and make a slave a man.

"Give a thousand men a pike, and make those men an army."

To Mary Day Brown

The Timbucto Mission
North Elba, New York
FROM: The Frederick Douglass House, Rochester, New York.
Dear Wife:

I am, praised be God, once more in York state, but whether I shall be able to visit you anytime soon, I cannot now say. Still, I take comfort in the feeling that I am so near.

The anxiety I feel to see you & the children once more I cannot describe. Also, I want exceedingly to see how that little company of sheep look about this time.

Unfortun'ly, the cries of my poor sorrowed & despairing brethr'n whose tears are ever in my eyes & whose sighs are ever in my ears may prevent my enjoying the happiness I so much desire.

But: courage, courage, courage! The Great Work of my life I may yet see accomplished & then be permitted, God helping, to return & rest at evening.

P.S. I shall send you some newspapers soon to let you see what different stories are told about me. None tell the truth as I know it.

Dred Scott v. *Sanford*
(Racism in Judicial Robes)
1857

THE CASE

Dred Scott—a slave whose Missouri owner takes him along when he moves to the free state of Illinois, then to the free territory of Wisconsin, eventually back to the slave state of Missouri—sues for his freedom on the basis of his having been for several years a resident on free soil.

THE DECISION
(Edited Transcripts)

We think they—negroes, the negro African race—are not included, and were not intended to be included, under the word "citizens" in the Constitution, and can therefore claim none of the rights and privileges which that instrument provides for and secures to citizens of the United States.

On the contrary, they were at that time considered as a subordinate and inferior class of beings who had been subjugated by the master race, and, whether emancipated or not, had no rights or privileges but such as those who held power might choose to grant them.

In the opinion of the court, the language used in the Declaration of Independence shows that neither slaves nor their descendants were then acknowledged as a part of the people, nor intended to be included in the general words used in that memorable instrument.

The Constitution makes no distinction between property in a slave, and other property.

The right of property in a slave is distinctly and expressly affirmed in the Constitution.

It is the opinion of the court that any Act of Congress (viz. the Missouri Compromise) which prohibits a citizen from owning property of this kind in federal territory, is *not* warranted by the Constitution and is therefore void.

Neither Dred Scott nor any of his family was made free by being carried into that territory, even if carried there by the owner with that intention.

Negroes, being members of an inferior order and altogether unfit to associate with the white race either socially or politically, have no rights which white men are bound to respect.

> —ROGER B. TANEY, age eighty, scion of a
> prosperous, slave-owning, Maryland tobacco-
> farming family, and—for the moment—chief
> justice of the United States

Taney's decision effectively renders Negroes the *only* people *on the face of the earth* barred from *ever* becoming American citizens.

Two months later, John F. A. Sanford, Dred Scott's former owner, expires in his bed in Room 46-A of the St. Louis Home for the Mentally Incompetent.

He is wearing arm and leg restraints at the time.

ABRAHAM LINCOLN

I never made any bones about being anti-abolition. Imagine for a moment the alternative: Abolish slavery, free the slaves, and . . . what? Stand idly by while emancipated cheap-labor slave-niggers swarmed North by the tens of thousands to elbow from their plows and anvils white workingmen from Maine to the Mississippi? Stand by while those same niggers aspired to polite society, rubbed elbows with our best people, clamored for the vote, fornicated with our women, in time debauched the gene pool of the North as they had hitherto the South with their enfeebled mongrel spawn?

Thus my delight in the passage of the Fugitive Slave Act. The North already was cursed with its share of legal Negroes. It scarce could withstand an onslaught of illegal ones as well.

The fact is, where slavery existed, it existed under the law. It was perfectly legal. It had of judicial constraint to be coddled. I was not prepared to blame the law-abiding slaveowner for behaving precisely as I, in his shoes, would have behaved myself.

Embracing anti-slaveryism, on the other hand—which is to say, opposing the *extension* of slavery *outside* of those states where it already existed—was a thornier matter altogether. Not that I approved of slavery *personally*. Sleuth the record; you'll find I bemoaned it as "a cruel wrong," the demise of which I hoped might be hastened by confining it to an attenuated enclave in the South even as the rest of the nation expanded west toward freedom. (Had the Lord seen fit to robe me in all earthly power, I confess I should not have known what to do with the slaves, save to ship the lot back to Africa, and Godspeed—and good riddance.) But personal conviction and political wisdom seldom coincide, and as I was for the moment willing to leave bad enough alone, so I was content to let sleeping dragons lie.

Until *Dred Scott*. *Dred Scott* made that impossible. *Dred Scott* awoke the dragons and set them to snorting fire with a vengeance.

"Any Act of Congress which prohibits a citizen from owning property of this kind (viz. slaves) in federal territory, is *not* warranted by the Constitution and is therefore void."

That was the phraseology, more or less, and try as I might to put some less sinister spin on it, that wording was a betrayal—a *Southern* betrayal, I might add—of the Founding Fathers, the Declaration of Independence, the Judeo-Christian Ethic, the democratic tradition, and the Union as a whole. If slavery was a cancer, not only was this tolerating the disease, it was guaranteeing its metastasis.

There lurked, I decided, a pernicious logic at the heart of *Dred Scott*. Namely, once make it illegal to bar slavery from a United States Territory—all those vast new territories establishing themselves out West—and it became as inevitable as two and two are four that the nation must in time become more slave than free. And once let the nation become *mostly* slave, and in time the nation must become—by election, acquiescence, or imposition—*wholly* slave.

Dred Scott was nothing more than the abolitionist nightmare turned on its head, the abolitionist nightmare minus the abolition.

I declared myself thereafter both anti-abolition *and* anti-slavery.

JOHN BROWN

Poor old agonized Abe. Heartsore and soultorn and all for what?
You know what they called him down South, don't you: High Ape of the Black Republican Free Love Free Nigger Party.

For all that, I reckon Lincoln was a great man. Which is to say, as great as any practical politician can ever be.

What he never was was any sort of folk god.

Queer how history insists upon narrating itself into saints and sinners, heroes and villains; makes the mongrels invisible; shoulders the misfits to its margins.

See, there's nothing I can say about him. Nothing that matters. Because he's not real. He doesn't exist. He's strictly private domain. Entirely public domain.

He's fairytale. He's folklore. Quicksilver. Teflon.

Father Abraham. Honest Abe.

Here, he lies.

R.I.P.

Slinging the newspaper to the floor in high dudgeon, the old man turns to Frederick Douglass and exclaims, "The highest court in the land is become but the Devil's Workshop, and *Dred Scott* is that Devil's masterwork!

"Should God now send famine, pestilence, and war upon this guilty, hypocritical nation, we need not be surprised, for never before did a people so mock and despise Him.

"*Dred Scott?* No, Frederick. Dread *God.*"

One year before the Ferry.
One year and counting

down.

Slave Rebellions:
  Spartacus, Roman Empire
  Toussaint L'Ouverture, Haiyti
  Nat Turner (with *fifty* men held *all* Virginia five weeks)

Guerrilla Warfare:
  Francis Marion v. Great Britain
  Schamyl v. Russia
  Mina v. Napoleon

See *Life of Lord Wellington,* Joachim Hayward Stocqueler, 1852, pages 71–75 (Mina), also page 102 (reliable hints), also page 196 (important instructions to officers), also page 235 (these words: "deep and narrow defiles where three hundred men could check an *army*").

—JOHN BROWN, "Notebooks" (1858?)

In slave quarters, so it is said, she is better known than the Bible (on account of she circulates more freely).

There they call her Moses.

The old man calls her General.

"General," the old man begins when he visits her in St. Catharines in Ontario, "I come to ask a favor." (St. Catharine's is a major terminus of the Underground; more than one thousand fugitive slaves make their homes there.)

She knows.

"I know," she says.

Most believe she's mystic; she won't say they're far wrong.

Since the day ol' Boss McCracken stove-in the side of her head with a makeweight for having the sand to step in the way of his fetching after one of the fieldhands who'd made his break to run off the place, ever since then she'll be going along doing the unthinkingest things—toting water, lugging wood, pitching hay, splitting rails—doesn't seem to matter what—sitting talking, walking across a room—when all of a sudden—*pffft!*—lights out, out cold on her feet, like a wind snuffed out a candle flame.

Save she's not snuffed out atall. Not hardly. She's seeing things is what—transports, raptures, auguries, visions. And hearing things besides—harps and such, choirly sounds, whoosh of angel's wings, heavenly hooves a-cleating. But voices mostly. Moses', say. Or God's.

She hears the voice of God right frequent.

Their understanding of one another—John Brown's and Harriet Tubman's—is implicit, immediate, and perfect.

He recounts for her his escapades in Kansas. She describes for him her shagtailing it off the ol' plantation down the Bucktown District out Maryland's Eastern Shore, and how the last minute she lost her nerve until His voice told how the hour was nigh and to trust to Him, and how when she got so hopeless turned round and tangled up in the swale and the brush and the bracken, why—*pffft!*—didn't she have herself a vision of Sweet Jesus smiling kindly, of Jesus pointing true, of Christ Jesus pointing ever north a-lighting up her way.

And didn't the voice sound then all-knowing and Fatherlike and lift her up and urge her on: "Come, My child. Take hold My hand. Arise and follow My footsteps to the Promised Land."

And so she'd made it. Maryland to Pennsylvania. Slave to Free.

He enumerates for her the support he's drummed up on the Seaboard. She calibrates for him her work on the Underground:

—10 years a conductress

—19 raids on plantations

—303 slaves brung off single-handed and ferried north to free land (that's over $170,000 worth, so they tell her)

—a $40,000 price on her head, dead or alive

"General," says the old man, "I believe you to be naturally manlier than any man I have ever met. Your life shames my sex by half, and credits your own twice over."

"Ain't my life," she says flatly. "Never been. Outta my hands. All in His.

"Doin' His will is all. Listen to dat voice is all. 'Go back down and bring dem off,' it say. 'Hasten-up South and usher dem through,' it say. 'Why you dally, gal,' it say, 'while de rest still back dere a-waitin'?'

"What dat voice say? Lawdy, I tell you. I tell you what it say. It say 'Moses, you go down dat Egypt land, you lead dem peoples out.'

"So I do. Best I can."

The old man's eyes are glistening. "General," he says, "I have in mind some business, and could greatly use your help."

"I know," she says.

"I need men," he says. "Money, arms, munitions—these I can get plenty of. But men." He shakes his head. "Men, *white* men, even the ones who favor my measures in secret fear association with me. I try not to blame them. I do not succeed.

"Still, you see how it is. It is men I need more than bread itself. God-fearing men. Negro men."

"What business?" she asks, eyeballing him clean through.

"Deadly business, I'm afraid," he says gravely, meeting her eye squarely with his own. "Deadly, serious business. Business more terrible, I should think, than either of us has yet had occasion to taste.

"Should it succeed—and I mean to see that it does—the Union must cleave in two. God willing, of course."

The Moses of her people does not blanch. She neither questions that the old man means what he says, nor wonders at his mettle to accomplish it. But she knows more than she is letting on, and she is not so sanguine by half. "How *dat* free de slaves?" she asks. "They all still left chained down yonder."

"Because such a split the government never will permit. And then, General, then there must come a collision the like of which the world has never known."

"Dat so?"

"It is decreed by the Lord," he replies. "In Daniel 11, verses 14 and 15. 'Many shall rise against the King of the South, and the robbers of thy people shall exalt themselves to escape the vision, but they shall fail. And the King of the North shall come and throw up siegeworks, and take even the most well-fortified cities, and the forces of the South shall have not the strength to withstand, not even its picked troops.'

"You see, decreed, and you and I must do nothing but act in true faith and play our parts, or perish for the trying.

"Now I am asking, General, will you play yours?"

"Half a mind to," she says. "You aim to team up, dat it?"

The map he unfolds before her is attached to a scrim of cambric

India-inked with crucifixes at more than a dozen places south from Virginia to Florida (St. Augustine), and west from Florida to Texas (San Antonio).

Along the map's right-hand margin a fringe of slipstitched paper tabs lists state and county populations—culled, so he discloses, from the U.S. Census Report of 1850—under the headings black/white, slave/free, adult/child, male/female.

"Each cross signifies a federal fort or arsenal," he tells her. "We strike the target, then slip away into the mountains here," he indicates the Appalachians, "or the swamps here and here," he indicates the Great Dismal and the Okefenokee. "As we move south we raid the plantations nearabout, spreading the word as we go. The slaves will rally."

"And I be along take dat flock off by Rail?"

"Most. But others'd stay on as recruits. Join the fight."

"Fight? How? What with? Bare hand? Brickbat? Stick and stone? Slave's got no notion with shooting arms."

"Pikes, General. Pikes by the thousand. Pikes ready and waiting for steadfast hands to hold them."

She feels her head gone all swimmy.

"General, the South is a powderkeg. The talk in Congress is all for secession. The right spark, the likely place, the proper time," he pounds a bony fist into a calloused palm, "the South must blow sky-high."

"Do tell."

"So General," he folds the map as if it were silk brocade before slipping it back into his pocket, "can you round up the men for the work? Would you be willing to hook on your team and wait on my call? Will you join me in doing the Lord's work, though our triumph be like the last victory of Samson?"

"I've a mind to," she says. "Reckon dere's plenty be willing."

"Well then," he says, "I only wish I had more to offer in the way of relief to ease your labors." Removing a roll of bank notes from the pocket of his trousers, he peels it off bill by bill, sliding them one after the other across the tabletop like a croupier doling out winnings. "Recruiting can be a costly business."

Folding the stack of bills in half, the woman called Moses shoves the fifty dollars' worth deep into the billows of her skirts.

"Good," he says. "When the hour draws nigh, I will find some way to send up word."

"When you reckon dat be?" she asks.

"Lord knows," he replies, his smile a gash.

Reckon it was the month before he come to St. Cat's.

I was ramblin' through a wilderness sort of place. All rocks and bushes and brushlike. Dat where I spied the serpent first off, when he raised up his hatchety head 'bove dem rocks.

'Cept dat head turn rightaway to an ol' man. A white man it was. A white man with de longest, whitenest beard—like a white torch, dat beard—and eyes like to walk straight through me out de other side.

Well, it kep on a-lookin' and a-lookin', all wishfullike, like it was fixin' to speak, to ask somethin,' save right den two others rose up, one to left, one to right. Smaller dey was, younger and cleaner-shaved—no beards on dem—but white too, white-skinned jus' like the ol' one.

"What you want with me?" I asked dem three.

Jus' den a slew of people, all mens dey was, not a woman no-wheres, dis whole mess a mens come a-swarmin' round, and beat on dem heads with sticks and clubs and such, 'til all three was laid out dead, and de ol' one a-lookin' at me wishful de whole time through.

I pondered and pondered—musta had dat same vision a dozen times—but more I did, less it seemed sensical.

'Til the day he come by my house in St. Cat's. Den I seen it right off. Dat head? Dat ol' one with the beard? Dat head was the spittin' image of John Brown hisself.

Later, heard he had two sons got killed down de Ferry.
Heard neither had beards.

JOHN BROWN

She was the best and the bravest, she was stalwart, and it would have been rank privilege to fall fighting beside her.

Surely it was only the Lord's interposition that kept her from my side in the hour of my most desperate want.

From St. Catharine's he traveled to Chatham, also in Ontario, where he orchestrated a clandestine political convention upon the pretext of organizing a Negro Masonic Lodge, it producing:

The Provisional Constitution and Ordinances for the People of the United States

Adopted May 8, 1858, at the Negro Convention
held at Chatham, West Canada
as written and recommended by John Brown

Preamble

Whereas slavery is a most barbarous, unprovoked, and unjustifiable *war* of one portion of its citizens upon another in utter disregard and violation of those eternal truths set forth in the Declaration of Independence:

Therefore we, the oppressed people of the United States—the *prisoners* of that *war*—who by a recent decision of the Supreme Court are declared to have no rights which white men are bound to respect—along with all other people degraded by the law thereof—do *for the time being* ordain for ourselves a Provisional Constitution, the better to protect our persons, property, and liberties.

Said Constitution shall not be construed to encourage the overthrow of any state government of the United States. Rather it shall apply to a created community within the purview of, but existing sovereign and separate from, the government of the United States.

Our flag shall be the same that our Fathers fought under in the Revolution.

Forty-eight Articles comprised this "Constitution" which was unanimously approved and signed by thirty-four Negroes and twelve whites. Six were:

Article 39: **ALL MUST LABOR**

All persons shall be under obligation to labor for the general good. Those refusing shall receive a suitable punishment.

Article 40: **IRREGULARITIES**

Profane swearing, filthy conversation, indecent behavior, indecent exposure of the person, intoxication, quarreling, and unlawful intercourse of the sexes, shall not be tolerated.

Article 41: **CRIMES**

Persons convicted of the forcible violation of any female prisoner shall be put to death.

Article 42: **THE MARRIAGE AND FAMILY RELATION**

The marriage relation shall be at all times respected, and families kept together as far as possible, and broken families encouraged to reunite, and intelligence offices shall be established for the purpose.

Article 43: **ARMS**

All persons connected with this organization, male or female, shall be encouraged to openly carry arms.

Article 44: **RELIGION AND THE SABBATH**

Churches shall be established for the purpose of religious and other instructions. The Sabbath shall be regarded as a day of rest devoted to moral and religious instruction and improvement, relief to the suffering, instruction of the young and ignorant, and the cultivation of personal cleanliness.

He had invited Frederick Douglass, Harriet Tubman, and each of the Secret Six to address the convention. None of them bothered to attend.

He never sought an accounting for their absence.

He never received one.

What was the point?

The point?

The purpose of the convention. The rationale behind the drafting and ratification of this so-called constitution.

Why, to establish in writing, and in the best spirit of participatory democracy, a footing upon which to proceed.

Where?

Where? I'm afraid I don't follow . . .

Well, you state an intention to proceed. Proceed where? Proceed with what?

Why, proceed southward I suppose, proceed to the mountains.

And you felt it necessary to have an *ersatz* constitution snug in your pocket before you went ahead?

I do not accept "ersatz," but yes, I did.

Why? Why bother? Why not just get on with it?

Because never in my life did I act in such a capricious and cavalier manner, merely to get on with it, as you say. I acted always from principle and from principle alone. This is something most people have yet to reconcile themselves to. When it comes to John Brown, they much prefer their little fictions.

I once made a statement, a now rather notorious statement as it turns out, something along the lines of: "The credo that all men are created equal is but the political echo of Our Saviour's commandment to love thy neighbor as thyself. Taken together, they comprise John Brown's Private Doctrine, and rather than have one jot or tittle of that doctrine violated in these United States, it would be better that a whole generation of men, women, and children die a violent and bloody death. Men are nothing. Principles everything. I mean this altogether literally."

After the affair on the Pottawatomie, they called me a murderer. After the debacle at the Ferry, they called me a terrorist. At my trial, and thenceforward, they decided that surely I must be a lunatic. These were nothing but convenient labels conjured up by discomfited people who wished to avoid facing the unpleasant truth.

The unpleasant truth was, I never was any of those things. The unpleasant truth was, I was right, slavery was wrong, and no violence I ever committed, no blood I ever spilled, no madness I ever participated in can compare to the violence, bloodshed, and madness not only perpetrated against the millions of poor Negroes held in bondage, but visited upon the country in the years following my death.

I understand that President Lincoln later dismissed my effort at the Ferry as both "peculiar" and "absurd." He is entitled to his opinion, but how then describe the half-decade of wanton fratricide over which he presided? Two of my sons perished at the Ferry, but what explains the butchery of 620,000 of the nation's sons in the course of the war?

Life abounds with peculiarity and absurdity. What of it? It abounds with any number of things, few of them noble. Men have made of God's world a compost heap and of His America a boneyard. They hung me, murdered Lincoln, and between times slaughtered 620,000 innocents for no earthly reason save that a handful of sexually threatened white folks could not find it in their hearts to behave civilly toward a good many more black ones.

Too bad.

Although I hold no brief for gazetteers, it was the editor Horace Greeley who in the aftermath of the Ferry stepped forward to defend it as "the work of a madman for whom I have not one word of reproach." That is a comment I would be hard put to edit. "Madman" aside—perhaps given the outcome of the affair it did indeed seem to him mad—he got it exactly right. He understood, you see, that John Brown, mad or otherwise, counted as nothing alongside the utter sanity and rightness of the principle from which he acted.

I never met Greeley. I wish I had. Among newspaper people of my acquaintance such sagacity too often was lacking.

Horace Greeley, President Lincoln, the Civil War, Harper's Ferry, I fear we range rather far afield. My question went to the dubiousness of your so-called constitution.

All I have said is germane to the point. Minus the constitution, or some other document of **principle,** *the business I had in mind would soon enough have degenerated into base ruffianism. I had seen it in Kanzas—anarchy, banditry, brigandage—and you can be certain that neither side was exempt. No, I knew that once the lines were drawn and the gauntlet flung it was inevitable that emotions would take over, the battle-blood would rise, the best-laid plans would go awry, circumstances would spin out of control, situations mutate, the picture blur, caprice reign, evil flower. The constitution was calculated to regulate, restrain, order, and discipline—both in the field and in camp.*

I would not tolerate loose talk and un-Christian behavior in my men any more than I would condone unmanaged violence and unpremeditated killing—save, of course, in instances of self-defense. I would not have it.

Purity of moral purpose.

Yes. That is it exactly. I would at all times occupy the moral high ground, or I would fold my tent, furl my flag, and quit the field.

Those who read the document too literally, as a statement of political ideology or an outline for the practical governance of some imagined mountain commonwealth, miss much of the point.

The preamble appears to border on a declaration of war.

You might say that. **Holy** *war.*

Yet it was kept a secret from the world at large. Indeed, the entire episode smacks of occlusion. The convention was called clandestinely, the constitution got up under the rose, your intention to raid the federal arsenal at Harper's Ferry *in advance of* retreating to the mountains deliberately withheld from the delegates. While in Chatham you even employed an alias, did you not?

[He nods.] *Nelson Hawkins. It was a practical necessity. My critics have condemned me for being insanely secretive, but I had no alternative but to proceed strictly on a need-to-know basis. And this was a great handicap. I would much preferred to have printed recruiting posters and hung them on doorknobs and lampposts from Boston to Chicago, or dispatched riders to raise the alarm of my coming in slave quarters from Washington to New Orleans. The explanation for my not doing so is clear. In the beginning we would be hopelessly outnumbered. Until such time as those slaves we might free or who rallied to us could be armed, the element of surprise was one of the few tactics we might employ to our advantage.*

It was always my intention to declare war in a more public forum once circumstances permitted. Unfortunately, as you are aware, they never did.

*In any event, I kept no secrets from God. With Him, I shared everything. Before Him, I stood fully revealed. **He** knew what I was about from the outset, and from the outset **He** approved.*

Then let me ask you this: Why resort to so extreme a measure without first exploring other avenues?

Such as?

Such as seeking to arrive at some common ground, some reapproachment with the more progressive elements of, say, the new Republican Party, Mr. Lincoln, and his circle.

But Lincoln was utterly hopeless. He was, well . . . might I strongly suggest that you read on.

Keeping Faith with the Fathers:
Father Abraham
(Edited Transcripts)

Equality

I am not, nor ever have been, in favor of bringing about in any way the social and political equality of the white and black races.

There is a physical difference between the white and black races which I believe will forever forbid the two races living together on terms of social and political equality. And inasmuch as they cannot so live, while they do remain together, there must be the position of superior and inferior, and I as much as any other man am in favor of having the superior position assigned to the white race.

The Negro is not my equal in many respects—certainly not in color, perhaps not in moral or intellectual endowment.

I have never seen a man, woman, or child who was in favor of producing a perfect equality, social and political, between Negroes and white men.

Free them and make them politically and socially our equals? My own feelings will not admit of this, and if mine could, those of the great mass of white people will not. Whether this accords with justice and sound judgment is not the sole question, if indeed it is any part of it. A feeling, well- or ill-founded, cannot be disregarded. We cannot make them equals.

Negro equality? Fudge! How long, in the government of a God great enough to make and maintain this universe, shall there continue knaves to vend and fools to gulp so low a piece of demagogism as this?

Segregation

You and we are different races. We have between us a broader difference than exists between almost any other two races. Whether it is right or wrong I need not discuss, but this physical difference is a great disadvantage to us both, as I think your race suffers very greatly, many of them by living among us, while ours suffers from your presence. In a word, we suffer on each side. If this is admitted, it affords a reason why we should be separated.

As immediate separation is impossible, the next best thing is to keep white and black apart where they are not already together. If white and black people never get together, they will never mix blood.

There is a natural disgust in the minds of nearly all white people to the idea of an amalgamation of the white and black races.

I will to the very last stand by the law which forbids the marrying of white people with Negroes.

As God made us separate, we can leave one another alone and do one another much good thereby.

There is an unwillingness on the part of our people, harsh as it may be, for you free colored people to remain with us.

But for your race among us there could not be war, although many men engaged on either side do not care for you one way or the other. Nevertheless, I repeat, without the institution of slavery and the colored race as a basis, the war could not have an existence. It is better for us both, therefore, to be separated.

Deportation

There is a moral fitness in the idea of returning to Africa her children. May it indeed be realized.

I believe it would be better to deport them all to some fertile country with a good climate which they could have to themselves.

With deportation, enhanced wages to white labor is mathematically certain. Reduce the supply of black labor by deporting the black laborer out of the country, and by precisely so much you increase the demand for and wages of white labor.

Emancipation

The promulgation of abolition doctrines tends rather to increase than abate slavery's evils.

In relation to slavery, let it be again marked as an evil not to be extended, but to be tolerated and protected.

I have no purpose directly or indirectly to interfere with the institution of slavery in the states where it exists. I believe I have no lawful right to do so and I have no inclination to do so.

Why this fuss about niggers? We have no idea of interfering with slavery in any manner. I am standing up to our bargain for its maintenance where it lawfully exists. But sustain the popular sovereignty men and Negro equality will be abundant, as every white laborer will have occasion to regret when he is elbowed from his plow or his anvil by slave niggers.

I have no prejudice against the Southern people. I surely will not blame them for not doing what I should not know how to do myself.

Much is said by Southern people of the affection of slaves for their masters and mistresses, and a part of it, at least, is true.

My paramount object is not either to save or to destroy slavery. If I could save the Union without freeing any slave, I would do it.

John Brown

John Brown's effort was peculiar. In fact it was absurd.

Ensconced at the kitchen table bare-chested and in his stocking feet, the old man clutches the foolscap with both hands, and eyes rivet at words that have assumed the immutability and obdurateness of an echelon of marble pickets posted across a bridge. No matter how hard he stares—and he has been staring with sufficient hardness that for the past hour he has succeeded in staving off nature's increasingly insistent call—they refuse to shrink before his gaze.

They refuse to step aside and let him pass.

1. Invade Virginia
2. Secure safehouse
3. Await arrival of recruits
4. Take Ferry
5. Arm slaves
6. Retreat south to mountains
7. Construct base of operations
8. Launch forays

It is four in the morning and he has been awake since—well, he never did get to sleep, not properly, though he must have dozed off a time or two because one moment his gums weren't bleeding down his beardfront and the next they were and for the life of him he cannot recall the moment. His eyes feel as if they've been pecked at by a flock of starving gulls, as if they must look like a pair of half-gnawed plum tomatoes.

Inside his bloodied beard he is sweating. He smells chives, day-old onions, the dank of damp mulch. A housefly drizzes past his ear. His beard itches. His nose twitches. He feels infested with lice. Ignoring the cramp in his right hand he redoubles his grip on the paper and renews his interrogation. The fire splooshes cinder in the potbelly stove at his back. A comma of sweat sleighs down his spine. He stares harder. Surprisingly, his groin is only slightly moist, but the sweat has broken full-blown across his forehead. The salt sting fish-hooks his varicosed eyes.

The letters blur, stop being letters, teardrop to dollar signs.

Laying the paper aside he rankles both hands through his jack-strawed hair. To execute and sustain the kind of protracted enterprise he has in mind will by his reckoning require a bankroll of several thousand dollars. Unfortunately the convention at Chatham has all but cleaned him out. He is not just strapped, he is broke. The circumstance is one with which he has a long-standing acquaintance —it often seems to him that he has been broke the better part of his adult life—and ordinarily it would not faze him. But this is no ordinary circumstance. This is in every conceivable way an extraordinary circumstance. If ever there was a wrong time to be renewing the acquaintance, surely this is that time.

Hoisting to his feet he snatches the list off the tabletop, compresses it with his left hand to a ball, shuffles to the stove, levers the lid, and feeds it to the flames.

"Water to wine, marble to ash," he thinks to himself, wondering why he thought to think that. Still, there is no denying it, as the lid clangs closed he feels buoyed.

Nelson Hawkins boards the eastbound train packing a loaded pistol in each of his pockets.

No, that is not entirely accurate. The two inside the breast of his Prince Albert frock coat bulge with six freshly printed copies—three per pocket—of his Provisional Constitution.

Shrugging off the frock he folds it in half across the roll of his arm and lays it lightly across the seat beside him before lowering the window shade and leaning back to brace himself against the lurch of the train.

He is decked out discreetly in derringers.

He sports his pants legs roomy and tugged down around the tops of his boots to conceal the handle of his Bowie. The handle, which is fitted with a brass pommel, is made of grooved elk antler which for no reason other than pure contrariness he is more partial to than stag.

He is en route to prevail upon the Secret Six, the Men without Fists, and he aims to reach his destination if it require guns blazing each step of the way.

He is too close. He has come too far.

Lord knows, only God can stop him now.

They meet in an attic.

Or rather, behind the latched door of a storage room in the attic.

Someone sees to a lamp.

They are in Boston late at night, in accord with his request, in a hotel but a short remove from the Negro quarter near Faneuil Hall. The cluck of horse hoof on cobblestone issues from the street below with the constancy of a clock ticking time.

None of them hear it.

The walls have rats which skitter with the light. The clatter of their paws sounds like the rattle of ossicles inside a shaken gourd, like a hank of barbed wire being yanked through pipe.

The ballroom is two floors below. When the rats calm, the sound of violins can be heard filtering up, seeping through the door.

Thinking to himself how odd it is that he should prefer the pawing of rats to the sawing of violins, the old man makes a show of depositing with each of the Six a copy of his constitution as they with much dyspeptic grumbling lay claim to such berths as they can improvise—a hogshead in the corner, a pallet on the floor, a burlap sack well stuffed with unshelled peanuts wedged against a wall, a steamer trunk by the window, a spool of coiled dockrope. When each of them has come to roost, as it were, he summarizes for them the document's contents, sketches the proceedings of the late convention at Chatham, and outlines what he describes as "the Virginia Plan."

He does not mention Harper's Ferry.

"Sirs," he says at last, contriving just the right note of portentousness, "all is in readiness. I have sufficient men. I have ample arms. But unless assistance is rendered me at once, I have not the means to proceed further.

"When I leave this place," he laces his fingers and glances heavenward, "I pray that it will be with not a penny less than one thousand dollars."

When a low-whistling George Luther Stearns—as chairman of the Massachusetts State Kansas Aid Committee typically his most deep-pocketed supporter—suggests through a sharp intake of breath that such monies as they may contribute be directed instead toward a resumption of his activities in Kansas, he is taken entirely aback, although he succeeds in appearing altogether contrariwise.

"Kanzas, Mr. Stearns? But it is my intention to beat up a slave quarter in the *South*. That and no other is my fixed purpose. The whole language of Providence whispers me 'Try on!' and if having tried I succeed, I assure you sirs," he pendulums his glance left to right around the room, "the whole country from the Potomac to New Orleans will be ablaze.

"Gentlemen, you hold the purse. I am powerless without you. It is your prerogative to withhold your aid of me as you see fit. But should you do so, it will but delay, not prevent me. Only betraying me to the enemy can accomplish that."

"Mr. Brown," sputters Stearns, clearly horrified, "I can assure you that no man in this room would ever stoop to so vile a . . ."

"You see," the old man cuts him off with a look fit to smithereen glass, "I have had but this one opportunity in a life of nearly sixty years, and as I could live ten times as long and never have another, I will not be thwarted. Sooner or later, gentlemen, I *will* go forward. I mean to carry the war into Africa."

"Very well then, Mr. Brown," says a vastly bemused Gerrit Smith. "I believe we have ascertained your position. If you would be so kind as to step outside? We will inform you of our decision directly. Thank you, sir."

As the old man sees himself out, each of the Six—save Smith, who is too much troubled by the gout to bestir himself, and the young cleric Wentworth Higginson, who perched astraddle his hogshead is engrossed in the application of an emery board to his thumbnails—rustle to their feet and undertake to pace the floor. The storeroom is not capacious; the jostling at once becomes problematic.

"So, what say you, gentlemen?" remarks Smith bluffly. At sixty-two, he is both the oldest, and more important in this instance, the wealthiest of the cartel. "What answer ought we give our friend? What wisdom offer?

"Chev?"

Chev is Samuel Gridley Howe, so-called owing to his having received the Chevalier of the Order of St. Savior from the king of Greece for his surgeon's service in the Greek War of Independence some thirty years before. His wife, Julia Ward, will shortly author the words to the "Battle Hymn of the Republic," thereby so eclipsing her husband's reputation that he will sink into a neuralgia-ridden depression from which he will never recover.

This evening, Chev appears wound even tighter than is his custom.

"Well, Gerrit, it is a singular and most startling proposition, I must say. The Virginia Plan did he call it. My, my. Desperate in character, dubious in method, its success wholly uncertain. And yet, yet, I believe it will succeed. Absolutely. If the nation is to survive, I believe that it must."

"I disagree," interjects a bespectacled Theodore Parker.

Well now, this *is* a surprise. Howe and the balding Unitarian minister are soulmates and bosom friends. Indeed, the childless Parker once requested of Howe, presumably in the spirit of that *transcendent* friendship, that he persuade Julia Ward, as a gift to him and his wife, one understands, to conceive a child—a request, it bears mention, which Mrs. Howe was only too delighted to decline. The men here cannot recall the pair ever wrangling over anything more momentous than who ought foot the dinner bill.

"But Parkie," pleads Howe, "surely you do not mean to say that you believe the plan foredoomed."

"Foredoomed, Chev? No, not foredoomed. From time to time miracles do occur. Yet I cannot conceive that the slaves shall rise, or if they do, shall fight. The race is utterly docile. Were it otherwise, they should have thrown off their shackles long since.

"Still," he turns to Smith, "however ill-fated, I might wish for our friend to try on, for I suspect the mere attempt is more the point than his success or failure. Indeed, it may be precisely from his failure that our success will spring."

Higginson, who has pocketed the emery board, barstools down from the hogshead with an athlete's effortlessness and, arms akimbo, unfolds to each of his splendidly proportioned six feet. The firebrand pastor with the heartthrob good looks is a notorious gym rat; he can bench-press twice his weight and execute without apparent tax a one-armed handstand. His chest is as broad as a park bench.

Much the most militant of the lot, he has lately been involved—sub rosa, naturally—in the recruitment of what he calls "the Army of Mobile Retribution," several hundred exotically accoutred minutemen capable of scrambling on the moment to the site of such slave insurrections at the South as he is convinced shortly must erupt. Higginson conceives of the old man much as the old man conceives of himself, as the lit match struck by God to ignite the powderkeg of civil conflict.

"I concur with the Reverend," he says matter-of-factly. "It is scarcely a question of feasibility, as I am confident Mr. Brown would agree, but of morality, of right and wrong. That the old man suffers on his side from a certain lack of reason, I shall not argue, but he most certainly is possessed of an abundance of right, and I for one am always eager to invest money in treason where treason is no longer treason, but patriotism."

Leave it to Higginson to twist home the shiv. The man's knack for blunt-spokenness is too well honed by half. The room appears palpably to constrict beneath a collective cringe.

"Well," sighs Stearns, "I would be loathe to go quite *that* far Went, but it *is* an intriguing experiment, I daresay, and doubtless far from the last that necessity shall place in our path before slavery can be toppled once and forever."

"Fine then, fine," stammers the beardless Franklin Sanborn, "but I insist that he tell us no more of his plans." At twenty-six, the

Connecticut boys' academy headmaster is by far the youngest—and most skittish—in the room. "Indeed, I fear that he has told us too much already. Can we not direct him to give us no more guilty knowledge, no incriminating reports of further progress? Is it not wisdom to suggest that from this moment forward we allow his actions alone to speak for themselves?"

"Oh, agreed, agreed, a thousand times agreed," enthuses Howe, oblivious to the expression of disgust scrawling itself upon Higginson's face. "I am with Sanborn utterly. It is simple prudence. The less contact we have with him henceforward, the better for us all.

"As to the money, I suppose he must have what he requires. But surpassing that, I wish to know neither what he is about, nor where he is going, nor when he intends to go there. Let us of these matters remain perfectly ignorant, hence out of harm's way."

"As you wish, Chev," says Smith. "Still, you see how it is. Our dear friend is unswerving in his course. Our choices are clear—betrayal, desertion, or support.

"I confess to a certain queasiness myself. Will the slaves rise? Is it in them to fight? Can the business be accomplished with so few men? Can they hold off all those who must be certain to pursue them? And what if our friend should fail? If he should be captured? What will he tell? What might he be *compelled* to tell?

"That said, I remain undaunted. I shall not stint. I know no truer Christian in all the world than that old man, and I will not give him up to dash himself upon the rocks without lending such aid as I am able.

"Sanborn, would you be so kind as to butler our friend back in then?"

By the time the old man reenters the room, Smith, with a companionable if altogether manly assist from Higginson's right forearm, has succeeded in heave-ho-ing to his feet.

"Mr. Brown, it is the earnest prayer of each of us that you might carry forward with your work as expeditiously as possible. To that end," he reaches into the apron-deep pocket of his topcoat and hoists out a drawstrung leather cinchbag, "you will find there, I believe, four hundred dollars in gold."

Before the old man can utter so much as a word in gratitude, Stearns, never one to be outshone, hornpipes forward with an envelope containing—as the old man discovers when he opens the packet later—twelve hundred dollars in new-issue banknotes.

"Check your Hartford account on Monday," he whispers cryptically, placing a hand on the old man's bony shoulder and babying it with a squeeze.

"God bless you, sir," says Howe warmly, breasting up to extend a hand.

"Yes indeed," enjoins Parker close on his heels. "May God bless you and keep you and speed you all the same. I, we, all of us pray that the Lord may smile upon your endeavor and crown your labors with laurels."

"We do indeed," chimes in Sanborn. "We do indeed pray that."

Higginson patrols the rear, but before he can properly pay his respects, it is the old man who elbows past the others to address him.

"Well, Mr. Higginson," his voice sounds ironed flat, "as I suspect that this may well be the last we shall see of one another in this world, I pray you in my absence to carry the good fight forward."

When Higginson swears an oath and recoils in protest, the old man raises his hand like a pledge and shakes his head. "No, no, you must listen. I do not say so lightly. As there is every prospect that I shall not return alive, you must promise that if the Lord so wills, you will plow on undeterred."

Higginson's eyes are lipped with tears. "My word, sir. I will. As God is my witness."

"Good then. I will pray for you, son. I will keep you in my prayers."

"And I you, John Brown," says Higginson, clasping the old man's hand in the both of his. "And I you."

Referring to his account (#001273) at the Cashier State Bank in Hartford, he discovers that it has been replenished to the amount of eighteen hundred dollars.

He withdraws five hundred and fifty, jackrabbits by carriage up to Collinsville, and places five hundred upon the countertop before the forgemaster.

"What's this then?" asks Blair.

"Your payment in full, sir," says the old man. "Per our contract."

The forgemaster appears nonplussed. "But the order is but part filled."

"What's that, sir?"

"Well sir, it's like this. You want 'em right, or you want 'em fast?"

"Both, sir," says the old man sternly. "I insist that I shall have both. The use I intend for them cannot wait.

"You have been paid in full, Mr. Blair. I wish delivery in full. I wish the items properly crated and clearly marked. You will mark the crates on each of their outer sides by hand stamp, label, or some such, in this fashion." He slides a scrap of paper across the counter-top like a dealer dishing out a playing card. On it Blair reads the words:

Hardware & Castings
Via R. Rd. to Cumberland Valley Depot
Oakes & Caufman Warehouse

"You will ship the crates by freight to this name and address," here he hands Blair what appears a professionally embossed business card, "and you will make such arrangements as are necessary to ensure that they arrive at that address no later than the first of August.

"Can you accommodate me, sir?"

"I guess you'll get what's coming to you," mopes Blair. "I ain't no piker."

After the old man has gone, Blair scrutinizes the address on the card.

> Nelson Hawkins Esq. & Sons
> c/o J. Henrie
> 225 E. King St.
> Chambersburg, Pa.

Cantankering something indecipherable, he rolls his eyes, shakes his head, shrugs his shoulders, and jams the card deep into the pocket of his dungarees before curmudgeoning it again.

"Fucking lunatic!" he crabs, and disappears into the backroom.

(It's W. A. Phillips, special correspondent of the *New York Trib.*)

"Mr. Brown, sir, a word if I might."

(Knew Phillips in Kansas where we palavered a time or two, where he coined the nickname "Osawatomie Brown." Regular mythmaker, Phillips; useful man.)

"Mr. Brown, a word, sir."

(Well, why not? Final interview before the Ferry; farewell words to a fissioning nation.)

Ask away Mr. Phillips. But be brief sir, be brief. I have other affairs to attend to.

Mr. Brown, what now?"

War.

[Reeling] But—*war*, sir? Why?

The Republican candidate for president wins in November. The South secedes from the union and sets itself up as a rival nation aided by Europe. War follows as does night day.

But war, sir. Surely *war* can be avoided.

It cannot. We are on the eve of the greatest war in history. I do not fault your skepticism. Even our best people do not understand this. Our so-called leaders have compromised themselves at such length that they no longer believe the power of right and wrong can wreak change upon this earth. I know better, and I intend to act upon what I know with all the power that God has given me.

And what power might that be, sir?

Why, you need only recall Spartacus and his slave war against the Roman Empire.

But Roman slaves were captured warriors, many of them seasoned gladiators. Our Negroes are a peaceful, pliant, docile race, incapable of resentment much less reprisal against their owners.

You have not studied them right, and you have not studied them long enough. Why, in Africa their men were the fiercest of warriors, a good many of them tribal chieftains. No, human nature is the same everywhere. It hungers after freedom. Given the right opportunity and the proper leadership, it will fight to attain it.

Mark me well, Mr. Phillips. The white people of this country can undertake no more critical business in the years ahead than to enlighten themselves upon the subject of the Negro—his history and folkways, his culture and personality, his character and customs.

And why is that, sir?

Because nothing could be clearer than that the future of our nation must be largely determined by the fate of the Negro. Either we accept the Negro as one with us and become as a people the stronger for it, or we reject, persecute, and revile him, and stand the price. And sir, you must write in your newspaper so that none can mistake it—that price, to black and white alike, will be unspeakably steep.

Begging your pardon, sir, but when you say 'accept the Negro as one with us,' how exactly do mean?

Do you know your Latin, Mr. Phillips?

Not so you'd notice, I'm afraid.

*Well then, take the Latin verb **miscere**, meaning "to mix," append it to the Latin noun **genus**, meaning "race," and you have my meaning wholecloth and in detail.*

But sir [horrified], surely you do not mean to suggest . . .

But I do, Mr. Phillips, as God is my witness I do. Were the choice that a daughter of mine marry an industrious and honest Negro, or an indolent and deceitful white, I would urge that she choose the former, and rejoice in such mulatto grandchildren as might issue.

Then sir, I daresay your sentiment exists exclusive to yourself. I am aware of no citizen of these United States—which is to say no *white* person—who shares anything approximating it.

*No, of course you don't, though I take it you **are** aware of the thousands of slaveholders who in private thrust their baser nature upon any number of African Negresses while in public scorning them as scarce fit to lick their chamber pots. Who furthermore sire by those Negresses tens of thousands of mulatto progeny whom they decidedly do not rejoice in, but rather enslave to their personal profit.*

A scandal, I grant you.

No sir! A sin. A sin against God and a crime against humanity. Whatever else the South may be, it has always been a vast brothel whose Negro women are capriciously reduced to cloacae at the hands of white fornicators, adulterers, and sodomites. I ask you, sir, how in good conscience deplore miscegenation when the entire South has for two hundred years winked at the rampant defilement of Negro women? How revile race mixing, when from Richmond to San Antone little brown and yellow babies suckle tonight at black teats?
Am I to take it, Mr. Phillips, that you find it more acceptable that a white man rape a black woman than that he ask for her hand in marriage?

[Reddening] You are to take it that the overwhelming majority of white people are perfectly content to leave the overwhelming majority of black people alone. You are to take it that ending slavery is one thing, and marrying Negroes another.

Oh, but they are absolutely one and the same.

Now you have lost me utterly.

Simple syllogistics, Mr. Phillips, simple syllogistics.
To wit, and I will go slowly:
Abolition equals freedom.
Freedom equals justice.
Justice equals equality.
Equality equals integration.
Integration equals miscegenation.
Free the slave today, and tomorrow, or the day after, or the day after that—the timing will take care of itself—we must mingle blood with him. As the nation can today no longer survive half slave and half free, so tomorrow it will not survive half black and half white. Abolition and miscegenation, or continued enslavement and mass rapine. That is the choice. There can be no other.

I must disagree, sir. Why, even as I sit here I can conjure . . .

Two. You can conceive of two others, am I correct? Abolition and segregation, or deportation en masse from the country.
Both are chimeras, sir. The first is unworkable in theory, the second impracticable in fact. Segregation contradicts equality. Deportation defies logistics. No, if the slave is to be liberated, and I intend to do all in my power to ensure precisely that, then it is inevitable that miscegenation will follow, and it serves no useful purpose to pretend otherwise.
To be perfectly frank, the prospect does not cheer me, but what cheers me less is the alternative: to free the slave by law, yet disown and ghettoize him in fact. Down that path, Mr. Phillips—and that path has a name, sir, and that name, sir, is apartheid—lies our undoing as a nation, and we can only pray that God will grant us the good sense not to take it.
In the meantime, the issue remains a good bit less entangled. The slaves must be freed, and I intend to free them though it require the raising of holy hell itself.

Black as aubergine.
   As poppyseed.
   Batwing.
   Bark.
   Their fear; eyes behind the peepholes augured from the hood.
   As the heart of the matter.

When in 1661 the Virginia House of Burgesses passed legislation aimed at stemming the plaguelike spread of the dread "abominable mixture and spurious issue," the remaining Southern colonies marched in lockstep.

But the laws apparently contained certain loopholes, for an arcane and esoteric vocabulary shortly arose as a way of tracking with mathematical precision the progress of that "mixture" through the national bloodstream.

This was the nomenclature of Negrophobia, of the secret life of slavery, an American phenomenon unprecedented in all the world.

sacatra: $7/8$s a Negro

griffe: $3/4$s a Negro

marabou: $5/8$s a Negro

mulatto: $1/2$ a Negro

quadroon: $1/4$ a Negro

octoroon (or mustee): $1/8$ a Negro

sextaroon (or meamelouc): $1/16$ a Negro

demi-meamelouc: $^1/_{32}$ a Negro

sangmelee: $^1/_{64}$ a Negro

Under the law of course, whether ***sacatra*** or ***sangmelee,*** a Negro was identified not by the *amount* of Negro blood but by the *presence* of Negro blood. A person $^{63}/_{64}$ths white, for example—that is, all of whose progenitors were of white descent save a single great-great-great-great-grandparent—would still be considered Negro.

Apparently, at least in the eyes of the law, Negro blood was once regarded as some extraordinarily powerful stuff. As Tennessee Circuit Court Judge John Henry Holliday put it in the course of handing down one of his rulings: "If intermarriage is allowed, a hybrid yellow mulatto man will come into being who will be the most despised man in human history, a mutant outcast and pariah who will be the battering ram which will splinter the government and undermine our civilization.

"All niggra attempts to breed up his inferior intellect and whiten his skin must be resisted, for whenever and wherever the white man has his blood polluted and skin muddied by the blood of the niggra, the white man, his intellect and his culture, must wither and die. This is as true as two plus two is four."

(Said John Brown upon reading the judge's remarks in the newspapers, "And they call *me* a lunatic.")

As a nation we no longer traffic in such overtly pathological termi-
nology. (Well, save perhaps "mulatto.") We are more enlightened
now, less paranoid.

Instead we have:

jaybee
moke
hod
and shade

snowflake
tarbaby
burrhead
spade

jemima
sambo
rastus
spook

spearchucker
buckwheat
jigaboo
cooze

remus
jungle bunny
splib
and coon

shine
and gange
and geech
and boog

cuffee
juba
jit
and dinge

darkie
schvartza
blackamuffin

Which if more "colorful," are at least less precise.

It is a midsummer's night, the night before his leave-taking, and his unbattened bedroom window is as wide-open as a dog's yawn; a host of fireflies patrols his head. The old man's face in repose appears aglow beneath a blinking halo of lightning bugs.

Perhaps their flashing wakes him, perhaps not, but he starts, his eyes fetch open, and after a moment's loss he bolts upright in bed tossing aside his sweat-dankened sheets, these sheets so redolent of winding cloth; moonlight chutes through the window.

Noticing the fireflies, he dismisses them as a product of his dream. He remembers now: there were fireflies abroad that night, flakes of light by the fields full, and down by the creek in the gulches. (Or were they bats? More likely they were bats.) It occurs to him that the ones he imagines here in his bedroom may be the souls of those men sent to haunt him.

Hugging his knees to his chin, he begins soundlessly to rock, to shake off the nightmare, to undream himself, in so doing jostling awake Mary who props herself by both elbows before hoisting up beside him.

"Father, what is it?" she whispers, and when he does not answer, asks full voice, "Is it the morrow then?"

She cannot see the fireflies; perhaps the moonlight blinds her.

"No, no! Not that!" The words are less spoken than extracted, as if he must pry them free before he can wrench them forth, as if he must wrestle each of them into being one by one. Still held in thrall by the shellshock of his dream, he struggles to find his tongue. "That . . . business."

"Yes? What business?"

"Back there. The fireflies. The blood."

"Blood? What blood? Blood where? What business, Father? What grieves you?"

"In the night. Everywhere. On the water." He cups his hands to his eyes and shakes his head as if trying to unstop a waterplugged ear. "The creek. Oh God, forgive me."

"Kanzas?" Her voice arpeggios in amazement. He has spoken to her of those days on but two occasions, neither akin to this. He dreams so seldom.

"There, there. That's all done for now. Done and hard done. You had a dream is all. Go on back to sleep then."

"No!" He scuttles from the sheets onto the wide plank floor to kneel beside the bed. "We must pray."

"But Father, 'tis the middle of the night."

"Come Mother, come kneel beside me."

"But . . ."

"Mary, for the love of God, help me!"

It is less the desolation in his voice than the sound of her own name that startles her into compliance. She honestly cannot remember the last time he called her by it, save that it was so long ago, the familiarity—it distresses her to think it—embarrasses her.

"Dear God," he monotones once she has pleached her hands and bowed her head beside him. But the words fail him. He feels the need to pray, knows he should pray, *must* pray or risk forfeiting all, but for the life of him he cannot think what to pray for. Forgiveness? Mercy? Salvation? Success?

"Dear God," he tries again, "let there be no more bloodshed. I beseech You to let Thy will be done, let *Our* will be done, to grant the slaves their freedom without more death and suffering."

It is too much to ask, he knows. His own presumption appalls him. He must do better.

"Let Thy will be done in this manner and in the days to come do with me as You please. Take my life in exchange. Take it for Your greater grace and glory. Amen."

"And amen," mouths Mary, feeling not for the first time unworthy of her husband's company as one by one the fireflies wink out.

The next morning the old man awakens before daybreak to whittle his great beard down to bristle, whisking the shorn whiskers into an envelope which he arranges like a memento on the bedstead beside the head of his sleeping Mary.

Then, stifling the impulse to kiss her on the cheek, he catpaws from the room without a wish to wake her.

He descends the mountainface on horseback flanked by his sons Owen and Oliver, each of whom leads by the reins a single dray mule.

Tied athwart Owen's is a portmanteau, and among the 404 incriminating documents therein is one of recent vintage entitled "John Brown's Declaration of Liberty," a two thousand-word opus two hundred of which are:

> We demand our liberty and natural rights as faithful citizens of the United States, and intend to obtain those rights or die in the struggle to obtain them. The natural object of government is to protect the Right and defend the Innocent. When government fails in this while furnishing protection and encouragement to the man-stealing, woman-defiling slaveholder, then it has transcended its limits.

> The history of slavery in the United States is a sin without parallel in the history of the most barbarous ages. We therefore before the Supreme Judge of the World do solemnly declare that *all* the slaves are hereby as free and independent as the unchangeable Law of God requires that *all* men shall be. And that as free and independent citizens of the United States, they have a perfect right, and sufficient cause, to defend themselves against the tyranny of their oppressors.

> For the support of this declaration we rely on the protection of Divine Providence and mutually pledge to each other our lives and our sacred honor.

Nature is mourning for its murdered and afflicted children.

Hung be the heavens in scarlet.

The old man is away off the mountain before he thinks to spare a thought for his long-suffering Mary. More than likely she is just now awakening to his absence. And knowing his wife, thanking him for the extra shut-eye.

Mary Day Brown

I knowed what he chose to tell, not a word more, and what he told was less'n what he didn't.

Been home less'n a fortnight when he left, saying this time he mightn't be back.

Never known him to carry on so.

"Mother," he told me that last night before we gone off to bed, "it is all up to God now. Whatever happens, you must accept it as His will.

" 'Yea though I walk through the valley of the shadow of death, I fear no evil, for the Lord my God is with me.' We must try to remember the Psalmist."

"Father," I heard myself saying then, "when does it end? Tell me and I will believe you."

I'd never talked to him so before, never raised the question.

"It ends when it ends," he said unruffled. "It ends when the Lord in His wisdom ends it, when He enables me to end it, and not a moment sooner. It ends when the last slave is freed.

"You see, Mother, I cannot say. I cannot say because I do not know. I do not know how long slavery can endure. I believe it cannot endure much longer. I believe it must not.

"You must pray for me awhile longer, that is all. You must pray for my success and for that of my boys."

"I *will* pray," I answered. "I will pray as I have always prayed. I will pray for God to spare you."

He didn't tell me what or when, but where he told me. He told me Harper's Ferry.

Could've been the moon for all I knowed.

Know a heap more now.

Know it ain't no moon.

SONS AND DAUGHTER

Salmon Brown

I did not want to go along and I did not go. I told the others before they left, "You know Father. He will dither and dally until he is trapped. He will insist that circumstances be perfectly in order and the situation arranged so that every *t* is crossed and every *i* is dotted before he will consent to make a move."

Had he acted with alacrity, he might well have succeeded.

But he was Father.

Ruth Brown Thompson

It was both Father's weakness and his strength to see things as they ought to be and should occur, and on that basis go into action, making no allowance for things as they really were or might occur. He was not always practical. He was very seldom practical.

Jason Brown

He was walking straight into the arms of the enemy. It was suicide pure and simple, and I was having none of it.

John Brown, Jr.

His success in Kanzas combined with his extensive reading upon the subject fed the fiction that he was a sort of genius about guerrilla warfare. I wanted no part of the Ferry and I took no part. The reason is simple enough: I knew Father.

As a military thinker, he made a first-rate shepherd.

TERRA DAMNATA

Eighty-one miles due west of Baltimore, fifty-seven northwest of Washington, the town of Harper's Ferry occupies a chevron of land inlaid on the floor of a river gorge wedged into the cleft of a camelbacked mountain ridge.

Bandshelled by molars of tree-caped rock, the angle of the chevron—called "the Point"—juts into a cummerbund of swift-moving water at the confluence of the Potomac and Shenandoah Rivers where the former sweeps through the Blue Ridge range.

North and east across the Potomac looms the 1,307 sheer vertical feet of Maryland Heights, south across the Shenandoah rises the 886-foot upslopes of Loudoun Heights, and west and to the rear leapfrogs the staggered crags of Bolivar Heights.

Surmounted at every turn by escarpments, morros, precipices, and promontories, walking the cobbled streets of Harper's Ferry inevitably produces in one the feeling—depending on mood, weather, and point of view—of being either lifted up and hugged fast, or cooped up and pinned down; of being part of something larger and loftier than oneself, a bishop striding his basilica, say, or as dwarfed into insignificance as a sow bug scuttling the bottom of a garbage pit.

In any event, it is irresistibly the kind of place that invites one to cup one's hands to one's mouth and hallo at the top of one's lungs to discover if one can hear the echo as it caroms off the clifftops. (One cannot, save on foggy days, and even then, barely.)

In the summer of 1859 a brace of toll bridges spanned the two rivers. The one across the Potomac, commonly called the B & O Railroad Bridge despite its likewise accommodating horse-drawn carriages, wagons, and pedestrians, was a nine hundred-foot simple truss bridge enclosed chute-style by a locust-wood slant roof and sidewalls, an architectural quirk which made it impossible for those in town to ascertain what was coming *at* them—when what was coming at them was coming at them across that particular bridge—until it was virtually *upon* them.

That summer as well the town itself was a scar. Drab, cramped, unshorn, its warren of colorless buildings—weatherbeaten brick and mortar cottages, low-rent hotels, cheap eating houses, dingy saloons, shaggy merchandise and squat manufacturing shops—straggled forlornly along the ferric, cinder-strewn riverbanks beside a pair of railroad spurs (the Baltimore & Ohio along the Potomac, the Winchester & Potomac down the Shenandoah), or clung haphazardly to the ledges, tiers, and terraces that pitched fitfully up Bolivar Heights to the Harper Cemetery Overlook.

The neighborhood's jamble of depots, warehouses, loading docks, lumberyards, mills, foundries, blast furnaces, pig iron mines, stone quarries, ore banks, and coal dumps was of interest to the old man owing solely to the added presence of:

a) the United States Armory (a clutch of twenty brick buildings recently refurbished in the "factory gothic" style and arrayed in a double row inside a walled and gated compound sandwiched between a barge canal and a train trestle propped upon the brow of the Potomac);

b) the United States Arsenal (slanchwise across the street);

c) Hall's Rifle Works (a half mile up the Shenandoah on Virginius Island).

———

The nearest town of any size was Charlestown, the Jefferson County seat located eight miles southwest down the Charlestown Turnpike.

Home to the Jefferson County Jail, the Jefferson County Court-house, and the Jefferson County Jefferson Guard Standing Militia, its situation was infinitely less fetching than was the Ferry's, a fact that when the time came—and it was coming now with the celerity of seasoned cavalry—the old man would have ample opportunity to ponder.

Youth is easily deceived because it is quick to hope.

—ARISTOTLE

They worshiped the very water they believed that old man walked on.

—OWEN BROWN

On the Fourth of July, Nelson Hawkins—describing himself as an itinerant New York cattle buyer—pays thirty-five dollars gold for an eight-month lease on the R. F. Kennedy farmhouse, a two-story former collier's dwelling enclaved three hundred yards off the nearest public road, four miles west of the Ferry amid the Maryland Heights switchbacks across the Potomac River. Included in the price are a milch cow, a buckskin mule named Dolly, a mongrel pup named Cuff, two shoats content to root the trough beneath the front porch, a dozen cords of firewood, and a nearby storage cabin.

As hideouts go, it will do.

As hideouts go, it had better.

Communicating word of his whereabouts to Frederick Douglass and Harriet Tubman by way of John Junior—whom he recently has arm-twisted into acting as his chief recruiter and arms runner despite his eldest son's "melancholic incapacity disqualifying him from anything engrossing in nature"—the old man sets purposefully to waiting. He expects eighty, prays for one hundred, dreams of two hundred, will settle for fifty, is resolved to forge ahead if he can

245

scrape together fifty, with at least fifty good and God-fearing men is convinced that in collaboration with the Lord he can perform a miracle.

He meets with Johnny Cook, his resourceful, if distressingly indiscreet pistoleer, who for the past several months has been casing the neighborhood. Cook sketches for him the layout of the armory compound, arsenal, and rifle works, stressing the absence of armed guards and soldiers; ennumerates the habits of the watchmen; details the schedules of the workers; lists the type and number of citizen-owned arms (two squirrel guns and five shotguns).

"I'll go tell the slaves you're here," says Cook, spurred as always by impulse.

"You will put a snaffle on it, son," decrees the old man. "Not a word. Not a whisper. Once the business is begun, they will swarm like bees to honey. You go on now and lay low. No alerts son, no tocsins. I forbid it. Follow?"

The munitions funneled down from Ohio by John Junior—198 Sharp's carbines, 200 Maynard revolvers, ten twenty-five-pound kegs of gunpowder, and one six-pound paterero, as well as sundry percussion caps, rifle primers, cartridge papers, and unmolded lead —arrive at the farmhouse the very day as the first of the recruits.

The fifteen crates of weapons and ten kegs of powder the old man orders unloaded from the bed of the battened buckboard and stacked by torchlight throughout the night like caskets along the walls of the parlor. The men he stashes in the garrets, haymows, barn lofts, root cellars, storm cellars, cribs, coops, keeps, and storage sheds strewn about the property, though not before he has impressed upon them the necessity of "keeping invisible" so as to avoid piquing the suspicion of neighbors and passersby.

"During daylight hours you must make do with a chamber pot," he tells them without apology. "The outhouse keeps for after dark."

These then are the men—or more nearly, the boys—who comprise John Brown's Invisibles. "My young Turks," he takes to calling them with all the affection he is capable of mustering, feeling certain the Lord has decided long since which on his account will be required too soon to make of their youth untimely forfeit. He can accept that if he must—he knows full well that he must—but the prospect scarce cheers him.

They are so, *so* quick with life.

THE LIEUTENANTS

Aaron Stevens, twenty-eight. Professional soldier, swordsman, dragoon, Indian fighter. Mexican War veteran at fifteen. Campaigner against Apache in New Mexico. Court-martialed and imprisoned for beating superior officer senseless. Escaped and lived with Indians prior to fighting in Kansas under alias Charles Whipple, brigadier general Second Regiment, Kansas Free State Volunteer Mounted Militia. Outspoken atheist fond of quoting Paine's *Age of Reason.* Six feet, two inches of volatility. Arms like dock rope, shoulders like ceiling beams, chest as broad as a canoe. Old man calls him "My Hercules."

"We are in the right and will resist the universe."

John Henry Kagi, twenty-four. Schoolteacher, newspaper reporter, lawyer. Astute as he is cold. Fought with Stevens in Kansas. Habitually amuss, unshaven and uncoiffed, slouch hat dented and cockeyed, pants legs one in one out of boot tops, satchel slung by shoulder strap overspilled with papers. Passionate for anagrams and acrostics. Teetotaler and dead shot. Old man calls him "My Greeley."

"I am as opposed to slavery as I am to murder, nor acknowledge the least distinction between the two."

John E. Cook, twenty-nine. Yale alumnus, New York City law clerk, Sunday school teacher. Saw action in Kansas. Sister married to governor of Indiana. Garrulous to point of logorrhea. "Earnest, but wayward," says old man. Sentimental adventurer, shameless womanizer, cocksure high-strung fancier of fancy sidearms; style-over-substance man, save with a pistol: does not miss.

"It is the crime of crimes and I hate it to the bottom of my soul, with each chamber of my heart, in every fiber of my being."

THE SONS

Owen Brown, thirty-five.

"The welfare of man is the first great law. Let all, irrespective of complexion, be governed by it. The alternative is a world of horror."

Oliver Brown, twenty.

"If we succeed, someday a United States flag will fly over this land. If we do not, it will be thought a den of scoundrels."

Watson Brown, twenty-four.

"Here is my opportunity to do for others and not live wholly for myself."

THE NEGROES ("THE COLORED MARTYRS")

Esau Brown (aka Shields Green, aka Emperor Green), twenty-four. Son of an African prince. Fugitive slave from South Carolina. Acquaintance of Frederick Douglass. Quiet, fearless, steadfast.

Dangerfield Newby, forty-four. Most senior, save old man. Manumitted mulatto slave deported from Virginia, separated from wife and seven children. Aims to find and free them. Blacksmith. Biceps like croquet balls.

"Freedom must be more than just a word."

Ozzie Anderson (aka Chatham Anderson), twenty-four. Freeborn printer's devil from Chatham, Canada. Thoughtful, dignified, bachelor. Hangs sack of bran in lieu of punching bag from farmhouse rafters and works out in middle of night.

"What the swords props up, the sword must bring down."

Lewis Leary, twenty-four. Fugitive octoroon slave from Fayetteville, North Carolina. Harness maker and saddler. Plays a mean mouth harp; blues mostly, field shouts, some folk, a little jazz.

"Men must often suffer to aid a worthy cause."

John Copeland (aka Junior Copeland), twenty-five. Freeborn carpenter from Raleigh, North Carolina. Leary's nephew. Griffe—three-fourths black—reared in Oberlin, Ohio. Active on Underground.

"If I must die, I prefer it be trying to liberate my poor and oppressed people."

THE CHOIRBOYS

Dauphin Thompson, twenty-one. Baby blues beneath mop of golden curls.

Barclay Coppoc, twenty. Baby-faced, balding, consumptive, Quaker.

THE BROTHERS

Will Thompson, twenty-five. Dauphin's brother. Easygoing, affable, walking bearhug. Practical joker and gifted impressionist who so uncannily mimics old man he makes others quail at mere sound of his voice.

Ed Coppoc, twenty-four. Barclay's brother. Quintessential Iowa hayseed. Says mother upon his leaving, "When they get the halter around your neck, will you think of me?" Answers Ed, "Aw, Ma."

THE HELLIONS

Al Hazlett, twenty-two. Guileless, uncouth, dumb as dander. Behind old man's back, peerless abuser of profanity. "He is not trying awfully hard to climb the golden stair," as old man puts it. Veteran of Kansas.

"Shitfire, if I had ten thousand lives, I'd lay each cocksucker down for the cause."

Billy Leeman, twenty. Most junior and fullest of sap. Heedless, headstrong, all fight. Chain-smokes. Chews tobacco. Drinks to excess. At seventeen, in Kansas, skirmishes at shoulder of old man who favors him like a wayward son. Dauntless.

"My whole life is a war with slavery, the greatest whore that ever infected America."

THE LONERS

Charlie Tidd, twenty-five. Saturnine, sullen, sour. Querulous nature, willful disposition. Veteran of old man's Kansas skirmishes. None cooler under fire.

"If we succeed, and we shall not, the world will call us heroes. If we fail, as surely we must, we shall hang between heaven and earth."

Jerry Anderson, twenty-seven. Gaunt, morose, phlegmatic. Indiana born. Grandson of slaveholders. Veteran of old man's Kansas campaigns. Hellcat when aroused.

"Is it not a sin to recognize evil and do nothing about it?"

THE MYSTIC

Stu Taylor, twenty-two. Practicing spiritualist. Believes in stars. Believes in signs, omens, symbolings, dreams, portents, precognition. Visions he will be "first to fall at the Ferry."

"It is my only desire to fan the flame of freedom."

THE LATECOMER

Francis Jackson Meriam, twenty-one. Frail scion of affluent Boston abolitionists. Shows up unexpectedly day before action with forty thousand Sharp's carbine percussion caps, rucksack full of boatswain's whistles, six hundred dollars gold, wearing a glass eye.

"Me-quoths Lord Byron. 'They never fail who die in a great cause.' "

The pikes arrive in the dead of the night, handles and heads to their respective crates. The old man sets the Invisibles to affixing 954 ash-helves to 954 pikeheads while he sits down to write Mary: "This must be our last communication. It will not do to contact me further. It will never reach here in time & will do no good in any case. I will communicate with you ag'n as soon as I am able. It may not be possible very soon. God bless you. Pray thee all goes well.

"P.S. As you can foot the cost, get up a subscription to the *New York Tribune*, remembering that it may not report the truth in every detail as to real events."

By the time he skates the portmanteau out of harm's way under an upstairs bed, autumn is barbed upon the air well-cidered with the spice of quince.

Their powwow—clandestinely arranged through a go-between named Yaller Indian Dick—takes place on a Saturday morning inside the scoop of an abandoned granite quarry scurvied with standing water on the Conococheague Creek southwest out of Chambersburg.

While a pair of Invisibles patrols the lip of the rimrock, the two principals clasp hands bluffly and descend to a rock ledge that sticks like a tongue out over the brackish water where they sit side by side letting their legs dangle the edge.

"Thank you for coming, Frederick," says the old man. "I know it is no mere stroll down from Rochester."

"Not atall, John," says Douglass, working to conceal his distress at not only how much, but how badly the old man has aged. It strikes him that he appears not simply old, but atrophied. "I expect you are about to make it worth my while."

"Reckon that's up to you, Fred," says the old man obliquely. "I do have a proposition though."

"I would have been crestfallen had you not. Proposition away then." Douglass appears in high spirits. For Douglass.

"The long and short of it, Fred, is that I am after the Ferry."

"The Ferry?" The reference does not immediately register, but as it does, Douglass slackjaws. "You *can't* mean *Harper's* Ferry." The "Harper's" rubberballs off before doubling back along the quarry's walls.

Shushing him with the upthrust side of a forefinger, the old man nods. "The armory is there. The arsenal. A rifle works."

"Indeed," deadpans Douglass. "The *federal* armory. The *federal* arsenal."

"I intend to have at them," says the old man matter-of-factly.

"You intend to have at them." Douglass is floored. "Let me understand. You propose to attack—do not hesitate to correct me should I err—you propose to attack the government of the United States."

"I reckon that's much the measure of it, yes."

"But how? With what? When?"

"I have the men. I have the weapons. I have the design. I have the blessing of Almighty God. I have all these, and I have them laired down in Maryland prepared to strike as we speak.

"We'll be going in soon, I expect."

"A wing and a prayer," thinks Douglass to himself. But he does not say what he thinks. He says instead, "It is a mistake. It is"—he gropes for the right word—"foredoomed. Even should you succeed at the outset, which I believe unlikely in the extreme, you must fail at the endgame. Sweet Christ, John, once you involve the federals . . ."

"I transfix America," interposes the old man, eyes abeam. "I become a public sensation. I win the attention of the country. I create a national scandal. I gain a nationwide audience.

"I reenact the Boston Tea Party. I reenact the Tea Party only more . . . *magically.*"

Douglass sighs. "And magic is precisely what it will take, magic or some other act of sorcery. Involve the government, John, and you awaken the dragon. You invite to descend upon your head the collective wrath of the United States Military.

"In any event, Harper's Ferry is a steel trap, the perfect crypt. Once in, you shall not come out again. Not alive."

"I intend to take the leading citizens of the place hostage to ensure otherwise. Should the worst happen, I will use them to wangle my way out."

Douglass shakes his head. "It will not do. Not when they surmise what you are about. The government will blow the lot of you sky-high before it will submit to your holding the Ferry for so much as an hour."

"They will not harm innocent civilians," parries the old man. "They would not disregard the lives of God-fearing Christians and law-abiding citizens. They would not dare. Besides, we will have flown to the mountains long before the troops can be dispatched."

"But don't you see?" Douglass's incredulity is on the verge of tumbling into exasperation. "Even should you manage it, they will come for you. And they will not cease coming for you until they have you locked inside a cage"—he averts his eyes—"or hooded upon a scaffold.

"John, I beseech you, reconsider. I know you spare no thought for yourself, but think of the others. Think of your children. Think of Mary. I believe this can only end badly for all involved."

Now it is the old man who is aghast. *If Douglass should spurn him at this late date, there is no telling what may* . . . The prospect so discomfits him that he rises to his feet, knees crackling like the fire-snick of kindling.

"I need you, Fred," he says deliberately, perambulating as he does so the breadth of the ledge. "I must know that I can rely upon you." A thought occurs to him that had not suggested itself before: *Perhaps he lacks the spine.* "You have my sacred vow," says the old man quickly, "that if need be I will defend you with my life.

"Come with me, Fred, for when I strike, the bees will swarm and I must have you there as the honey to help me hive them. Come with me. Together we cannot fail." The old man is at his shoulder with a well-draped arm and a companionable squeeze. "Abandon me now, Frederick, and you oblige me to forsake all."

Douglass gazes wistfully across the stillwaters; he does not budge. "Why not take up the old plan? Why not bypass the Ferry for the mountains, assemble your base, subsist off the countryside, spirit the slaves off the lowland plantations, funnel them up on the Underground?"

The old man is pacing so furiously now that Douglass fears he may inadvertently pitch headlong into the waters below. "Later," he says impatiently, "that is all for later. At present, take stock. The country is primed to explode. All it wants is for some paroxysm, some upheaval, some *ignition* to reach its flashpoint.

"No, it must be the Ferry. The Ferry will rock the foundation. Perhaps the Lord will arrange that it trigger the grand rupture itself, the apocalypse and the tribulation to follow."

For the first time Douglass becomes aware that the old man is glossed with sweat. "Well then," he says, gaining his feet, "if it must be the Ferry, it must be without me. I shall not hinder you, John, but I shall lift not a finger in assistance. Perhaps, as you seem to believe, it is the height of gallantry to go forth against all odds, but in all candor, do you really think it wise?"

For a moment, for a moment at most—the windborne alighting of a shadow, more briefly even than that—the shoulders slump, the face fatigues, and the old man appears stricken. "But you miss the point, Frederick. It is neither gallantry nor wisdom that are at issue. Nor reason, nor scruples, nor high-sounding words.

"It is *time*, that is all. It is simply time." The words rain down like ice picks. "You see—or perhaps you do not see, perhaps you *cannot* see—for those who would face into the guns, history awaits just down yonder, and she's beckoning to us that she's ours."

And then something extraordinary: he smiles. And not just any smile. A brazenly *winsome* smile. He smiles altogether winsomely.

"You know me, Fred," he chirps, "never could keep a fair lady waiting."

———

Months later, having visited the old man in his prison cell, Mrs. Judge Thomas Russell was assailed by the always-wolfpackish Gentlemen of the Press. "Gentlemen, gentlemen," she remarked, motioning the curs for silence, "all I can tell you for certain is that he reserves no very *marked* fondness for Fred Douglass."

FREDERICK DOUGLASS

I could live for the slave. He could and did die for him. The tools to those who can use them. Each man for the cause in his own best way. I was always more distinguished for running than for fighting. I offer on that score neither self-reproach nor apology.

I acted as I thought proper. No man dare condemn me for it.

Besides, liberty won by white men would have lost half its luster.

JOHN BROWN

On that side, the less said the better.
I thought he had it in him to face into the guns.
I was wrong.
Dead wrong.

Sept. 24
Boston, Mass.
Mr. Hawkins, Sir:

Late word from here places General T. gravely ill and confined delirious to a New Bedford bed. In consequence, no reliance ought be placed in *his* recovery in time sufficient to appear in person upon the field at date certain.

Likewise those who labor in service of T. who have yet to depart their farms awaiting word of *his* recovery before they will consent to "go the whole way for the Lord."

For the time being I shall remain here in communication with other of our interested friends endeavoring as we might to "plow on undeterred."

Will keep you informed as we know more.

The tree of liberty must be refreshed from time to time with the blood of patriots. It is its natural manure.

—THOS. JEFFERSON

THE NATIONAL INTELLIGENCER
Tuesday, Oct. 18

Reported Negro Insurrection
and Capture of the Arsenal
at Harper's Ferry!

BALTIMORE—The following dispatch
has just been received. As it seems wholly
improbable, it should be read with the ut-
most caution:

(Monday, Oct. 17, 11 A.M.) FREDER-
ICK, MD.—There is an insurrection at
Harper's Ferry. A band of abolitionists
has full possession of the United States
Armory and Arsenal there. The outlaw
band is composed of 250 whites and a
smaller gang of Negroes.

BALTIMORE, 12:30 P.M.—The affair at
Harper's Ferry is more serious than at

first reported. There is a stampede of Negroes from Maryland.

BALTIMORE, 2 P.M.—The town of Harper's Ferry is in possession of the Negro mob. The Negroes arrest everyone they can catch and imprison them. They have threatened to burn the town. They number 200 blacks and whites commanded by a white man with gray hair, chin stubble, and moustache.

BALTIMORE, 8 P.M.—The insurgents are taking people from along the river, trying them, and carrying them off for slaves. There are now 500 to 700 blacks and whites engaged. All the principal citizens have been imprisoned or killed.

BALTIMORE, 11 P.M.—The following is from the special reporter of the *Baltimore News American:*

(9 P.M.) *Monocacy Bridge*—Luther Simpson, baggagemaster of the express mail train, gives the following particulars: "I was permitted to go up to the armory and see the captain of the insurgents who is named Ned Hawkins. I saw from 500 to 600 Ne-

groes, all armed, and 200 to 300 white men."

HARPER'S FERRY, 1 A.M. (Tuesday)—The troops have landed and are in the town. The insurgents are willing to surrender on terms of safe conduct out of difficulty.

HARPER'S FERRY, 2:30 A.M.—The rioters are entrenched in the armory and are commanded by Captain Brown of Kansas notoriety. They number seventeen white men and five Negroes. Capt. Brown avows that he will defend himself to the last. At least sixteen persons are known dead. Col. Robert E. Lee has arrived and promises to quell the rioters.

HARPER'S FERRY, 3:10 A.M.—No attempt has been made by the insurrectionists to pillage the town or to insult the females. No damage has been done by them to the railroads or to the bridges. Their purpose seems to have been to hold the town until several thousand slaves could be collected, then to make a stampede south. The mood here is to hang all the prisoners once they are captured in the morning.

HARPER'S FERRY, 6 A.M.—For the last hour all has been quiet. Three rioters lie dead in the streets, three in the river, and several more within the armory where they are in full force. Preparations are making for an attack upon them. They have just sent out a flag of truce.

HARPER'S FERRY, 8 A.M.—The armory has been stormed and taken after desperate resistance. The insurgents were brought out amidst calls that they be lynched. Many in the militia endeavored to shoot them as they passed by. Capt. Brown and his son both were shot in the fighting. The latter is dead and the former is dying. He acknowledges that he is the notorious Osawatomie Brown whose deeds in Kansas have stamped his memory with infamy.

HARPER'S FERRY, 11 A.M.—A scout has been made by Lt. J. E. B. Stuart and a company of Marines on the Maryland side where a search turned up several crates of weapons and other supplies. The most valuable article, however, was a portmanteau stuffed with documents of a particularly incriminating and alarming nature.

———

And now let us turn to the truth of the matter to find out what really happened.

Said the old man
beckoning like a doppelgänger

        Let us face into the guns

                said the old man
                beckoning like a revenant

and rip yourselves immaculate to flinders

Amen

A fanatic does not calculate.
—CELINE

I profess faith in miracles.
I believe miracles can occur.
I believe miracles must occur.
I believe miracles do occur.
I believe, further, that I am Chosen by Him to help them come to pass—
—so that as they stealth the terrain like Apache, their breath shows in white snarls, like crowns-of-thorns on the air above their heads, like hives of concertina wire.

As of this moment they are Invisible no longer. As of this moment they are *death on the wing.*

This the old man had told them as they had prepared to abandon their rookery and swoop down in the dark from the hills, so that now—

—four miles to the mouth of the bridge

—nine hundred feet across to the Point

—then turn and face into the guns

—then twirl and catch history beckoning

—they repeat it to themselves like children who require reassurance: "Death on the wing, death on the wing, death on the wing."

It has begun to rain, a frigid, strafing rain. As they slog, stroking with every fourth stride the oiled-slick barrels of the loaded Sharp's

265

carbines slung handily aslant their shoulders beneath their black woolen serapes, they feel it bouncing off the back of their necks like dimes. The night is shit, but it is shit that redounds to their advantage, screening their advance, muffling their sounds, herding folks indoors.

The old man is seated tailorwise as inevitable as the weather atop a casket of pikes in the bed of his horse-drawn wagon fretting after the telegraph lines which had better have been cut by now or they are all in for one hellacious evening. This, as farther up along the road along the tracks along the bank of the river, Johnny Cook and Charlie Tidd are at this very moment snipping through the lines with the old man's sheep clips, a task that in this burr-cold *braaaaangs* their gloveless hands to the bone like fistfuls of hornets.

Death on the wing.

He prays that they may believe it, for what the old man knows as certainly as he has ever known anything is that they are not enough, nor would they be enough twice over, and that unless the slaves flock in force and flock from the outset, they will require the aid of . . . something more.

This he has held back from them: They believe they are here to seize arms and munitions before lugging themselves off to the mountains. And so they are. But they are here also, and as much, to confirm that he is right, that John Brown knows better, that the slaves will fight for their freedom, that they would rather die with a pike in their hands than live with a strop on their backs.

If only Douglass had not betrayed him, only General Tubman not fallen ill.

The old man visors his eyes with the brim of his hand and peers through the rainslant from the back of the wagon. Impossible to see. Too dark. (The moon has long since capsized.) Shadows. Silhouettes. Breathsmoke. Too rainy. They're there, though. He can hear them even now. Footfalls like metronomes down the slish-sloshing lane.

It is approaching midnight as they reach the mouth of the bridge where the old man orders them to affix their cartridge boxes outside their ponchos and see to the cocking of their carbines.

Across the river a clutch of lights shines yellowly from the Ferry: a pair of saloons with wee hours. Only with difficulty does the old man delineate through the rainpelt the anacondas of smoke scrolling from their chimneytops like arm bones out of shirtsleeves.

"Those lights," he thinks. "Like fireflies." He lets his eyes inventory the dark knowing evenso that it is the middle of October and well past their season.

Aaron Stevens and John Henry Kagi slip as prearranged down the blackened throat of the bridge while all else stand fast awaiting their beacon. The horses nicker uneasily in harness, dipper their necks, spade at the earth with their hooves.

The urge to pray sharks through the old man like stepping on a nail. "Boys," he says out the back of the wagon, "won't you gather 'round to join me in a short one?"

And so in a voice as unsparing as the weather, he prays, "O Lord, stretch forth Thy hand from on high and deliver us from the clutches of aliens whose mouths speak lies. Use us to *execute* Thy judgment among the nations and fill them with the corpses of evildoers. Help us to tread them in our anger and trample them in our fury until their blood shall be sprinkled upon our garments, for we have come not to bring peace but a sword. We commend our lives to Thy hands and humbly ask upon them Thy blessing. Amen."

"Amen," they signify after him sotto voce, their breath whitening the air of impending engagement.

Deep inside the belly of the bridge a lantern appears beckoning, a bobbing cat's eye in the distance.

"There it is," he says. "This is it. Cook, the torches. We're onto them gentlemen. Let us fly. Death on the wing."

Detaching Watson and Stu Taylor as rear guard, when the old man gees the wagon forward it lumbers like a caisson, dollying up onto the wooden decking of the carriage path beneath the slanted roof of the bridge where the patter of rain, the clop of horse hooves, the clocketting of the wagon's wheels fill the bridge with a sound like fistfuls of brass knuckles a-knocking at the door.

He is here and he is coming.

John Brown is across on the bridge.

"Open it," growls the old man.

To either side of him stand Aaron Stevens, Jerry Anderson, Dauphin Thompson, Al Hazlett, and Ed Coppoc, and each of them has the barrel of his carbine trained through the wrought iron bars of the armory gate on the rounded basket of nightwatchman Danny Whelan's belly.

The gate is double-chained and padlocked.

"Will not," says Whelan, who in trying to sound defiant, succeeds only in sounding ridiculous.

"I'm not asking, son."

"Anyways, don't have the key. It'd be a-back yonder in the watchhouse."

"Not a move then. Not a peep." The old man turns to Hazlett. "Crowbar. Hammer. In the wagon. Follow?"

It's Stevens does the honors, the chain snapping beneath a single sharp jacking of the bar and a well-placed blow of the sledge.

Hazlett giddaps the wagon inside the gate where Jere Anderson and Dauphin Thompson catch the embrangled Whelan up by his armpits.

"Not a sound, son," says the old man, "or as the Lord is my witness, it must be your last."

"But . . ."

"We are here from Kanzas," says the old man. "This is a slave state and we aim to free every Negro in it. As of this moment you are our prisoner and the armory is in our possession. Should the citizens choose to contest the fact, then I must only burn the town and have blood." He rounds toward Anderson. "The watchhouse. Lock him up." Then to Hazlett who is slouched on the wagon seat, elbows V'd on his knees, reins laced lax in his hands, "Allie, take Ed Coppoc with you and hie yourselves across the street to the arsenal. You'll find no locks nor guards on watch. Let none approach too near. Follow?"

Hazlett leans down and sows a yard of chawslush nonchalantly across the ground in advance of hoisting off the wagon with a soup's-on grin.

"Now skedaddle," says the old man, "and keep your heads down, the pair of you."

If all is by the clock, John Henry Kagi and John Copeland will momentarily be securing the rifle works a half mile down the Shenandoah, and Oliver Brown, Will Thompson, and the mulatto Dangerfield Newby will already have taken possession of the Shenandoah River Bridge.

It registers with the old man that the rain has stopped.

A single gunshot whangs the dark.

The old man's head whipsaws so violently in the direction of the report, which issues from somewhere back by the covered bridge, that Stevens half expects it to detach from his neck and go hurtling off its shoulders.

"No guns!" barks the old man. "No guns! I said no guns!" He will not learn until later of Stu Taylor's ham-fisted attempt to shoot down bridge relief-watch Paddy Higgins when Higgins bolts his custody. "Aaron, you best take your five and make for the plantation. Now."

"Right, Cap'n," says Stevens, setting off to lasso the three Negroes, Ozzie Anderson, Shields Green, and Lewis Leary, plus Cook and Tidd besides, only to be brought back by a hand laid on his shoulder.

"Aaron." Stevens senses the old man's reluctance to let him go. "The word to what slaves you can, and Colonel Washington brought back unharmed. No blood, son, not if it can be helped. Follow?"

"I do, sir. I will."

"And Aaron."

"Sir?"

"Go with God."

Stevens makes as if to protest, stops himself, salutes instead. As the old man knows well enough, he holds no brief for the God business.

"My Hercules," thinks the old man, watchful of his back as he strides off. "The best I've got. Go with God, son. Go with God all the same."

———————

At 1:34 A.M., shortly after a panicked Paddy Higgins flags down the 1:15 Wheeling-to-Baltimore mail train before it can cross to the Maryland side, the old man hears three gunshots whicker on the bridge.

He cannot know it of course, but the last of them is a Sharp's carbine bullet that after plowing into Hayward Shepherd's back mows through his left lung punching a hole in his chest the size of a baby's fist just above the nipple.

For twelve years the soft-spoken, gentle-spirited, aptly named Shepherd has worked as baggagemaster of the railroad depot adjacent to the bridge.

Hayward Shepherd is a Negro, a manumitted slave, and Watson Brown has just backshot him in the dark for failing to "halt" on command.

Shepherd does not know what "halt" means any more than a hog knows from a holiday.

Coughing up weevils of blood and morsels of lung, Shepherd staggers off the trestle and collapses through the front door of the depot where he immediately convulses into unconsciousness.

Fourteen hours later, no more aware that his killer is an abolitionist than is that abolitionist, John Brown's son, that he has killed a Negro, Hayward Shepherd gives up the ghost.

———————

The 1:15 caterpillars a quarter mile back down the track, snuffs its lights, and squats on the trestle between the armory and the riverbank exhaling steam and bracking in the dark like the consumptive iron lung of an enormous iron elephant.

Someone is powerful after the infernal bellpull in the steeple of the Lutheran church. The old man grimaces as for the umpteenth time his gaze toggles up the Bolivar Heights to the rear of town. "Come on, Aaron," he supplicates beneath his breath, as if by sheer prayerpower he can make Stevens and his men materialize over that godforsaken ridgeline. "Please God, bring it home, boy."

In fact, the old man is fixed to be strapped with a problem infinitely more vexatious than the whereabouts of the supremely self-reliant Stevens, for Dr. John D. Starry, awakened by the gunshots, the persistent clonking of the churchbell, and the news of Shepherd's wounding, is just now rousting from bed three of his neighbors. One he will dispatch south to Charlestown, one north to Shepherdstown, and one to spread the word to detain all incoming eastbound trains. With all three he will deposit the identical alarm:

Harper's Ferry is occupied by armed Negroes. They are killing the citizens. Get up the militia. Come on. Be quick. Bring packs. P.S. Bring Packs.

It is well past 4:30 A.M. when Aaron Stevens, wearing a grin as gappy as a wedge of watermelon, trolleys through the gate into the walled-off armory yard at the reins of a freshly confiscated four-horse wagon.

In the bed of the wagon are ten Negroes, all liberated slaves, and one white man, their owner.

The former—we have their names—are Sam, Mason, Catesby, Henry, Levi, Ben, Jerry, Phil, George, and Bill.

The latter is a corpulent, middling-aged gentleman with plunging sideburns and a heavily waxed, yet walrusy mustache whose manifest girth is rivaled only by his apparent indignation at the fix in which he finds himself.

271

"Stevens!" gladtidings the old man, raising his lantern head high as he sidles quickly up beside. "Praise be!"

"And who might you be sir?" challenges the heavyset man lolloping stiffly to his feet in the back of the wagon as he tentstakes the old man with a scrutinizing look. It does not escape the old man that though the fat man's belly jowls well over at the waistband, his hands are balled defiantly into fists.

"Cap'n, this here is Colonel Lewis by-God Washington," says Stevens. "Colonel Washington, Captain John Brown, late of Kansas."

"Osawatomie Brown," says the old man helpfully.

"Not a clue," sniffs Washington.

The old man does not ruffle. "Sorry I cannot say the same about you sir, sorry for *you*, I mean. I know well enough who you be." In fact, Lewis W. Washington is none other than the great-grandnephew of the sainted George. He is also the wealthiest man and largest slaveowner in the neighborhood, and a part-time staff aide to Virginia Governor Henry A. Wise. "I am here to rid Virginia of slavery," says the old man matter-of-factly. "You are a man-owner, sir, and you are my prisoner."

Scarleting about the gills, Washington's jaw slowly unhinges before he recovers enough of himself to splutter, "Now see here!" The vein running diagonally past his right eyebrow protrudes like pipestem.

"There there now," says the old man. "Do not take it so hard. Rest assured that I shall be most attentive to you, for I may yet get much the worst of it, and then sir, then your own life shall be worth much the same as my own. You have my word. I shall be most particular in my attentions to you."

"Mr. Anderson?" Turning to Ozzie Anderson, he motions to the black men huddled in the rear of the wagon. "Arm these men with pikes and have them escort the colonel to the watchhouse. Then join Mr. Hazlett at the arsenal. You will find Mr. Coppoc there as well. Have him return here. Follow?"

Trampling on Anderson's response, the old man turns back to

Aaron Stevens. "Have you the article we spoke of?" Without a word Stevens hooks his arm beneath the wagon seat, hefting out a decoratively scabbarded sword looped with gold braid and tasseling. "So this is it then?"

"That it is," replies Stevens, handing it down like a newborn to the old man. "Bend an eye to its shaft."

Easing the saber from its scabbard, the old man walks the light of the lantern along the sweep of its blade. The curved surface, scrolly with rosettes, quatrefoils, and fleurs-de-lis, has been buffed to a spit-shine so keen it is blinding. Doing his best to squint-eye past the glint, the old man reads the words inscribed in a single line along its length:

> From the World's Oldest General, Frederick the Great,
> to Its Greatest, George Washington.

These words he buckles on at the waist.
He would quickdraw history from the hip.

———

After ordering the octoroon Lewis Leary and four of the liberated slaves out to the rifle works in support of Kagi and Copeland, the old man detaches Cook, Tidd, Leeman, and yet another four of the slaves over the covered bridge in the confiscated wagon to load the balance of the guns and pikes being readied by Watson Brown, Francis Meriam, and Barclay Coppoc back at the farm. He explains that they are to arm with pikes any slaves they may find rallied there —he anticipates more than one hundred—after which they are to return to the Ferry with both men and weapons "by 9 A.M. at the latest."

Six of the Invisibles—nearly one-third of his assault force—now lie on the opposite side of the Potomac River.

———

The old man permits the detained mail train to cross the covered bridge into Maryland and continue on its way. His parting words to its conductor, Andy Phelps, are: "Because there are women and children aboard, I am letting you pass upon your word that you shall hold your peace along your route about what is going on here.

"If you understood my motives, if you understood my past history, if you knew my heart, you would not blame me for what I am about to do."

———

The sky climbs the horizon on a ladder
each rung a hue,
tusky white to khaki gray.

Daybreak is backlit matte,
stray clouds are scuff marks.

The morning stinks
of recent rains;
it gargles
motile groundwater.

The day awakens with the sniffles.

It is another one of those formaldehyde mornings:
greeting the day
is like
shaking hands with a bone.

———

The old man collars and confines to the watchhouse each of the armory employees as they arrive for work at first light. His hostages eventually tally more than forty.

Dr. Starry gallops to Charlestown to spur its militia onward.

Grocer Thomas Boerly, who has staked out the corner of High

and Shenandoah Streets directly opposite the arsenal, discharges his shotgun at Will Hazlett who is crouched inside the gateyard no more than twenty-five yards distant. The shot is errant, spraying high and wide, but Hazlett's return fire is not. The single shot from his Sharp's carbine shovels roughshod through the burly Irishman's groin.

It takes Boerly two hours to die faceup in the gutter.

———

The mail train chuffs into the station at Monocacy Junction, Maryland, at 7:03 A.M. Debouching on the dead run from the engine, Conductor Phelps sprints to the telegraph office where he wires his superiors in Baltimore his description of "an abolitionist insurrection of 250 whites and a smaller gang of Negroes."

His superiors wire Washington, D.C.

President James Buchanan is asleep when word arrives at the White House.

His staff deems the news critical enough to wake him.

"What does Secretary Floyd recommend?" asks the president, flipping aside the bedcovers.

Floyd is John Floyd, the secretary of war.

"He is just downstairs," says Buchanan's aide. "I believe he mentioned a lieutenant colonel, Robert E. Lee of the Second Cavalry. And a detachment of Marines."

"Tell the secretary I shall be down directly," says Buchanan, swiveling on his butt before flopping his legs over the side of the bed.

Buchanan is a bachelor.

"In the meantime, have him arrange to have Colonel Lee report to me as quickly—and as quietly—as possible. Word of this to no one. Am I understood?" The aide nods and disappears out the door.

"Always the niggers," says Buchanan out loud, slipping his nightshirt over his head. "My whole life long, always the goddamn niggers."

Stevens hands the old man a written message from Kagi who still is bunkered down at the rifle works with Copeland, Leary, and the four slaves.

"We dare not dally a moment longer," it reads. "We must be over the bridge and into the mountains at once. Our purpose is accomplished. The country is terrified. The slaves will respond. Do not delay. Let us be off while we yet have the opportunity. Pray you, do not remain here."

Drafting Stevens's back as a desktop, the old man scrawls a message of his own perpendicular along the left-hand margin of the page. In consequence, the handwriting is difficult to decipher, but what it appears to say is: *All is well. Stand fast awhile longer. Send all slaves onto the armory.*

Then, having charged Stevens with seeing to it that the communiqué reaches Kagi, he orders out for breakfast, sending one of his hostages across the street to the kitchen of the Wager House Hotel with another, more legible note: *You will furnish forty-seven men with a good breakfast. Ham. Hotcakes. Potatoes. Eggs. Coffee.*

A short while later the food is delivered piping hot on lidded trays stacked on pushcarts truckled into the armory yard by hotel servitors. The servitors, busboys really, are slaves, and when they are invited by the old man to remain behind and take up pikes, they backpedal for the hotel by the nearest exit.

No one touches the food, which they uniformly believe has been poisoned.

———

Come spring, Harper's Ferry floods. Without fail, at least once each spring the rivers surmount their banks and spill into the streets. A nuisance, but there it is; to some, the price one pays for living in such a picturesque setting, to others, well, a nuisance.

Which is why, at some point lost to posterity, it had been determined that a storm cellar be quarried out of Bolivar Heights—on ground high and dry, remote from risen waters—where could be cached in the event of emergency certain articles of self-defense: rifles, guns, powder, bullets.

This cache the old man has failed to root out and the townsfolk have overlooked. Until roughly 8:30 A.M. on this day. Which is when somebody—a shopkeeper's wife, Jenny something-or-other—remembers.

At roughly 8:45, 9:00, 9:15, somewhere along in there, Kagi, Copeland, and Leary come under light fire out at the rifle works.

At roughly the same time, actually some short while before, the old man details Will Thompson over the covered bridge to reassure those back at the farm that "everything is going smoothly, in concert with our plans."

He does not prod them to hasten their pace because he does not feel the least twinge of anxiety about how events are unfolding. He feels utterly—not elated exactly—but easy, complacent, cocksure. So sure, in fact, that when a second note arrives from Kagi imploring him to evacuate "on the instant," he can scarce be bothered to peruse it.

Billy Leeman and Will Thompson arrive back at the armory from the farm with news that not a single slave on the Maryland side has yet rallied.

"It is only a matter of time," replies the old man serenely. "The Lord will provide. The slaves will rise."

It is now nearly four hours since the mail train has departed the Ferry, three hours since his premeditated act of mass aggression against a military installation owned and operated by the government of the United States of America has been broadcast abroad.

The old man is the picture of nonchalance.

The old man is the epitome of folly.

———

"They are risen," says the old man to Stevens. "Hush now. Listen. Can you hear them?"

Stevens hears something. It's a ways off, but it's gathering steam, building like kettledrums, and it's coming from inside the bridge.

If it's men—and it sounds as if it could be men, or rather the footfalls of men—it's more than a mere handful, and they're squandering no time on the crossing.

"Praise God, here they come," says the old man, hand on the hilt of George Washington's sword as he heels across the yard for the armory gate. "The slaves are up at last. Come, Stevens. On the double. Let us get out there and greet them."

It is sixty yards from the gate of the armory to the apron of the bridge. Stevens and the old man have covered perhaps one-third that distance when they catch sight of Watson Brown and Stu Taylor emerging from the tunnel on the backpedal, watch transfixed as first Watson, then Taylor drop to a knee, shoulder aim, fire, slew to their feet, and slalom full out for the armory.

Instinctively, the old man jacks the sword from its scabbard.

Which is when with his side vision he detects the blur of motion off his portside that prompts him to wheel that way as both Oliver and Dangerfield Newby come catering straight toward him across Shenandoah Street.

One moment Newby is there, and the next he is not, and the old man has neither heard the report nor seen the impact of the shot that sprawls him across the cobblestones in the middle of Shenandoah Street with his mouth oblonged and his eyes owled overbig and a six-inch gaming dart ice-picked through his brain and the life seeping out of him like water into parched earth.

Oliver races past the old man for the armory gate hard on the heels of Watson and Stu Taylor. "Come on, Father," he hollers as he chuffs by, "Newby is for God."

The drumroll inside the covered bridge is grown ominously near, a great onlumbering rumble.

"Appears we've lost the bridges," says Stevens coolly, saying the superfluous.

"Appears so," says the old man absently, still gandering down Shenandoah Street where a small but obstreperous crowd has straggled out from the Gault House Saloon to scrummage about

Newby's outsplayed corpse. "We will have to—sweet Jesus, Aaron! Do you see?"

Down the street they are having their sport. The kicks and the cloutings are well aimed and vicious: the head, the ribs, the privates. A few employ walking sticks or tree limbs. They look like firefighters trying to beat down flames.

The old man watches as one divests the body of clothes and boots and another bends to the carcass with a knife.

Where the hogs come from he cannot conceive, but suddenly they are glommed onto the corpse, a whole drove of them, half a dozen at least, squalling and snarfling, logrolling the body with their snouts into the gutter as the crowd shies off ha-whooping and guffawing with appreciable delight. He can hear not a few suweeing them on.

"Cap'n, I believe they will be coming off that bridge directly," says Stevens, nodding toward the covered span. "We had best get ourselves rearranged."

"Yes," says the old man blankly. "Quite so. By all means. Rearranged." He pauses, and in that pause hears choiring up as from the margins and along the fringes of the undifferentiated fanfaronade downstreet, a sound he recognizes at once as the bullying, self-satisfied singsong of the sideline taunt and the schoolyard chant:

> *Monkeys, apes, chimps, baboons*
> *Spooks, spades, spearchuckers, coons*
>
> *A niggra slave*
> *A niggra free*
> *A niggra's a niggra*
>
> *Same difference to me.*

Then horselaughs and sniggers, the gales mean-meant and monsterish.

"Ah Aaron," he says all swamp-eyed and soulful-voiced, "God hears it. God sees it. God knows and will weigh their crimes.

"But He it is who must forgive them, for I can never and shall not."

———

The onslaught is spearheaded by the Jefferson County Jefferson Guard, which crosses the Potomac River in rowboats a mile above the Ferry, skelters down to the covered bridge on the Maryland side, and barrels across onto the Point, bowling over Watson Brown and Stu Taylor in the process. It then deploys around the Wager House Hotel, effectively partitioning those at the farm from those in the Ferry.

Its action is seconded by the Charlestown Volunteer Grays who storm the Bolivar Heights from the rear, fly its slopes into town, and after bearpawing aside Oliver Brown and Dangerfield Newby, take possession of the Shenandoah Bridge. They then deploy to the rear of the arsenal around the Gault House Saloon, effectively partitioning those out at the rifle works from those at the armory and arsenal.

For the moment, both appear content to catch their breath; neither the Guard nor the Grays make so much as a feint in the direction of the armory.

———

"Have you a stick of chewing gum?" the old man asks Stevens, patting at his own breast pocket. They are standing side by side inside the armory yard outside the watchhouse. The rest of the Invisibles, Watson, Oliver, Leeman, and so on, are inside palavering with the hostages. "I could have sworn I had an open pack right here. Probably lost it back there in all the hoohaw. But see here? The pocket is still buttoned. Darnedest thing I ever saw."

Unbuttoning the pocket he tugs its wrongside out. "See? Not a stick." He shrugs, then worries the nail of his little finger at the seam between his front teeth.

"Gum?" replies Stevens matter-of-factly. "Uh, no sir, I surely don't." He's more partial to pistachio nuts himself. "But Cap'n? I believe now may be the time to consider the back door while the back door yet remains open."

"The back door?"

"There," says Stevens, gesticulating the barrel of his carbine down the flagstone sidewalk running past the finishing shop, the polishing shop, the boring mill, the stocking shop, and the fifteen other factory buildings lining the walls of the compound. "Over the wall and up the Heights." The backmost wall stands some six feet high and six hundred yards away.

The old man looks vacantly down the sidewalk, blinks, looks vacantly at Stevens, blinks again. "But Aaron, it would mean abandoning all."

"Yes sir, for now. To fight another day."

"But the others. Kagi. The farm."

"They are capable men. They will see to themselves."

"I know you for a cardplayer, do I not?" Cocking his head, the old man shakes his finger in Stevens's face. His tone is playful, almost antic. "Now don't deny it. I hear things, you know."

Stevens is caught off guard. "It's true enough," he replies beguiled. "I do enjoy a serious hand of poker on occasion."

"Well then, we still hold the aces, is that not the expression? We have the hostages. Let us weed out the more valuable, place them in the enginehouse, seal ourselves off, barricade the doors and windows, use the pikes to chip loopholes in the walls.

"So long as we hold the hostages we can wangle our way out if it comes to it. Not that it shall. Come to it, I mean. In the interim we shall connive a cease-fire. Dictate our terms. We can send Will Thompson out under a white flag.

"It will buy us time, the time we must have for the slaves to rise." When Stevens looks askance, the old man adds, "And do not doubt it, Aaron, rise they will."

"Pretty to think so," harrumphs Stevens.

"Bank on it," winks the old man.

He has never seen the old man wink before. The old man never winks.

It is the wink, such a winsome wink at that, that frightens Stevens.

Because armory worker Rezin Cross stands as tall as a flagpole and as broad as a grandstand, the old man arranges for Will Thompson to employ him as a human breastplate when he sallies out under a white flag.

"The terms are simple," he counsels Thompson. "We, all of us—that means those at the rifle works as well—are permitted to leave the town armed and unmolested. In return we permit them to take custody of the unmolested hostages. On this I give my word.

"Also, I want Newby's body. That I must have. That I insist upon. Follow?"

The old man watches Cross with Thompson at his back exit the compound through the armory gate; watches the pair summarily jostled off at pistol point; watches the white canvas flag as it is wrested from Cross's hand, torn from its ax handle, the material filleted with knives, knotted into a ball, and flung back across the wall, flat-tiring to a stop at his feet.

The ax handle duly follows, describing a perfect parabola as it cartwheels past his ear.

"The second time around must be the charm," he thinks.

This line of thinking proves flawed.

When a second flag is posted out with Aaron Stevens, Watson Brown, and armory superintendant J. M. Kitzmiller—a man too pint-sized to approximate a human shield for anyone more statuesque than a schoolgirl or a circus dwarf—Stevens is shot six times about the head, neck, and chest, and Watson has a portion of his vitals horsekicked out his back. Although he manages to stagger his way back to the armory, Watson is obliged to abandon the perforated Stevens who lies like an overturned sofa in a Potomac Street gutter fluming it for thirty feet with his blood.

As the old man stands helpless inside the armory yard, his brain labors without success to lock out what his eyes have just let in.

"Nooooo!" he roars, reeling for the gate.

As Watson lurches through the armory gate clutching at his brisket and houghing up blood, Billy Leeman, who has sponged up each detail of the turkey shoot from his vantage point beside the old man, lights out down the flagstone walkway. The old man musters a few "Leeman, stop!"'s even as he props his son inside, but they are unavailing; Leeman trampolines the rear wall without a stray word or a wayward glance.

Perhaps five minutes later, surely no more than ten, they hear the spank of gunfire signifying that twenty-year-old William Leeman is become a carcass strewn across a sandspit in the middle of the Potomac River.

———

His wavy long hair, black as jackdaws, furs the surface with each churn of the river as they throng the bank to use it to sharpshoot. It will be hours before the target lifts away from its snag.

As it driftwoods downriver, no one notices: it is missing its face.

———

Over on High Street, slaveholder and West Point graduate George Turner is just dismounting from his sorrel when he is shot and killed by one of the men—we don't know who, Al Hazlett probably— holed up in the arsenal yard.

His horse rears and bolts, dragging him a block and a half before his left boot untangles from its stirrup leaving him splashed across the cobblestones, his face a smear.

Out at the rifle works, Kagi, Leary, and Copeland find themselves pinned down inside a snare drum. Flushed from cover by an increasingly withersome gunfire, they attempt to crowhop the stepping-stones of the Shenandoah River out the rear of the factory, where Kagi is killed outright, Leary is mortally wounded, and Copeland is captured. He is about to be strung from the bough of a tree on the riverbank when Dr. Starry intervenes on his behalf.

On the train tracks trestling the brow of the riverbank a shirttail posse of citizen-snipers mascotted by the enormously popular, immensely overwrought, notoriously jug-eared Mayor Fontaine Beckham, sporadically pocks the armory yard with halfhearted rifle fire. When the mayor, armed with nothing more lethal than a straw boater, rubbernecks around the corner of the water tower which stands diagonally no more than thirty yards opposite the enginehouse, Ed Coppoc, who is prowling the enginehouse doorway, blows the back of his head off.

The straw skimmer explodes like pinfeathers.

"Drat," says Coppoc. "Only meant to wing him."

(When the old man later learns of Beckham having provided in his will for the manumission upon his death of each of his five slaves, he remarks, "Five free slaves for one dead slaveowner. I'd say a fair exchange all around.")

In the next instant, Oliver Brown, standing no more than an arm's length from Coppoc, is bellyshot. The kick of the impact lifts Oliver off his feet and tosses him like a sack of feed back inside the enginehouse where he toboggans to a sit, pawing at his blood-bloomed shirtfront as casually as a man picking lint.

"Look at me," he says disbelieving, blinking his eyes at the widening corsage of blood. "Look here what they've done. Father! See here?" His eyes flutter, spooling white in their sockets as he pukes up red scraps of himself and passes out.

When news of the mayor's death reaches the saloons in town, Will Thompson is steer-roped from his Wager House Hotel room by a mob spilt mainly from the Gault House Saloon, yanked across the Point onto the covered bridge, shot by an impromptu firing squad, and his body dumped unceremoniously between railroad ties into the Potomac where, hung up on the shoals, it is intermittently employed for target practice.

The Martinsburg Militia arrives by rail, debarks from its train a quarter mile above the armory yard, threshes its way through the surrounding joe-pye weed and bull thistle thickets, vaults over the back wall into the upper end of the armory yard—effectively shutting Stevens's "back door"—and in the teeth of a concentrated fire laid down by the Invisibles from outside the enginehouse, with relative ease corrals them inside. It then riflebutts the windows of the watchhouse next door and frees the hostages, save the dozen or so safekept by the old man inside the enginehouse.

———

Where behind barricaded double doors he plunges to his knees with his chin on his chest trying to piecemeal a prayer.

Outside it is raining. The slate roof leaks. When the rain quickens to a downpour the old man feels the raindrops plop against the nape of his beleaguered neck like the kisses of icy lips.

———

On the other side of the river, Johnny Cook, thinking he hears the chitter of a firefight, clambers up the Maryland Heights, shinnies up a hickory tree, and watches in despair as the Martinsburg militiamen swarm the Invisibles like Dobermans, cattledriving them back inside the enginehouse.

Unable to think what else to do, he hoists a finger to his windage, jams the gunstock to his shoulder cuff, sharp-eyes along the downslant of the barrel, and squeezes the trigger.

One shot and one shot only, and then he is tumbling through space, the branch on which he has been nesting having been shot out from under him, landing on his back with a crunch that he reckons for having busted something small but dear.

Dockwinging his way back to the farm, he chews it over with the others and finds himself in agreement: it is a dodge-out for Pennsylvania, and not a backward glance.

———

The kiln-brick enginehouse consists of three contiguous slant-roof bays, each separated by an interior brick wall. The twenty-four-foot-square bay in which the old man is Alamo-ed is hung with an inward-swinging, whitewashed, oak plank double door surmounted by a crescent of checkerboard windows.

Drafty, dimly lit, understocked with hand axes, rope-handle fire buckets, alderwood fire-hose spools, and a pair of rickshaw-style, hand-tub fire carts arranged by the old man as bulwarks, it is in effect and feel anything but a fort.

In effect and feel, it is wholly and utterly, a garage.

———

At this point, those showerstalled in the enginehouse are:

The old man (praying)
Watson Brown (bellyshot and delirious)
Oliver Brown (bellyshot and unconscious)
Ed Coppoc (at the double doors)
Stu Taylor (at the double doors)
Jere Anderson (guarding the hostages)
Dauphin Thompson (guarding the hostages)
Shields Green (piking out embrasures in the walls)
Freed slave Phil Luckum (assisting Shields Green)
The eleven hostages, including Lewis Washington (huddled
    in a batch against the rear wall)

———

Just then Stu Taylor gets a little heedless. He reckons the rain curtains him. When he shows too much of himself at the opened seam of the double doors, a single shot belts through the rainslant. A remarkable shot. It slugs into his throat, crumpling him to the ground like laundry down a clothes chute.

Stu Taylor cashes it in before his corpse clumps earth.

———

Aaron Stevens, eyes lidded, lies caped in his own blood in the bed of a Wager House second-story hotel room.

Standing over him is a local barfly, one Georgie Russell Crockett, aka—for reasons best left unenumerated here—Coonskin Wally. Wally sways in place. His cheroot is shrunk to a glowing stub and it is about to scorch both his fore- and middle fingers.

"Here's to you, nigger lover," slurs Wally, taking a slurpy pull off his pocket flask. "May yer dying be slow as hard shits."

At that moment, Captain Tommie Sinn of the Frederick, Maryland, United Guard Militia, fills the doorway. (The Frederick troop, like those from Shepherdstown, Winchester, and Baltimore, is lately arrived in town.) He is obliged to duck to avoid grazing his head on the lintel as he enters the room.

"Shut up and get out," barks Sinn. "If this man had a popgun, you would be out the window and down the street and your tail twixt your legs." Then to Stevens, "I must apologize sir. Riffraff, that sort. 'Tis a pity though."

"Pity?" whispers Stevens. His eyes remain closed.

"That we'll never go our few rounds. I would dearly have loved to spar some with you."

"Fight? But why?"

"Because, sir, even lying there all shot to pieces, you are without a doubt the finest looking piece of manhood that I have ever feasted eyes upon." When Stevens says nothing—what could he possibly say?—Sinn continues, "Is there anything I can do for you sir?"

"When I am crossed over," whispers Stevens, "my body north, away from this place."

"And your family, sir, if I might inquire, where are they?"

Aaron Stevens groans open his eyes. "Family?" he croaks. "Why, everywhere. They're everywhere. Everywhere that all men are free.

"They are down there. They are down there in your godforsaken engine house."

And blacks out.

———

He is beating it back as best he is able, but the old man has begun to flag. He can feel it well-deep in his bones: the ore in the marrow gone molten, the ligatures all sprang loose. It is as if—what?—the train of his thought has slowed to a chug? refuses to locomote altogether? Something like that. The point is, he feels no more capable of mustering an unchloroformed response at this moment than of heaving this engine house onto his shoulders and sprinting uphill for the mountains. He feels as limp as a windsock, as inthrall as a firefly fixed in amber.

For the first time it occurs to him: *I may be through. We may have had it. The string may be played full out.*

There are so few of them left.

His two sons are dying all around him. Stevens is as good as gathered to his Fathers. Kagi and Cook, who can say? It is nightfall and the slaves will not flock. It's wet and it's cold and it's pitch-black. The town is plumb hellrose on rum. The militia has got him surrounded. Stu Taylor lies stick-figured in the doorway. He is stuck with a *garage* for a last stand. He can feel himself melting like soapsuds. It is all too ridiculous for words.

O my God, why hast Thou forsaken me?

On the other hand, why on earth not? And who in the wide world cares? Could anything possibly be more beside the point?

No, the devil with all that, that . . . bellyaching. Get a hold and keep a-going. That's all that matters. Carry on and muddle through. Salvage what remains to be salvaged, and if there is nothing, invent it.

And so this is the task set before him: that if necessary he will conjure something from nothing—a hare from a hat, wine out of water—whatever—life out of death (that would be nice); that if it comes to it he will alakazam a miracle.

And so he thinks, not thinking clearly, that if he can just stay awake, if he can just outlast this suffocating weariness, if he can just weather it through to the sun, then—well, something—who knows?

Weather it through to the sun.

Weather it through to the sun.

Weather it through to the sun.

Because history is up there circling, and once asleep, the vultures will surely descend.

None of this is true, of course. The truth is that he would quit in a heartbeat if only he knew what quit meant. He has lived fifty-nine years, and he still has not the jot of an inkling.

━━━━━

Over at the arsenal, Al Hazlett and Ozzie Anderson wait until night is terminally fallen to dance their way through the drunken, increasingly unruly streets. Darting undetected for the riverbank, they scavenge a johnboat, row across, and make for the farmhouse, whereupon finding it deserted, they decide to bed down in the woods across the road. Before dawn the next morning they safari north for Pennsylvania.

As they slicker off overland, it still is raining.

━━━━━

At 11:03 precisely, Lt. Col. Robert E. Lee, his aide—the aggressively self-aggrandizing 1st Lt. Jeb Stuart—and ninety United States Marines, tympani across the covered bridge from Maryland into Virginia.

To a man they are unfamiliar with Osawatomie Brown, but without having been debriefed they know to a man exactly what they are about: they know that for those with the temerity to oppose them, they are tantamount to *death on the wing.*

The raffishly moustachioed, somberly handsome Lee is this Monday evening in his fifty-second year, seven years younger than his adversary. His undulate black chevelure has only begun to salt gray. Having been pressed into duty on the fly—he had been chatting up a childhood friend in an Alexandria apothecary's when the breathless Stuart had tracked him down—he is clad in his civvies, a three-piece, rain-drenched suit of cinder-flecked black bombazine courtesy of the windblown ride from Washington in the open-air engine cab. His ordinarily well-thought-out hair is all atousle.

Lee squanders no time entering the armory yard by the same door as had the Martinsburg troop some eight hours earlier. Never one plagued by the slows, he is sorely tempted to storm the engine house on the instant, but decides to delay until daylight to curtail the risk to the hostages. For this reason as well, he has decided to confine the assault when it comes exclusively to bayonet and saber.

Before he retires for the night, Lee bends to quill and inkwell to compose the following:

Colonel Lee, United States Army,
commanding troops sent by the President of the United States to suppress the insurrection at this place, demands the surrender of the persons in the Armory buildings.

If they will peaceably surrender themselves and restore the pillaged property, they shall be kept in safety to await the orders of the President. Col. Lee represents to them, in all frankness, that it is impossible for them to escape; that the Armory is surrounded on all sides by troops; and that if he is compelled to take them by force he cannot answer for their safety.

Handing the note to Stuart, he admonishes him to pocket it until morning when he intends that the Lieutenant should present it to "our friend in the engine house." Lee does not know John Brown from John Appleseed.

"He will not accept the terms, of course," says Lee, his honeyed drawl vintage Virginia gentry. "When he refuses, you shall step aside, remove your cap, and wave it above your head. This shall be the signal for the Marines to rush the doors. If all goes as I intend, it will be over with this Osawatomie person before he has the presence of mind to gather his wits."

Lee pauses a moment before adding pensively, "Lieutenant, just out of curiosity, what sort of name *is* Osawatomie anyway?"

———

He takes a step, and suddenly, altogether miraculously, he can feel it, right there underfoot, wedged along a seam in the stone-laid floor. Bending down, he ladles it up, salt-shakers out three sticks, braids them together, clews them up, stuffs the wad in his mouth like a magic trick.

This will help enormously. A wake-me-up, a pick-me-up, an old Kanzas trick, an Indian trick, chewing the coagulated pitch-pine of spruce trees, spruce gum as the aborigines call it.

As he chews he hums. Softly at first, but shortly working up a head of steam until he is humming full tilt at the top of his lungs, indeed, humming with all the brio of a kazoo marching band. He hums "Blow Ye Trumpet Blow," and "Ah, Lovely Appearance of Death," and "Sin Like a Venomous Disease Infects Our Vital Blood."

It is going to be all right. He can feel it. The sap rising. The blood well revved. That old second wind. Tip-top and shipshape. Back in the pink and on top of the world.

Absolutely incandescent.

Utterly indivisible.

"Father, please. Father, stop humming. No more. Water, Father. Please Father, water."

It is Watson.

"Watson, son, I believe you will get well." He does not believe he will get well. Not short of a miracle. He has bent to the wound. He has seen its like before. A lesser man would have succumbed long since. "Be brave awhile longer, son. We have no water here. All will be well. You'll see. God will provide."

He raises his voice to the dark. "Men, are you awake? Stand

alert. Stand steady by your arms. When they come, sell yourselves most dearly."

"Kill me!"

It is Oliver now.

"Oh God, let me die! Father, kill me! Kill me, kill me, kill me!"

"Quiet now!" he tasks. "You will get over it. I will not kill you. I will not kill you and God will not let you die."

Oliver's wound is nastier than his brother's, and Oliver is not nearly so doughty.

"I want to die! Oh God, I want to die right now!"

"Go ahead then!" snarls the old man effervescently. "But if die you must, then die like a man.

"In the name of God, die game!"

Shortly before dawn, not long after he has clove-hitched the double doors with firehose, he calls out to his son for the final time. "Oliver. Oliver, son, how goes it?" Receiving no reply, the old man says something that each of the hostages will take with them to their graves.

"No?" he says peppily, zippily, even zestfully. "Well then, I reckon he must be for the worms."

And resumes with appreciable gusto his humming.

———

At the crack of dawn,
comes knocking
the crack of doom.

———

First Lieutenant James Ewell Brown, aka J. E. B., aka Jeb, aka "Beauty" Stuart, comes a-knocking at the double doors of the enginehouse brandishing the surrender demand like a wanted poster in his right hand first thing Tuesday morning.

Beauty Stuart is this day neither bright-eyed nor bushy-tailed.

Indeed, while he may appear the very caricature of the dashing cavalier—what with his plumed hat, cavalryman's bootspurs and saber, flossy gold sashing, and so forth—he feels downright disheveled. And if there is anything Beauty Stuart cannot abide, it is dishevelment.

Beauty needs his rest, and last night he was sorely deprived. What is more, because he has risen so late he has not yet breakfasted, not a solitary cup of chickory, and so is in no gladsome mood for the abolitionist antics of the very lunatic whose fault it is for his feeling so . . . so amuss—this demented Osawatomie person.

On the other hand, that he finds himself here in the first place in the mizzle and the marl at seven in the godforsaken morning smack in the middle of this . . . this farce, this charade, this opéra bouffe, is entirely of his own making.

Indeed, he had had virtually to cajole Lee into letting him come, had had almost literally to twist his arm. And why not? As wretchedly as the affair promises to play out, as sordidly as it has progressed, he knows full well that if he acts his part with the proper— what shall we say, élan?—that there may be, that there most likely will be, that there certainly must be, that there had by God better be a promotion in it for him.

And so as he stands simmering outside the door of the enginehouse waiting for the madman inside to appear, it is this thought that the lieutenant labors to keep foremost in mind: *Captain's bars, Beauty, Captain's bars. Just hit your mark and they're as good as on your shoulders.*

———

It stacks up this way:

Ninety well-fed, well-rested, well-trained, well-paid United States Marines; two hundred militia supporting

vs.

One fifty-nine-year-old man, and four boys aged twenty-one to twenty-seven, none of them well fed, rested, trained, or paid; God supporting

Maybe.

———

The old man cracks the door a handwidth.

Without a word Stuart mailchutes the surrender terms through the opening.

The old man fishes it back inside, unfolds it, apprizes it by the light of the door slat, hands it back.

"This counter," he says evenly. "In consideration for not having put the town to the torch, for not having harmed a hair on the heads of my hostages, for not having knowingly fired on any unarmed man, for not killing you, sir, like a mosquito here and now" —his voice hoarsens—"for the loss by murder of two of my sons, I am granted with my men free passage across the covered bridge into Maryland where I release the hostages and am allowed to proceed on my way unmolested."

Stuart can feel his fists clenching and unclenching. If only there was some way to get at the scarecrowed son of a bitch, to wrap his meathooks around that scrawny chicken throat and . . . *Whoa Beauty, whoa. Tamp it down now, son. Remember, Captain's bars. Captain's bars, Beauty.*

"I am instructed to say that Colonel Lee will stand on his terms," fumes Stuart.

The old man raises the barrel of his cocked carbine and cuesticks it through the slit of the door not half a foot from Stuart's head.

"I will speak with your colonel."

"Sir." Beauty is boiling. "I am instructed to say that that is out of the question. I am instructed to request that you comply with the terms presented, and advise you to surrender on the instant and trust to the clemency of the United States government."

Hold fast now, Beauty. Just a few seconds more. Just hit your mark and hold.

"Clemency," deadpans the old man. "From the government. Of the United States.

"And what form, if you be authorized to hazard a guess, what form do you reckon that clemency will take?"

"Sir, enough! Do you comply? Will you surrender?"

"A hank of hemp perhaps? A scaffold? No sir! Your colonel will accede to my terms. If not, he is welcome to . . ."

The hell with you, old man! It's Captain Beauty now! Captain J. E. B.-is-for-Beauty Stuart!

Puddlejumping back and to the side, Stuart doffs his chapeau and semaphores a figure eight above his head as the old man thunks the door shut and readjusts the slack on the fire hoses.

On the command of Lt. Israel Green, fifteen Marines, twelve with bayonets fixed, three lugging sledgehammers, rush the double doors, bashing in unison at the oaken planks. With each whump the doors give and spring back, give and spring back. It is as if they are held in place by Bunyanesque rubber bands.

"Steady hand now," says the old man. "True aim." He is on one knee at the elbow of the dying Watson to the far side of one of the fire engine carts. With his left hand he feels for a pulse, with his right he clutches the cocked Sharp's. The hostages are huddled in a clot against the rear wall. Coppoc, Anderson, Thompson, and Green are cubbied behind and beneath the fire carts.

Lieutenant Green calls off his hammer team. "Ladder," he barks, leveling his light dress sword at the heavy-gauge roofer's ladder leaning against a wall of the watchhouse.

Reforming his men—seven pallbeared to one side of the ladder, seven to the other—Green raises his sword head high. "On my signal," he commands, flycasting the blade earthward. "Ram home!"

The ladder headbutts oaken planking dead-on on the dead run.

"And again," commands Green, clocking his saber skyward.

Inside, the old man has lost his son's pulse. No, no he hasn't. It's there. Here. Faint, fading, but yes, there.

"Here they come!"

The air shreds, peels itself inside out, rips itself in half.

Lumber yawps. Timbers argue. The door bows beneath an oaken crumple of sound.

But only at the bottommost right-hand corner does the planking splinter, split, and stove inward before dog-earing clean off.

Still, it is enough.

"Pour it onto them, men!" yells the old man, squeezing off a shot at the ragged flag of light near the base of the door. You would think he commands a battalion. He commands four quailing, cowering, cowlicked boys.

One by one, Marines in dress uniform shoulder through the hatch on their hands and knees, as inevitable as heartbreak. Private Luke Quinn is shot and killed. Private Matt Ruppert's jaw is shot off. Thirteen others duck through unscathed.

Thirteen is too many.

Dauphin Thompson, prone beneath a fire cart, is dragged out by his ankles and shish-kebabed through the throat and heart. Jere Anderson, crouched beside the same fire cart, takes a charging bayonet in the pit of his belly that doubles him up, lifts him off his feet, and propels him clear across the room where the blade chuds into the back wall pinning him like an insect. There, in his death-squirms, he pivots on the spindle of the blade until he is hanging upside down.

"There is Osawatomie!" yells Lewis Washington from the back of the room. "That is Osawatomie there!"

The old man is down on one knee still hunched over his son when some sixth sense tells him to move, *now!*

It is all that saves him.

He is shoulder-rolling to his strong side when Green's swordchop, intended for his head, catches him instead across the back of the neck and shoulders. Cutlassed to his knees, he drops his weapon to backscratch at the wound only to be hoisted supine when Green attempts to run him through with a thrust like the hurl of a javelin to his left breast. When the point of the ornamental blade snags on the heavy buckle of the old man's cartridge box and jackknifes double, Green pounces, straddling the old man's chest with his knees as he pummels his head with the pommel of the sword.

By then the old man feels softer than air.
By then the old man's plumb heavenly.

———

Robert E. Lee and J. E. B. Stuart stand side by side in the armory yard where the ground goes slightly hillocked sixty feet opposite the enginehouse. As the bodies of the dead and wounded are stretchered outside and triaged on the ground beyond the double doors, Lee latch-springs open the hunting case on his key-winder Waltham pocket watch.

"Two minutes and forty-seven seconds, precisely," he comments to Stuart, open-palming the timepiece in his direction. "I daresay that makes short work of our Mr. Osawatomie."

October 19, 1859
Headquarters
Harper's Ferry, Va.

Colonel R. E. Lee, Colonel Commanding
to Colonel S. Cooper, Adjutant General
U.S. Army, Washington City, D.C.

Colonel:

I will now, in obedience to your dispatch of this date, direct the detachment of Marines to return to the Navy-yard at Washington in the train that passes here at 1:15 A.M. tonight, and will myself take advantage of the same train to report to you in person at the War Department.

I must express my thanks to Lt. Stuart and Lt. Green for the aid they afforded me, and my entire commendation of the conduct of the detachment of Marines who were at all times ready and prompt in the execution of any duty.

The promptness with which the volunteer troops repaired to the scene of the disturbance, and the alacrity they displayed to suppress the gross outrage against law and order, I know will elicit your hearty approbation.

The result proves that the plan was the attempt of a fanatic or madman which could only end in failure.

A list of the killed and wounded, as far as came to my knowledge, is herewith annexed.

I am very respectfully, your obedient servant,

R. E. Lee

ROLL CALL OF THE INVISIBLES

THE FLED
Owen Brown
Francis Meriam
Barclay Coppoc
Johnny Cook (later captured in Pennsylvania)
Charlie Tidd
Ozzie Anderson
Al Hazlett (later captured in Pennsylvania)

THE CAPTURED
John Brown (wounded)
Aaron Stevens (wounded)
John Copeland
Shields Green
Ed Coppoc

THE KILLED
Dangerfield Newby
Billy Leeman
John Kagi
Lewis Leary
Will Thompson
Stu Taylor
Oliver Brown

Dauphin Thompson
Jere Anderson
Watson Brown

Watson Brown died of his wounds before dawn on Wednesday. His body was floured with rosin before being crated in chip ice and shipped by freight to the Winchester Medical School at Winchester, Virginia, some thirty miles southwest.

The bodies of Billy Leeman and Will Thompson were fished from the Potomac River, and the body of John Henry Kagi from the Shenandoah by the Marines. The body of Lewis Leary was removed from the rifle works. What was left of Dangerfield Newby was shoveled off Shenandoah Street and the cobblestones hosed down with a disinfectant composed of hot water, quicklime, and soda lye. The lot was tumbrelled to the enginehouse where it was arranged in echelons alongside the bodies of Dauphin Thompson, Stu Taylor, Jere Anderson, and Oliver Brown.

Like that of Watson Brown's, the bodies of Kagi and Anderson were supplied to the Winchester Medical School "to add their heads to the collection in our museum," as Professor of Anatomy A. E. Peticolas wrote, "and for exhibition and dissection."

The bodies of Leeman, Taylor, and the Thompson brothers were buried in an unmarked mass grave on the outskirts of town.

The bodies of Oliver Brown and the mulatto Dangerfield Newby were buried two miles away, on the banks of the Shenandoah River.

Newby's mutilated body was placed in the grave faceup.

Oliver's was tossed in after him, facedown.

The old man had from the outset declared it his intention to free *all* the slaves then living in the state of Virginia. According to the United States Census Report of that year, some 490,865.

He fell short.

The number we are supplied, the number confirmed on the record, is four; precisely four slaves liberated—or escaped—as a direct result of the assault on Harper's Ferry.

Each of the four fled north, two of them—Charles Williams and Reginald Ross—making a clean getaway on the Underground clear through to Canada.

The other two, history never heard from again.

Afterward, Lee and Stuart lock the old man bleeding and unconscious in the paymaster's office adjacent to the enginehouse tucked beneath burlap bags on a straw pallet arranged beside Aaron Stevens, who has previously been gurneyed over from his room at the Wager House Hotel.

As an increasingly rumblesome lynch mob catcalls outside, there occurs the following exchange:

Lt. Beauty: And so, there lies the celebrated Osawatomie Brown of Kansas, a man so infamous for his robberies and murders that if the people outside these walls knew his history, he would not be permitted to live five minutes.

Col. Lee: His wounds appear most grave. Perhaps we ought send for a surgeon to look after them.

Aaron Stevens: Yes, it is a sin that a man such as he should be so maltreated and neglected.

Lt. Beauty: If I were you, you son of a bitch, I would hold my tongue. The pair of you shall be treated exactly as the midnight thieves and murderers you are, not as men taken in honorable warfare.

Aaron Stevens: Only my present condition, sir, prevents me from taking you outside and thrashing you to within an inch of your perfumed life.

We do not have Stuart's reaction to Stevens's riposte. Perhaps Lee intervened and ushered the Beautiful One away before matters turned testy.

———————

The vultures descend at midday.

By rail from Richmond comes Governor Henry A. Wise; United States Senator James M. Mason (author of the Fugitive Slave Bill); and former United States Congressman Chas Faulkner.

By rail from Baltimore comes United States Congressman Clem Vallandigham of Ohio. By rail come reporters from the *New York Times, Herald,* and *Tribune,* the Associated Press, the *Baltimore News American,* newspapers in Richmond and Washington, D.C., as well as sketch artists and journalists from the *Atlantic Monthly, Harper's Weekly,* and *Frank Leslie's Weekly.* With Lee, Stuart, attorney Andrew Hunter, and Col. Lewis Washington, they cattlechute into the paymaster's office intending to conduct their drumhead catechism, only to inadvertently reward the old man with the one object he has coveted from the outset: a nationwide audience.

Having regained consciousness, he is lying on the floor with his head propped upon pillows plumped and fluffered across the frame of an overturned chair. Spatters of blood and gouts of flesh cling to his hair and beard.

They look like snow-borne roses.

His face is raccooned with gunpowder.

All and all he looks remarkably himself: an old man with a saber gash troughed across the back of his neck and a headache of such saber-toothed intensity that it makes his eyes tear.

"I would be happy, sir," says Lee, "to order the removal of the Press, if that would be to your liking."

"It would *not*, sir," says the old man emphatically, allowing no room for confusion in the matter. "I am eager to make myself and my motives clearly understood to any who would care to listen."

"Very well then," says Lee. "We will proceed."

The inquiry lasts three hours.

Mason: Where did your money come from?

From myself, most of it. I will not implicate others. I have been taken by my own folly. I allowed myself to be surrounded by being too tardy. I allowed the train to cross the bridge.

Vallandigham: Who sent you here?

No man sent me here. It was my own prompting, and that of my Maker—or of the Devil, whichever you please to ascribe to it. I acknowledge no master in human form.

Faulkner: How many men in all had you?

I came to Virginia with twenty-one men only, besides myself.

Faulkner: What in the world did you suppose you could do here with that amount of men?

I could not say. I will not discuss that here. I expected help. I was disappointed, disappointed in more quarters than you can know.

Mason: How do you justify your acts?

I think you are guilty of a great wrong against God and humanity, and it would be perfectly right for anyone to interfere with you so far as to free those you hold in bondage. I think I did right, and that others will do right who interfere with you at any time and at all times.

Lt. Stuart: But don't you believe in the Bible?

I do, don't you?

Mason: What wages did you offer your men?

None.

Lt. Stuart: The wages of sin is death.

*Young man, I would not have made such a remark to you had you been a prisoner, and wounded, in **my** hands.*

Faulkner: Do you consider this a religious movement?

I do. It is in my opinion the greatest service man can render God.

Faulkner: Do you consider yourself an instrument in the hands of Providence?

I do. Yes. Most definitely.

Faulkner: But upon what principle can you justify your acts?

Upon the Golden Rule. I pity the poor in bondage that have none to help them. That is why I am here. Not to gratify any personal animosity, revenge, or vindictiveness. It is because of my sympathy with the oppressed and the wronged that are as good as you and as precious in the sight of God.

Vallandigham: Did you expect a general rising of the slaves in case of your success?

*A **general** rising? No, sir. Nor did I wish it. I expected some to rise. I expected to gather them up from time to time and place to place and to set them free.*

Vallandigham: Did you expect to hold possession here until some rose?

I do not know that I ought to reveal my plans. I will only say that I am here a prisoner because I foolishly allowed myself to become one. You overrate your strength if you suppose you could have taken me if I had not allowed it. I was too tardy after commencing the opening attack.

Colonel Lee: Why did you not surrender before the final attack?

I did not think it was in my interest to do so. We did kill some men in defending ourselves, but I saw no one fire except in self-defense. My orders were strict not to harm anyone not in arms against us. I could have killed the lieutenant here as easily as a mosquito when he came to the doors.

New York *Herald* Reporter: If you have anything further you wish to say, I will report it.

I claim to be here to carry out a measure I believe perfectly justifiable, not to act the part of an incendiary or ruffian. I wish to aid those suffering great wrong, that is all.

I wish to say this furthermore. I wish to say that you had better—all of you people at the South—you had better prepare yourselves for a settlement of this question, for it is coming up for settlement sooner than you are prepared for. You may dispose of me very easily—I am nearly disposed of now—but this question is still to be settled, this Negro question I mean. The end of that is not yet.

Stuart: Brown, suppose you had every nigger in the United States, what would you do with them?

Set them free, of course.

Stuart: To set them free would sacrifice the life of every man in this community and throughout the South.

You are wrong, sir. You could not be more wrong. That is precisely the kind of infantile logic that you must rid yourselves of if you are to avoid bringing down the apocalypse upon your heads.

Stuart: I think you are fanatical.

*And I **know** you are. Whom the gods would destroy, they first make mad, and you, sir, you are mad.*

Colonel Washington: Is this failure of yours likely to be followed by similar attempts by your friends to create disaffection among our slaves and bring upon our homes the horrors of a servile war?

Only time can tell.

Wise: Mr. Brown, the silver of your hair is reddened by the blood of crime, and it is meet that you should eschew these hard allusions and think upon eternity.

Governor, I have from all appearances not more than fifteen or twenty years the start of you in the journey to that eternity of which you so kindly warn me, and

whether my tenure here be fifteen months or fifteen days or fifteen hours, I am
equally ready to go.

Try to understand, sir, there is an eternity behind, and an eternity before, and
the little speck in the center, however long, is but comparatively minute. And so I
say, you be prepared. I am prepared. All you slaveholders, prepare yourselves.
It behooves you more than it does me.

———

"He is the gamest man I ever saw," declares Wise admiringly, emerging from the paymaster's.

"Or at least the bravest ever to head an insurrection," appends Vallandigham.

Lee shrugs and shakes his head. "A fanatic, sir, or a madman."

"A niggra-loving, murdering polecat, that's what," mutters Stuart. "A goddamned, common, garden-variety murderer."

"I don't know, Lieutenant," muses Lee. "A murderer? Perhaps. But common? No, I think not.

"I daresay not so common at all."

ROBERT E. LEE

The painful discipline that the Negroes underwent was necessary for their instruction as a race. I know this to be true in my soul. No man, therefore, had the right to interfere in that discipline, more especially as it was ordered by a wise and merciful Providence.

John Brown tried not only to interfere, but to interfere by force of arms. That he thought he was right to do so, that he believed he acted under the authority and with the blessing of God, does not make him less wrong to have done so.

That said, I am glad that we did not have to kill him. He was executed by the state of Virginia, and that was just and proper, but I would not like to have killed him myself.

He was an old man, and he was an honest man.

And, oh my, however mad—and I believe him to have been *barking* mad, a perfect Negrophile—let no man doubt it, he *was* game.

An Indecent Haste

A week to the day after having been swordchopped in the neck, the old man was indicted in Charlestown by a grand jury of the Jefferson County Circuit Court. The indictment listed one count each of murder, of treason against the Commonwealth of Virginia, and of conspiring with slaves to commit treason, adding with a flourish that he was an "evil-minded and traitorous person not having the fear of God before his eyes, but being moved and seduced by the malignant counsel and instigations of the Devil Himself."

To each of the charges the old man pled not guilty.

Queried by the court respecting his need of counsel, the old man replied without malice, "Do not trouble yourselves. As I am to have no more than a mockery of a trial, spare yourselves the bother. I am ready for my fate. I asked for no quarter at the time I was taken, and I ask for none now. If you seek my blood, you may have it. It is yours."

The proceedings commenced the day following, were over in less than four, and were as he had predicted, mockery from beginning to end:

The old man was prohibited from arranging for private counsel and his court-appointed local attorney from preparing even the semblance of an adequate defense.

As he was not a citizen of Virginia and consequently owed it no allegiance, neither could he reasonably be prosecuted for having committed treason against it.

311

The delirium by which Charlestown found itself gripped precluded the possibility of seating an impartial jury, yet a change of venue was never contemplated much less filed for.

The federal court was successfully denied jurisdiction over the case by the state of Virginia despite the alleged crimes having occurred on federal property.

Still suffering the effects of his wounds, the old man reclined for the duration of the trial on a cot at the front of the courtroom, a sovereign presence, his head turbaned in cotton batting, picking at his teeth with a hat pin.

There was, briefly, nominally, a half-hearted attempt made by his lawyer, without his permission, to mount an insanity defense, but he was having none of it.

"It is a miserable artifice and pretext!" he protested from his cot. "If I am insane, I should claim to know better than God himself, but I do not so claim. I cannot, therefore, be insane, and I reject any effort to spare my life on that score. It is not I who am insane, but these proceedings."

Having previously boasted to Governor Wise that he would have him "arraigned, tried, found guilty, sentenced, and hung, all within ten days," Special Prosecutor Andrew Hunter, whose son Harry had instigated the lynch-mobbing of Will Thompson on the covered bridge, concluded his final summation with the words, "Let retributive justice send him before that Maker who will settle the question forever and ever."

In the end, the jury—all of them men, most of them slaveowners, all of them citizens of a slave state—deliberated slightly more than forty minutes before returning a verdict of guilty on all three counts.

At which the old man rolled over in his cot, and like a smoker stabbing out a cigarette, jabbed the hat pin into his left palm, emitting not a sound.

"It was a kangaroo court meting out drumhead justice with indecent haste," wrote one observer. "It was not a court at all. It was an inquisition. It was a star chamber. It was a judicial charade. It was a legal farce.

"It was an outrage."

Whatever else it may have been, it was that. It was that, at least.

> And when he was most in jail
> Crummy among the crazy in the dark
> Then he was most of all out of jail
>> —CARL SANDBURG, *Osawatomie*

On November 2, 1859, John Brown's public hanging was penciled in for December 2, 1859.

He was flabbergasted. After the breakneck clip at which the trial had galloped, it had not occurred to him that he would be permitted to wallow a spell in jail.

Not that he was apt to wallow. Not hardly.

"Nothing is more disagreeable than to be hung in obscurity," Voltaire had once observed, and now the old man had been awarded a month's reprieve, a month to make hay, a month to sell his case to the country and magic-hat victory from defeat, an entire month to mastermind his candidacy for martyrdom.

Being able to count among one's friends the likes of Ralph Waldo Emerson and Henry Wadsworth Longfellow was scarce a liability.

"He will make the gallows as glorious as the cross," declared the transcendentalist upon receiving the news.

"His death will mark the date of a new revolution," chipped in the poet.

And even Victor Hugo, writing from exile overseas, forecast that "his murder will penetrate the Union with a secret fissure which will tear it asunder."

Supplied the newspaper account of a sermon delivered by the New York City preacher Henry Ward Beecher—"Let no man pray that John Brown be spared; let Virginia make of him a martyr"—he scribbled in the margin, "Yes! Good! Exactly!"

From his Jefferson County Jail cell he commanded audiences, conducted interviews, fraternized with visitors, brunched with friends. Soldiers, clergymen, politicians, attorneys, pilgrims, tourists, curiosity seekers, northern morale boosters (though not a one of the Secret Six), above all the Gentlemen of the National Press who dutifully reported his every God-couched utterance—during the next month, thousands of visitors filed day and night past his prison cell.

Furnished at his request with secretaire, quill, and inkwell, he composed dozens of letters—to friends, family, well-wishers, critics —103 in all, not a one of them remarkable for its brevity.

He was sleeping three hours a night now, often far less. He was sleeping cuffed in leg chains.

"I feel the presence of God in this cell," he wrote. "I feel His calming peace. He dwells with me hourly. He walks with me & He talks with me. I feel His power guiding my pen across this paper. He who once put a Sword of Steel into my hand has replaced it with this Sword of the Spirit & may it prove mighty enough to pull down strongholds."

He was becoming a mystic.

He sang to himself as he wrote his letters each of the Hymns to the Silence.

He saw himself in his mind's eye standing with the Sisters of Mercy looking for the Veedon Fleece or ascending each of the steps of the Van Lose Stairway.

When he dined it was on the Body of Christ. When he bathed it was in the Blood of the Sacrificial Lamb.

He hummed himself to sleep each night listening to the Music of the Spheres; he dreamed of the Avalon Sunset; he communed with the Ancient of Days.

He began to inventory himself each morning for stigmata.

When Wentworth Higginson wrote from Boston suggesting that

he kidnap Governor Wise and hold him hostage until a prisoner swap could be arranged, the old man replied, "You are truly a friend in need, but the truth is that I am worth infinitely more to hang than for any other purpose. I did not keep to my own plan at Harper's Ferry & so I was whipped, but I see now that God's plan was infinitely better. A few moments hanging by the neck & all is recouped.

"The scaffold holds for me no terrors. Let them hang me. I forgive them. They know not what they do. I see only the beckon'g of a Rosey Dawn & a Better Day. To last words then: Labor always to better the condition of those on the underhill side."

Then he signed the letter, "Y'rs for God & the Right."

Higginson's scheme to spring the old man was but one of many. Certainly the rumors flowed as thick as creek mud between summery toes: 9,000 desperate men from Ohio; 5,000 from Philadelphia armed with pikes, rifles, and four cannon; 8,000 from Detroit with new-style carbines capable of firing ten shots a minute; and on and on; 2,500 unstoppables from New York, 500 noble sons of liberty from Pennsylvania, 1,000 armed men from Cleveland, 500 guerrillas from Kansas, an indeterminate large body from Wheeling.

Governor Wise wrote Andrew Hunter: "Desperadoes have occupied depots of rendezvous! There is an organized plan at the North to harass our whole slave border at every point! The hellhounds aim to invade this state and commit rapine on our women! I tell you, these Devils are trained in the Indian art of predatory war!"

New York Tribune Editor Horace Greeley could not get over it. "Brown seems to have infected the citizens of Virginia with delusions as great as his own. It seems impossible for them to get over the terror that his seizure of Harper's Ferry has inspired, their expectation that a Grand Army of Abolition is about to invade them from the North. *They really believe this!*"

Indeed they did; believed it because they could not feature the alternative—that this old man and his bobtail band of . . . of *adolescents*, was it, was all, had acted of their own accord and strictly on their own. And so they thought—and who to blame them—"When you reckon the rest'll show up?"

Hearing of the old man's plight, a Chattanooga, Tennessee, widow, herself up in years, was moved to communicate with the old man a scant twelve days before the end.

"Altho' vengeance is not mine," read the letter, which owing to her being illiterate she had been obliged to dictate to her daughter, "I was gratified to hear that you were stopped in your fiendish career at Harper's Ferry with the loss of your two sons.

"You can now better appreciate my distress in Kansas when you entered my house at midnight and took my husband and two boys out of the yard and in cold blood kilt them dead in my hearing.

"You can't say you done it to free the slaves. We owned none and never expected to.

"I do so hope you meet with your just reward."

Included on a separate page was this postscript:

"My son John is now grown up and very desirous to be at Charlestown on the day of your execution so that he might adjust the rope around your neck, for permission of which he has lately applied to Governor Wise."

The letter was signed Mahala Doyle.

The old man chose not to write back.

PROCLAMATION

In pursuance of instructions from the Governor of Virginia, notice is hereby given:

That from now until Friday next, *strangers* found within the county of Jefferson and counties adjacent who are unable to satisfactorily account for their presence, will *at once* be arrested.

That during the same period, *strangers*—and especially parties approaching under the pretext of being present at the execution of John Brown, whether by railroad or otherwise—will be met by the military and turned back or arrested *without* regard to the amount of *force* that may be required.

No women or children will be allowed to come near the place of execution.

> Wm. B. Taliaferro
> Major-General in Command

Nov. 26, 1859

As she disembarked from the train in Harper's Ferry, Mary was solicited by the Press for her thoughts regarding the imminent execution of her husband.

She replied without appearing much to ponder the matter: "Well, does it seem that freedom will gain or lose by this? I have had thirteen children, and but four remain, and if I am to see the ruin of my house, I would wish only that it be of some benefit to the poor slaves."

At that, a round of disembodied applause sounded from the direction of the station house.

"One with God is always a majority," she said, her eyes searchlighting. And disappeared on the wing of Robert E. Lee down the platform.

P.S. By the by, yesterday I was sentenced to be hanged. It appears that I am to be publicly murdered on Dec. 2 next. Do not grieve. I feel as happy as Paul when he lay in prison knowing that if they killed him it would advance the Cause of Christ. God bless.

———

Under escort of the Fauquier County Cavalry she arrives in Charlestown by closed and curtained carriage at 3:30 P.M. the day before the execution.

It is cold, it is mizzling, and as the countryside is quite literally ablaze, there hangs like a pall on the air the pungent smell of charred peat. Arsons—of barns, silos, stockyards, hayricks—have become so commonplace in the wake of the old man's sentencing that at night, the sky glares as garish as wartime.

"The slaves, madam," the sergeant of cavalry offers, observing her sniff the air and crinkle her nose. "Fear they've been on something of a rampage here of late." He proffers his arm as she hikes her skirts in advance of footstooling down from the carriage. "No thanks to your husband, meaning no offense."

"None taken, I'm sure," she replies. The weight of the moment weighing, she strutters uncertainly past the gaggle of uniformed guards posted at each flank of the half-dozen inward-turned cannon, mounts the steps, and disappears through the front door.

Before she is admitted to her husband's cell, she is discreetly frisked by the jail's matron.

The old man, having been alerted to her arrival, stands waiting beyond the door absent his leg chains for the visit. Their embrace is less an affectionate hug than a prolonged cling, a wordless cleaving unto.

"Dear John," she quavers at last, "so hard a fate. How go your wounds?"

"Ach," he says, drawing off, "not for me. For yourself though, eh? And the children."

She believes him. His voice commands uncommon strength, a strength for which she is grateful, upon which she is content she may draw.

Offering her a chair, he sits opposite her at the writing table, reaches across the tabletop, sockets her hand in his own. Her flesh feels so alien that he finds himself reminding himself, "This is Mary. Remember? This is Mary. Your wife."

"Our children," she says softly, fishing a kerchief from her sleeve to dabble some at her eyes. "Oliver. Dear Watson. I should want them to come home."

"I'd not think it likely they'll let you get away with them. But do not grieve on it. They are home to Himself." When she appears vague, he adds, "Second Corinthians, verse 6. 'While we are at home in the body, we are away from the Lord, and we would rather be away from the body, and at home with the Lord.'"

"Oh yes," she says, making an effort to brighten. "'Tis so, I know it. And yet still," for a moment she is bygone, "my dear boys.

"But how for yourself? After, I mean."

"Ach," he shakes his head, "what matter? Pyre it here for the ashes and then," he shrugs, "a phial, a cigar box, a coffee can, an old boot . . ."

"But I have permission."

"What's that?"

"'Tis true. Governor Wise. I applied after him to release your remains."

"And he was agreeable?"

"More. He said he would not have your corpse soil the soil of Virginia."

"Wise bird, Wise," he says wryly. She can tell he is well pleased. "If that's how it's to be then, put me out by the big rock, the old granite out the frontyard. I confess it would solace me greatly to rest at peace in the mountains, so nearer my God to Thee."

She smiles, pleased to have pleased him, in her experience seldom a ready thing.

"Mary?"

"Hmm?"

"I know it has not been so easy. With me, I mean."

"Now Father."

"No, no. I make no apology. My work. It could not be helped. I could not shirk the Lord. Still, it went hard with you and the children, harder than I should have chosen had not the Lord chosen me."

"Perhaps," she says. "Perhaps 'tis so, though not so you'd be thinking. Sure there are others who hoe a row far harder. Besides, when did you hear complaints?"

"Never. Not once."

"Well then, what I had or had not I had of my own free choosing. Who should want for more?"

Then footsteps down the corridor, and the key as it jangles the lock.

"Ma'am?" The jailer's name is John Avis. "Sorry ma'am, but we've got to be getting you back before we lose the light."

Rising from the table hand in hand they snailpace over to the door.

"Go on now, Mother, go ahead, and remember always to be of good cheer. Tis all for the best, as you shall shortly see."

It is then that from his face pours a gaze of such tornhearted woesomeness that she believes he must break down a-crying.

"Why, whatever is it, Father?"

"You must be careful, Mary. When comes it. Promise me that you will be careful, that you will take care of our family. Promise that all will take good care."

"Of course, John. I promise. We will. When comes what?"

"Why, the war. When comes the war."

"Yes, well, of course, Father, of course. God bless you now, God bless. God be with you, John."

They do not kiss farewell. They do not lock hands or moist embrace. But as she turns away on Avis's arm, the old man is openly weeping.

Governor Wise had solicited each of the slave states to bid for the privilege of providing the rope used to hang him.

Kentucky prevailed; a finely braided, clothesline-gray, Lexington hemp.

Coiled and knotted into a noose, the macabre item was for three days placed on public exhibition during strictly constabled daylight hours dangling explicitly from an exposed tiebeam inside the carriage room of the cellar of the Charlestown County Courthouse.

They jostled past in droves, winking and pointing, departing resentful of having been admonished not to touch.

Later, as he was dismantling the scaffold, carpenter David Cockerell, who had donated the lumber for its construction, unfastened the artifact from its hook and, as if in repayment, dropped it down his apron front.

In the years to come, after his baby daughter Jannie had come of a certain age, she was often to be observed in the family's frontyard, skipping rope.

As the body lives so does the spirit, and both must be born, and broken, in order to reach the light.

—BERYL BAINBRIDGE, *The Birthday Boys*

When they come for him he is praying.

Accordioning from his knees he approaches Aaron Stevens who for the better part of the past month has been his cellmate.

"I feel in my soul," says Stevens, hoisting from his cot as they clasp hands, "that you are going to a far better world."

"Oh, certainly," says the old man bluffly. "I *know* it." He presses a freshly minted quarter into Stevens's palm as a keepsake.

"Give my love to our friends on the other side," says Stevens.

"That I will, should I see them as I expect. May we meet in heaven, Aaron."

"Well, good-bye then, Cap'n."

The old man watches tears brim Stevens's eyes. "Now, now," he scolds, "no regrets. Bear up, bear up and do not flinch."

Flanked by Jailer John Avis and Jefferson County Sheriff John Campbell, the old man is ushered down the corridor, out the door, and down the steps where he is hefted into the back of a horse-drawn wagon belonging to Seth Ambrose, the local undertaker. As Avis and Campbell clamber up after him through the flopped-open tailgate, the old man perches himself atop the lid of the walnut coffin crated there, patting it as one might a horse's neck.

"I had no idea that Governor Wise thought my execution so important," says the old man to no one in particular, beguiled by the array of soldiery—upward of one hundred cavalry, infantry, and militia—assigned to cortege him to his hanging fields.

As the undertaker tongue-clucks the wagon forward and the procession jounces down the cobblestoned street, the old man cannot help but notice that the town seems almost deserted. "But where are the citizens?" he inquires.

"They are being kept at bay by the military," replies Avis.

"Ah. A pity." He pauses. "And the Press? Certainly those gentlemen must be allowed to see for themselves."

"The Press as well."

"Ah yes, I see. I think it wrong."

Avis does not trouble himself to shrug.

The morning is skittish and blustery, but for the first time in days it is not raining. The suns plays hide-and-seek, peekabooing around cloudwracks the color of bruised beets. The earth is shadow-flown. Breath shows on the air in whitened puffs mussed by windgusts. It reeks of char.

"A beautiful country," says the old man. He is clad in prison-issue: black cassimere coat and trousers, black slouch hat, collarless cotton shirt, garnet-red bedroom slippers. "I never had the pleasure of seeing it before."

"It is, isn't it?" says Avis, pausing a beat before adding, "I must say, you do not seem much afraid."

"No, reckon not," says the old man. "Never been. Physically, I mean. Not an ounce, even as a boy.

"You know, I applied after your governor that if I was to be publicly murdered, I much preferred to be crucified upon a cross than to be hung upon a scaffold. And do you know what he told me? Can you hazard a guess?"

"Why, no sir. I must say I cannot."

"Well, he wrote to me that perhaps in that case I ought not only to be hung, but to be hung between two Negroes. He intended it as an affront, of course, though I must say I chose to take it for quite the highest compliment I have ever been paid."

325

"Really! Well, sir, you do appear in altogether finer fettle today than am I."

"But Mr. Avis, I have every *cause* to be." When the jailer looks at him askance, he adds, "I am going home, you see."

Fishing in his pocket, the old man withdraws a scrap of folded-over paper. "Here, you will do me the honor of accepting this in trust."

"I will," says the jailer, taking the slip from him and depositing it absently in his coat pocket as the wagon veers from the cobblestones and bumps up and over the curb into the open field. "Well, here we are then."

Descried from this distance, risen across this treeless pasture, the scaffold resembles an enormous folding chair absent its back panel. The soldiery, both on foot and on horseback, is omnipresent. A brace of brass cannon wings the gallows east and west. There are assembled in this farmer's field two thousand men under arms, among them a covey of cadets from the Virginia Military Institute mother-henned by a notoriously unpopular professor of mathematics and science named Thomas Jonathan Jackson.

Jackson eyes the undertaker's wagon as it jostles over the fallow upland and rattles to a halt before the scaffold where the grizzled old man in the dented black hat and red slippers bounces from the opened tailflap before appearing eagerly to take the ten steps to the pine deck two at a time.

"Mr. Avis," says the old man, removing his hat and handing it to the trailing jailer. "Thank you." He extends his hand, which Avis clasps firmly. "Good-bye."

Below, Ambrose bobsleds the casket from the bed of the wagon, wrestling it to the ground before towing it to the foot of the stairs even as Avis slips a white satin hood appliqued in lace over the old man's head—a pillowcase with unraveled side seams actually—that drapes like a smock to his shoulders. When zephyrs snatch at the bag's borders, they flap like scarves until Sheriff Campbell safety-pins them down.

(Had he not chosen to shave his beard before leaving Timbucto, it might at this point have been observed as Melville imagined, extruding beneath the hem of the hood, foxtailing wierdly in the wind.)

"You are not standing on the drop," says Campbell. "Come ahead some."

"I cannot," says the old man beneath the hood. "I cannot see. You must lead me."

Avis guidedogs him to Campbell who calfties one rope around both of his ankles and figure-eights another around his wrists behind his back. Looping the noose over his head, he snugs its coil against his neckbone and hitches its hempen lead line to the hook extruding from the gantry beam overhead.

"Be quick, won't you?" chafes the old man. "I do not wish to be kept waiting any longer than is necessary."

But ten minutes later, observes Jackson, he still is standing there, standing stock-still as the soldiers below—one of them a twenty-one-year-old consignee to Company F of the 1st Virginia "Richmond Gray" Militia Regiment named John Wilkes Booth—parade and counterparade like some ill-practiced marching band until at length they approximate the semblance of a double hollow square—a box boxing a box—around the scaffold.

"You must be tired," offers Sheriff Campbell.

"Only of waiting, sir," replies the old man sharply. "Please, I wish to meet my Maker now."

"Ready!" calls an officer from below, but the word is finned off by the wind. "All is in order," he tries again. "We are ready!"

"It is almost an end," says Avis to the old man. "We will take our leave then. Good-bye."

"Good-bye—*again*," says the old man testily.

Avis and Campbell descend the stairs. Before they can reach the bottommost step, Ambrose has slipped the hatchet to Campbell who without missing a beat proceeds directly to the nearest stanchion where with a single, sure-handed thwack, he chwumps through the hitching of the guyline running from the trapdoor.

A hinge skrees.

The trap thlunks.

The old man hurls through the mouth of the open hatch like a sack of washers.

He does not struggle, but his hands clench, his knees hasp, and his arms wingspread up behind his back.

It is 11:08 A.M.

No one cheers.

━━━━━━

Avis does not give a second thought to the old man's scrap of paper until later that evening when, about to retire, he flops his coat over the back of a chair and it dollars from a pocket.

"So," he thinks, bending down to scissor it up between his fore- and middle fingers, "what have we here." Folding it open he reads what is written there in a hand uncannily redolent of its author— craggy, but sure:

> I, John Brown, am now quite *certain* that the crimes of this *guilty* land will *never* be purged away, but with Blood. I had, as I now think, vainly flattered myself that *without* very much Bloodshed it *might* be done.

"*Without* bloodshed?" Avis fleers to himself. "Well, *that's* a god- damn lie.

"Out of wholecloth to the end, eh, old man?"

Crumpling the note in his fist, his inclination is to feed it to the potbelly, but something, some impulse he will never adequately ex- plain to himself—or to others—stops him.

Uncrumpling it once again, he irons it out a time or two over the top of his bedtable.

Later that night, preoccupied with his wife's deteriorating health and hounded by the thought of a host of nagging details at work— the bedding wants delousing, the privy out back could do with a good scrub—he does not dream about John Brown.

John Brown was hung today at about half past eleven A.M. He behaved with unflinching firmness. I hope that he was prepared to die, but I am doubtful. He refused to have a minister with him, and I fear that he may receive the sentence, "Depart ye wicked into the everlasting fire."

His body was taken back to the jail and then sent to his wife at Harper's Ferry. When it arrived, the coffin was opened and his wife saw the remains, after which it was again opened at the train depot, lest there should be an imposition.

—STONEWALL JACKSON, *Memoirs*

Tomorrow, when they place his remains aboard the train, will be the *last* we will hear of this Osawatomie Brown.

—ROBERT E. LEE, *Letters*

Mary bore his body north from Virginia swollen with preservatives and salted down with lime. The corpse lay inside an unsanded, walnut plank coffin, its lid nailed shut beneath a canvas tarpaulin unfestooned by black crepe or bunting and battened down with leather belts appropriated from a pair of book-crammed steamer trunks stored in the attic of the Harper's Ferry Public Library.

As topography dictated, they traveled by wagon, locomotive, wagon again, skiff, sleigh, and on the homeward leg—the twenty-five miles or so between Elizabethtown and the farm—wagon once more. It was early December and churchbells chonged through the blown slant of the sleet through which could often be discerned the canted, craning shapes of the thousands of Negroes thronging the exequy.

His body was laid to rest beyond the southernmost tip of Lake Placid in the Adirondack Mountains in the shadow of a granite boulder the size of a symphony stage—but only after the lid first had been pried back for final viewing by the light of a coal oil lantern which revealed a wreath of fiery red ringing his neck where the rope of the noose had wrung it.

Someone commented, a bit rashly perhaps, how much it resembled a collar of blood.

The elevation thereabouts is well over four thousand feet; before the week was out it was being remarked in certain circles how John Brown had been furnished a head start on heaven.

To his children, final letter:

Dear family:
I admonish you always to remember—
Be good haters.

ACKNOWLEDGMENTS

I wish to thank Allen Peacock, Jacques de Spoelberch, Steve Hedgpeth, Phil Pochoda, Jack Edwin Olds, and George Ivan Morrison.

Also, the staffs of the Library of Congress, the Otto G. Richter Library of the University of Miami, and the Harpers Ferry National Historical Park.

———

Richard Boyer's *The Legend of John Brown* and Stephen Oates' *To Purge This Land with Blood* provided useful points of departure. Charles Johnson's *Middle Passage* and Barry Unsworth's *Sacred Hunger* inspired my description of the slave trade. Part of the text of Allen Wilkinson's "manifest" is from Truman Nelson's *The Surveyor*. The phrase "rifle-ball words shot from a rifle-ball tongue," on page 143, is a paraphrase of a line from the poem "History as Cap'n Brown," by Michael S. Harper. Some of the mystic referents cited in the context of John Brown's incarceration are taken from the oeuvre of George I. Morrison.

Any errors of fact, as all sins of omission, are strictly my own and entirely premeditated.